Robert White

Robert White is an Amazon best selling crime fiction author. His novels regularly appear in the top ten downloads in the Crime and Action and Adventure genres.

Robert is an ex cop, who captures the brutality of northern British streets in his work. He combines believable characters, slick plots and vivid dialogue to immerse the reader in his fast paced story-lines.

He was born in Leeds, England, the illegitimate son of a jazz musician and a factory girl.

He hated school, leaving at age sixteen.

After joining Lancashire Constabulary in 1980, he served for fifteen years, his specialism being Tactical Firearms. Robert then spent four years in the Middle East before returning to the UK in 2000.

He now lives in Lancashire with his wife Nicola, and his two dogs Tia and Spud.

Novels

Rick Fuller Thrillers:

THE FIX
THE FIRE
THE FALL

THE FOLLOWER
THE FELLOWSHIP
THE FIGHTER

MADE TO BE BROKEN
TOOTH FOR A TOOTH

Det Sgt Striker Thrillers:

UNREST
SIX
DARK TRIAD

Stand alone novels:

DIRTY
BREAKING BONES

Tooth for a Tooth

A Rick Fuller Thriller

Book Eight
(The Politics of Murder Pt 2)

By

Robert White

www.robertwhiteauthor.co.uk

ISBN: 9798843233884

For my wife, Nicola

Acknowledgements

As most of you Fuller fans will know, this series was never intended to be as long or as complex as it has turned out to be. Rick, Des and many other heroes have fought long and hard against their various enemies, some taken from the pages of history, some totally imagined. Either way, their endeavours have caught the imagination of many thousands of readers all around the globe, and for that I am truly grateful.

Book seven, Made to be Broken, turned out to be the most popular Fuller yet and is now followed by this tale, Tooth for a Tooth, the penultimate book in the series.

I can say honestly that book nine, Cross to Bear, will be the last.

There will be no more.

With each story, I have found Fuller more difficult to write. Whether that is due to my wandering mind, or as the tale sprints ever closer to its inevitable conclusion, the need to do Rick justice and create the best work I can, who knows, I really can't say.

So, once again, I have my wife to thank for her good advice. A Special Forces veteran that I only ever knew as 'Hugh,' for bringing me the character of Des Cogan, and my small but illustrious team of Jacqueline, Debbie and Vassil who do all the behind the scenes work.

Thank you for your continued support. I wish you all well.

ROBERT WHITE

*"While seeking revenge, dig two graves -
one for yourself."*

DOUGLAS HORTON

ONE

St Michael And All Angels' Cemetery, Headingley

He'd expected rain.

Not that the forecast had offered any, just that he'd anticipated it. After all, these practices, these rituals, somehow demanded bad weather. But no, this day, against all forecasts, the sun shone, and the sky was the clearest blue. The first shoots of spring filled his nostrils. New grass, new blooms, new life.

It was his first visit since... since.

Not that it was even the right day, not the true anniversary. This day, three years back, was her funeral, the day she was laid to rest, here, in this quiet, serene place. Three years since the kind words, since what remained of her friends and family had gathered, since hands were shaken, tears shed.

The actual date of her death, the date her life was snuffed out, was actually three years and nineteen days ago. A date burnt into his memory.

He'd wanted to be at the graveside on that very anniversary, but... but he figured other more deserving mourners may have coveted that very same opportunity, and his mere presence may have enraged those that still thought him responsible for their tragic loss.

Was he?

He'd asked himself that question so many times.

Responsible or not, the guilt and the pain never left him.

As he trod the ancient uneven stone path that he knew would take him towards her plot, he checked his footing. Spring may well have been in the air, but thick green moss still covered much of the lopsided pathway, and it was slippery enough to send a man clattering to the floor should he not take care where he trod.

He'd decided to wear his George Cleverly brogues for the first time. Stout and handmade, she had bought them for him as a gift for his birthday.

Was that four or maybe five years ago?

Either way, they had sat in their dust bag all that time, unworn.

It was as he was selecting his clothes for this sombre trip that he'd noticed them. He had held them in his hands, turning them over and over, his stomach churning in concert, heart breaking.

They were just a simple pair of shoes, yet they painted such a clear picture of her. He recalled the moment she'd nervously handed them to him, knowing how particular he was, knowing how flippant he could be. She had smiled and wished him many happy returns, her loveliness filling the room, overpowering any gift she could give.

And now, on this day, it somehow felt just right to wear them. She, a practical Yorkshire lass, trapped inside that stunningly beautiful exterior, would have wanted him to get use from them.

They were a tiny part of her, and he knew that simply having them on his feet was one more demon bested.

As he drew ever closer, he noticed that a white marble headstone had been added to the grave. The sun caught it and spikes of brilliance danced across its face. He could just make out the delicately carved name.

Lauren.

He stopped, squared his shoulders, touched the knot of his tie, took the longest, deepest breath.

He could do this.

Ten more strides and he was there. All around the grave he saw evidence of previous visitors, loved ones who had been thoughtful enough to take the time to remember her. Their flowers of course were wilted, the nineteen days between her anniversary and now taking their toll the way only nature could.

He knelt and began to lift away the curled up brown bunches, laying them to one side. Someone had left a small Teddy Bear, dressed as a nurse. It had a tiny note tied around its neck. 'Forever Young,' it said.

He sniffed and sat the bear up against the headstone.

There were few weeds to deal with, those early comers, those better placed, had dispensed with such things.

He'd brought a single red infinity rose; the beautiful petals held inside a clear glass box. The girl in the shop had said it would last for three years. A solitary black ribbon, tied in a bow around the glass held a card, somewhere to write a message.

That had caused him a problem. He'd sat for the longest time.

Whom exactly was he writing it to? The next visitor?

Or was it there simply to make the writer feel better?

He placed the box next to the bear and stood, head bowed. Fuller had never been a religious man, and at times like these, often felt slightly ineffectual. Des had his God to pray to and the Scot believed in the afterlife, where Fuller... well Fuller didn't give credence to such things, and therefore, in his mind there was no one to leave a message to. Consequently the card had remained blank.

She would have expected that too, he thought.

Rick was dragged away from his rationale by the sound the shuffling of feet. Off to his right an old boy in a grey overcoat was laying flowers at a grave that had obviously been around for quite some time. The man, like Fuller, had cleared away the old dead offerings before placing his own new blooms in pride of place.

"Grand day," he groaned, struggling to lift his creaking frame upwards.

Fuller managed a nod and a brief smile, hoping that may be the end of the conversation, but the old guy wasn't done. He hobbled over.

"Your Mam?" he asked, gesturing towards Lauren's headstone.

Fuller didn't quite know what to say.

"No," he said quietly. "A friend."

The elderly chap shuffled his feet again to steady himself on the turf. He grabbed at Rick's elbow.

"Sorry, son," he said, looking up into Fuller's face. "My eyes aren't what they used to be. I should have noticed the dates on the stone... she were awfully young, eh?"

"Awfully," said Rick.

"My Florence," said the guy, thumbing in the direction of the other plot. "God took her too soon n'all."

"I'm sorry to hear that," said Fuller.

The man rummaged in his pocket and found a handkerchief. He wiped rheumy eyes before blowing his nose. Once he'd finished, he tapped Rick on the arm.

"You'd be a military man then?"

"Was."

"Aye, and it still shows n'all… I were too. 45 Commando."

"You'd have seen Aden then," said Rick still staring helplessly at Lauren's headstone.

"Some of it."

"I lost my old man there."

"Dark times, son. Have you seen much yourself?"

"Too much, Sir… way too much."

Both men fell silent a while before the old boy asked, "She was a friend y' say?"

Rick nodded.

The old man turned down his mouth.

"Aye, and some by the look on yer face I'd wager. Now…Listen to me, son. I'm about ready to join my Flo." He wrinkled his nose. "Won't be long at all, I'm all busted up inside wit' cancer. But I'm ready, tha knows? I'm not scared. Tired o' life on me own is what I am. I've been layin' flowers in this place now for twenty seven years. Sittin' here, talkin' to her, tellin' her about me day, then goin' home to an empty house."

He shook his head, caught Fuller's eye again.

"It's no way t' live son. Take my advice. If you can find it inside yourself… move on, let her go."

"And what if I can't?" asked Rick.

The old man looked at his feet a moment, then back at Fuller.

"Can I ask… how did she die, so young I mean?"

"She was murdered."

"Oh Lord," he said, hand on mouth. "That explains something."

"Explains what?" snapped Fuller.

There was an edge to Rick's tone. He hadn't been able to keep it out. He screwed up his eyes, rested a hand on the old man's bony shoulder.

"I'm sorry I was sharp then, Sir," he said. "It's all a bit…"

"Hey, no worries, lad," smiled the old boy, turning and hobbling away. "None of my business anyways."

"Have a good day," called Rick, again lost for words.

The man stopped and turned.

"Let me just say, son, fer what it's worth like, whoever did it, I mean, did for your lass there, leave 'em be. Don't let it eat you up. Whoever said revenge was sweet lad, never tasted it… G'day t'you."

TWO

Stirling Lines, Hereford 14ᵗʰ February 1992

Fuller was balancing a large aluminium teapot and five pint sized mugs on a tray as he walked into the briefing room. Boiling, brown, over brewed, liquid dribbled from the spout as he went.

"Fuck me, it's the tea lady, the tea lady," offered Jimmy Two Times.

"All he needs is a frilly pinny," smiled Butch. "Be pretty as a picture then."

"I'm the man of your dreams, Butch," said Fuller. "You know I am."

Cogan worriedly checked his watch. He'd promised his wife, Anne that he'd be home in time to take her into town to do a food shop. It was a task he hated, but an essential part of keeping his increasingly irritable wife happy. This day had been listed as a simple training session. Fire a few rounds in the killing house, clean a bit of kit, maybe get some in.

'Be finished for dinner, hen,' he'd promised confidently as he'd kissed her goodbye. But as he watched his patrol leader balancing the teapot and mugs, he figured his pledge could be about to be broken.

Fuller slid his heavy tray carefully across a small round Formica covered table, then strode purposefully to the corner of the poky room to recover milk, a bowl of sugar and a teaspoon. He sniffed at the warm bottle of sterilised, decided it was just about okay and poured a few drops into four of the five mugs. Then came the sugar, none for himself, one for Des, two for Jimmy and four for Butch. He wasn't sure how many the new CO took, so he left his mug well alone.

Des, Butch and Jimmy were Fuller's patrol. Three immensely talented military men, tough and uncompromising, ruthless even. Attributes needed for the enormously difficult missions they would be asked to complete as part of the anti-terrorist arm of 22 SAS.

Fuller may not have known anything about his new boss, but he knew his patrol well, knew all their struggles, their strengths, their fears, and how much sugar they took in their tea.

Jimmy 'Two Times' Smith was named after the character in the film Goodfellows, as he sometimes repeated himself when he spoke. All the patrol had visited the cinema to watch the Scorsese classic and the name had stuck from that very evening. He'd suffered with Tourette's as a child and in his early teens had been plagued with tics. As he'd matured, his condition eased enough to join 2 Para alongside Des Cogan. Jimmy was a genuine hard man, sometimes stubborn, always reliable and immensely fit. He had followed Des, Rick and Butch into selection for the Regiment, and since his successful entry into 22, his only noticeable symptoms were an occasional sharp sniffing tic and the urge to repeat himself when in situations that stressed him out.

Like a briefing for instance.

That meant Jimmy didn't like to talk much, especially in a room full of people who may just take the piss out of him. Jimmy just wanted to get the job done, less talk, more action, which was just fine by his patrol leader, Richard Edward Fuller.

Dave 'The Butcher' Stanley, or Butch to his friends, was a whole different ball game to Jimmy. A big, brash, supremely strong and confident Yorkshireman. Another Para, whose nickname had come about as a result of his actions in the Falklands War. He'd been one of the lads found with Argentinean ears in their mess tins after the battle for Goose Green. The maroon berets had cut them off the enemy's dead bodies and saved them as war trophies. Did this bother Fuller? No. He wouldn't lose one wink over any of it. In the history of war, nothing had ever changed. From helmets and swords to scalps and skulls, fighting men had always taken trophies, and the Regiment needed hard men like Butch.

Of course, what no one had any way of knowing, was that years later, Butch would be killed in a helicopter crash in Iraq whilst working for a private security firm. He would be just forty two. Jimmy however, would be a different matter. After being turned by some deeply dangerous individuals, he would meet his fate in 2006, on the water, somewhere between Puerto Banús and Gibraltar at the hands of Lauren North. A sad end for a man with such promise.

The four were all part of A Squadron, Air troop. Four of sixteen men all expertly trained in free fall and high altitude parachute operations. Yet it wasn't the patrol's parachuting skills that were required this day. Fuller and his men had completed several operations in Northern Ireland over the last few months, and their anti-terrorist experience was becoming a matter of Regimental folklore. They had shown their abilities in urban conflict situations to be second to none. Fuller, Cogan, Stanley and Smith, were nothing less than a four man killing machine.

Des flopped in his chair and took a slurp of his tea. The Scot hadn't shaved for over a week and was sporting the beginnings of a full set. He scratched it absently.

"So, what's all this about then pal?" he asked Fuller. "Anne will have my guts if I dinnea get home te bring in the messages."

"Why do you call groceries, messages?" asked Butch.

"Why de ye call a piece 'n cheese, ye snap?" countered Cogan.

"Fuckin' weegie," muttered Butch, lifting his mug. "Tha' should be taught proper English before tha's allowed over't border."

Rick shook his head.

"Now, now, children, play nice," he said. "All I know is the new CO called as we were leaving the killing house. He said to muster here and make him a brew. So here we are. If I were a betting man, I'd say it's got something to do with what's been happening in East Tyrone."

"Aye," agreed Butch, lifting his mug. "The Paddies are running fucking riot over there again. They did another RUC base the other night. Used some big calibre stuff too. Russian made kit is what I heard."

"Aye," said Des. "That Gaddafi has a lot te answer fe. He's movin' all his Russian made kit into the South. Hates the Brits he does."

At that, the door opened and in strode Lt Col Cedric Holmes, the squadron's brand new 'Rupert.' This rather derogatory nickname for an officer apparently originated within the old Cavalry regiments of the Royal Armoured Corps, where their recruitment was often based upon their connection to old military families of the aristocracy, rather than their propensity for skill or common-sense. Special Forces CO's rarely lasted longer than three or four years. Some, of course were experienced fighting men and were well respected for their work in the field. However, Holmes' background was so far removed from the men he commanded, he was instantly at a disadvantage. Born into an army family, his father being a Major General, he'd begun his education at Cheltenham College Junior School, followed by a spell at Eton before taking a degree in Politics at Cambridge, where he was a keen member of the Pitt Club. Holmes was the kind of man who never really took his eye off his own career, rather than see the bigger picture.

Whatever this man's talent, or lack of it, all four troopers instantly got to their feet.

"Sit, gentlemen," said Holmes snappily. "Where's my tea, Fuller?"

"Right here, Sir," offered Rick. "Sugar?"

"As it comes," said Holmes, dropping a buff coloured folder onto the next table away from the possibility of tea accidents.

Fuller noticed that the front of the file was stamped in large red lettering, 'Top Secret Eyes Only.' He shot Cogan a look. His friend may not be going food shopping after all.

"So gents," began Holmes. "Settle down, this won't take long."

He opened the folder, took a sip of tea, grimaced and glared at Fuller.

"Let's hope you chaps are better at soldiering than making a decent cup of cha."

Butch sniggered and mouthed the word, 'prick' behind his hand. Fuller kicked his shin.

"Children," barked the CO. "Right listen in. On 3rd June last year, our chaps from Mobility Troop had a little skirmish over the water in Country Tyrone. The boffins from Six had sent through some intelligence that three IRA players were to kill an off-duty Ulster Defence Regiment soldier in the town of Coagh that very night. As it happened, 22 ambushed their car and all three were..." he considered his words carefully. "Terminated.... Adding to that ray of sunshine was the information that one of the three, Declan Ryan, was the same man who had led the shocking attack on Derryard checkpoint two years previously."

Fuller, Cogan, Stanley and Smith, knew all about Derryard. It had been just before Christmas 1989 when the Provos attacked a British Army permanent vehicle checkpoint complex manned by the King's Own Scottish Borderers. The PIRA unit assaulted the small base with heavy machine-guns, grenades, anti-tank rockets and a flamethrower, leaving two soldiers dead and two wounded. One of the fallen, Chris McAvennie had lived in Cogan's hometown, attended the same school. Des didn't know him well, but he knew he had a wife and four kids. Not a close friend, but close enough for it to sit badly in his gut.

"So, that was a good result, Sir," offered Des. "Three less players te worry about and no casualties fer us, eh?"

Holmes cocked his head, raised his brows and shrugged. It was an expression that told the team everything they needed to know about the man. Dead soldiers, dead terrorists. They all meant the same thing to him. Getting the job done and earning his next pip, crown or ribbon was all that mattered to this guy.

Des glared at his CO. Ruperts like Holmes, men in suits that worked in underground bunkers in London, what the fuck did they care? What did they know about death and dying?

"The who's, the why's and the wherefores don't matter, Cogan," said Holmes indifferently. "I mention it only because it was a very clean and tidy op, the way I like things done."

He sniffed.

"But now the boys from Whitehall have come up with further pearls of wisdom. Pearls that need instant attention."

He turned a page.

"And you chaps have been selected to complete this next little task. So... let me begin with some poignant history regarding this small piece of the Emerald Isle... Since 1985, the East Tyrone Brigade have been at the forefront of a campaign against the British forces and their allies."

Holmes took another sip of his tea and pulled another face.

"Despite some heavy losses over the years, these buggers have gone on to attack nearly 100 police and military facilities, and let's not forget the Ballygawley bus bomb."

Des was nodding slowly. He was well aware of the Ballygawley bus bomb too, although, he couldn't understand why this officer should be trying to educate four men on the history of the Troubles. Four men who had lived and breathed them since their teens. There wasn't a soldier alive that had served in that part of the world that didn't. In the horrific attack on Ballygawley, eight soldiers from The Light Infantry had been blown to bits, and twenty eight others wounded, many with life changing injuries. Because of that attack, all troops going on leave from East Tyrone were then ferried in and out by helicopter, the road being deemed too dangerous.

The only plus point to the tale, was that some months later, 22 had caught the Ballygawley bombers in another ambush near Carrickmore and slotted all three.

Cogan was getting somewhat tired of Holmes' tedious history lesson, and it showed. After all, he and his teammates had spent far more time getting shot at over the water than you could shake a stick at.

"So what exactly is this job, Sir?" asked Des, unable to hide the impatience in his voice.

The Lt Col peered at the Scot over half-moon glasses.

"I was getting to that, Cogan," he snapped. "I considered you may need a little background first."

Fuller drained his mug.

"We have fifteen tours between us here, Sir. That's fifteen with 2 Para alone, before we took selection. We know the ground, and it's bloody history, Sir. Know it well. Maybe the intel would be of a little more interest?"

Holmes looked as if he'd swallowed something extremely unpleasant.

"I see... very well," he straightened his tie, sniffed again. "For some time now, MI6 have had eyes inside this Tyrone Brigade, but until recently, our man has never been privy to actual operations... now he has. Our reliable information is that the day after tomorrow, February 16th, the Tyrone Brigade are planning to attack The Royal Ulster Constabulary security base at Drum Manor. The attack is due to take place at 2200hrs. The Brigade will use a stolen car and a lorry. We understand that there will be multiple attackers and that they have access to a DSHK heavy machine gun and armour piercing ammunition. They intend to mount that on the stolen lorry. The rest of the attackers will be armed with AKM assault rifles."

"Fuck me, they mean business," offered Butch, finishing his tea.

"Exactly," said Holmes with a weak smile. "That's why we are going to leave them to it."

Des nearly choked on what was left in his mug. "Leave them to what?"

"Leave them to it, Cogan. Our chap on the inside has all the intel. We will make sure that every man is out of harm's way at the base, and let these morons shoot their bolt, so to speak. Once they have done their worst, they will drive to Granville, a village just two miles from their target where their getaway cars will be waiting... and of course, you chaps."

The CO stood, tapped the loose papers of his file back into place and closed the cover.

"You'll be flown into Galbally Security base by helicopter, then the boys from 14 Int will get you to the FOP (forward operating point). From there it's a short tab to St Jude's Church, where you will lie in wait for your targets. This is a dress down affair chaps, jeans, leathers and balaclavas seem to make a man fit in just right in Dungannon. Extraction will be exactly the reverse of your approach. The Det will collect you, and you should all be home safe for breakfast on the 17th."

Holmes stopped in his tracks and pointed.

"Now, there's been a lot of talk in the media about this so called shoot to kill policy, and this chap Stalker has been nothing but a bally nuisance. So, with that in mind, no matter what the scenario, even if you are under fire, you will call out the challenge. Give these boys the opportunity to surrender. Am I clear?"

Holmes was met with silence. He wasn't sure if that was due to indifference or shock. Either way, he pushed his file under his armpit and made to leave.

"So… I expect a good result, chaps. Are we all on the same page?"

There were mumbles of 'Yes Sir' from the four troopers as the CO tripped out of the room, nose in the air.

"He's a fuckin' delight," said Butch standing and stretching.

"Typical Rupert, Rupert," said Jimmy, sniffing profusely.

"I've never liked the idea of an ambush," offered Des. "And if this lot do throw their hands up…"

"Which we know they won't," pointed Fuller.

"But *if* they did," said Des. "That fool hasn't made any provision to take prisoners. What are we supposed to do with them, stand in the fucking car park until a number six bus comes along?"

"There'll be no need for any of that, Des," snapped Butch. "Rick's right, these boys won't surrender, and that prick knows it. And another thing. I won't be announcing my position to a load of murdering bastard Paddies by shouting some poxy challenge, policy or no fucking policy."

Rick eyed his team. Des was on the money, no one in the Regiment liked an ambush, but sometimes the end justified the means. These men were heavily armed terrorists responsible for the deaths of dozens of British soldiers and if you lived by the sword, well, you had it coming. Butch's anger was common too. There were very few men who had not lost a friend or a relative whilst serving over the water. The Troubles were a dirty business, and no one involved had clean hands, not even the SAS.

"Let's get some kit sorted," said Fuller.

Before the team could leave the briefing room and head for the armoury, another face entered the room. This one was younger and in civilian clothes. He had short cropped blond hair, swept to one side, and a complexion that most supermodels would have died for. He silently handed Rick a large brown envelope, turned on his heels and was gone.

"Six," muttered Des.

"Poof," spat Butch.

Rick gave Dave Stanley a withering look, pulled out a single photograph from inside the envelope and lay it between the empty mugs. It was an aerial shot of St Jude's Church, Granville, Dungannon. The church was a modern building with a large carpark to its front and open fields to the rear. The cemetery that served it was separated from the main structure and grounds by a narrow lane, Cloghog Road, this lane also serving as the church carpark's entrance.

"So... the players will approach from here, this roundabout on Cleaver Road," began Fuller. "Then turn right into Ashfield Road, then left into the carpark." He tapped the picture with his nail. "Now, I reckon that these boys will have bolted that DSHK to the roof of the truck for stability."

"And they'll no want te lose that baby," offered Des.

"Exactly," pointed Rick. "They'll need to unbolt it or dismantle whatever they've constructed to hold it in place. And there is our chance. We can dig in..." he tapped again. "Here... in the surrounding fields until just before the Provos arrive. Then, there's enough bushes and the like surrounding the carpark to get us in cover." He studied the shot again. "That said, I think we need someone in the cemetery... about here, to give us a full arc of fire."

"How far away is that ye reckon?" asked Des.

Fuller took another look. "Even if they parked at the far end, furthest away, I'd say, sixty, maybe ninety yards."

"Piece of pish," said Des. "I'll de that. I can take out individual targets with single shots, whilst you lads rake the rest."

"Sounds like a plan," said Butch.

"Let's crack on then," said Fuller.

The British Special Forces have always adopted the latest weaponry and have often been at the forefront of hi tech warfare. However, this job, this slaughter of men, required nothing more than a keen eye, a steady hand and overwhelming firepower. Of course, it helped to know exactly what you were up against, and on this occasion, the intel was very specific. The players would be very well armed.

The DSHK heavy machine gun Holmes had mentioned was a fearsome weapon, the abbreviation hailing from its two Russian creators, Degtyaryov who designed the original weapon and Shpagin who later improved the cartridge feed mechanism. It was a Soviet heavy machine gun with a V-shaped 'butterfly' trigger, firing an armour piercing 12.7×108mm cartridge. The gun, like much of the weapons and explosives used by the PIRA in the late eighties and early nineties, had probably found its way to the Province via Libya and was easily mounted onto the back of a truck or pickup. The AKM assault rifles mentioned, were a modernised version of the AK47, still an old weapon, being designed in the late 50's, but lethal in the right hands, delivering a 7.62 hi-velocity bullet at a practical rate of 100 rounds per minute. The AKM also accepted the lighter curved 30 round mags popular with the Provos, and Fuller suspected that Butch was right, challenge or no challenge, these men would not give up. They would fight to the death and let's face it, they had the kit to do just that. Whatever Holmes said, this little job was not a walk in the park and would be anything but clean.

Knowing exactly what he was up against, Rick selected four M16 A2's as the team's assault rifles. The weapon was relatively new to the Regiment and fired a 5.56×45mm cartridge. It didn't have the range and stopping power of the 7.62mm the Provo's had, but it possessed better and more modern sighting. More importantly, at 7.9 pounds even with a loaded 30-round magazine, it was especially lightweight. This, of course was crucial when you had to carry all your own weapons across kilometres of cold muddy fields before you got to fire them.

Next came small arms. Rick pulled three Sig Sauer P228 compacts, and one single Browning High Power for Des as that was his preferred handgun. He considered a sniper rifle for the Scot too, but at the distances they would be operating at, the M16 A2 would be more than adequate.

As the ambush would take place at night and in a rural location, Rick was keen to get his hands on some night vision kit, but when he was offered the Yukon Tracker goggles, changed his mind. They were bulky and awkward, and it was almost impossible to gain a sight picture whilst wearing them. Therefore he went old school and pulled a Very gun and a box of white signal flares. After all, you can't shoot what you can't see.

Four sets of covert body armour came next, all complete with ceramic plates, as the standard Kevlar was no match for the 7.62 rounds the Irish would be firing. Finally he fitted four comms sets with new batteries and the patrol were ready to walk through their plan.

ROBERT WHITE

Jimmy and Butch set up traffic cones at the end of the runway to sim-ulate the church building, car park perimeter and entrance. Another set some ninety yards away, marked out exactly where Rick wanted Des to dig in at the cemetery. One of the biggest dangers when creating an ambush was crossfire, and all the patrol members needed to know exactly where each was, so once the contact began, he didn't draw fire from his own men. Rick then borrowed a car, a few lads from mountain troop to play terror-ists, plus a very grumpy civvy wagon driver and his seven and a half tonner, then, the role play began.

Over the next two hours, Rick walked his crew through every possible scenario, every eventuality and each time, every single terrorist ended up the same way.

Dead.

THREE

Kensington, London

He wasn't accustomed, or comfortable being naked in a strange bed.

He rarely slept nude, even in the confines of his own apartment. He'd been so used to sleeping in all manner of clothing and kit, it had become almost a comfort. From stab vests to NATO helmets, he'd dozed in most of it. Kipping in hammocks, burnt out vehicles, disused buildings, anything to give some modicum of shelter from the cold or cover from his enemies.

And this had held firm long after his discharge from the Regiment. At worst he was a t shirt and boxers kind of guy. After all, if someone came calling in the middle of the night, someone with evil in his heart and murder on his mind, it wasn't wise to be left swinging in the breeze.

He rolled to his left and took in the picture by the side of the bed.

It was devastation. His shoes and socks had been kicked or pulled off and flung across the room. And as for his suit trousers and jacket, they lay in two crumpled heaps, pulled inside out. Two thousand pounds of Savile Row superiority discarded like sweat shop specials. He couldn't see his shirt, tie or boxers for that matter, and was doing his best to recall where they may be. Finally, the fuzz of the champagne cleared, and he remembered. He and Rose had showered together before they had slipped between her crisp Egyptian cotton sheets.

He knew her Kensington apartment well. The million pound Victorian maisonette was situated directly opposite the Natural History Museum on the tree lined, Queens Gate, just a stones' throw from Earls Court. He'd had both good times and bad in these opulent rooms.

Loved and murdered.

He checked his Rolex and settled once more onto his back. Rosemary

Longthorn Grey, the UK's youngest ever Home Secretary stirred, ran her hand across his bare chest and nuzzled herself in close.

"Good morning, Mr Fuller," she breathed. "How are you feeling?"

"Tender," he managed. "Crystal is the devil's work."

"I thought it was yummy," said Rose, raising a long leg and running her foot upwards from his shin to his knee. "It made me very naughty."

Fuller had been seeing Rose for almost two years, however, her schedule, messy divorce and London location meant that they saw each other on the rarest of occasions.

"You've always been naughty," he countered. "Booze or no booze... Shall I make the coffee?"

Rose took in a long deep breath, savouring Rick's scent, feeling the warmth of his strong yet scarred body next to hers.

"Do we have to move just yet? What time is it?"

"Just after six, and your security team will be here in thirty minutes."

She kissed his cheek, held him close. "There just aren't enough hours, are there?"

Fuller turned and stroked Rose's raven hair. "I've organised with Des and Jack to take a week away from the business at the beginning of June. Why don't we do Dubai?"

Rose sat up, displaying her nakedness. "You think we could work it out?"

"I can."

She pouted. "Well, if the PM can run off with his new girlfriend during a major political crisis, I'm sure I can have at least a long weekend."

"I'll make the coffee then," he said, swinging his legs from under the sheets.

Rose watched admiringly as he ambled to the kitchen. "Nice buns," she giggled.

Two cups and a shower later, both were dressed and ready to go their separate ways.

"My team will be outside now," said Rose, finding her briefcase. "Damn, I'm already five minutes late. Bloody select committee all morning too."

"What did you do?" asked Fuller.

"It's all about the early release programme."

"I wanted to mention that to you myself," he said, suddenly stern faced.

Rose stood.

"I really haven't the time now, Richard. I know you're..."

"You have no idea what I am," he snapped. "That bastard raped and murdered Lauren and he's free as a bird. He served seventeen months in a cushy hospital for fuck's sake."

Rose shook her head, rested a hand on his tense shoulder.

"It was a medical decision, Rick. Not a legal one. It never came across my desk."

"Well it fucking well should have done."

"That's as maybe, but I don't make the rules, I just follow them."

"Yeah, until it suits you," he sneered. "How many times do you think I've been employed by people in dark offices carrying buff files with red stamps? How often have my services been required when people like you are frightened to get their hands dirty? Have you forgotten the Russians so quickly?"

She checked her watch, gave him a loving look. Rose knew all about how the corridors of power worked and just how ruthless those that dwelled there could be. But in the case of Larry Simpson, the reality was, no one in those darkened corner offices were sufficiently concerned about the ex cop, or his heinous crimes, to put the wheels in motion and deal with him.

Because Simpson had been diagnosed as being unsound of mind at the time of the offences, once the medical experts considered him no longer a threat to society, there was no longer a medical or legal reason to keep him incarcerated. Those were the facts. However, Rose knew that trying to explain those hard truths to Richard Fuller over morning coffee would be impossible.

"Rick, I have to go. I'll call you later huh?"

He stood and fixed his gaze on her. His usual comforting deep chocolate eyes turning glassy, cold, fish like. There was sheer hate in his voice.

"I've had more than a year of this, Rose. A year of him walking around the streets of Manchester. He even got invited to the fucking CID Christmas party, can you believe that? He's not mentally ill now, is he?"

"I don't want to know how you found that out Rick."

"You don't want to know anything, do you Rose?" Fuller was shaking with rage. "Well, if you and your guys can't help me with Simpson, I'll deal with him myself," he said, teeth clenched. "And you know what that means."

Rose swallowed hard.

"Don't do anything stupid with this, Richard. I mean it. You lay hands on Larry Simpson, and I won't be able to help you. Listen, Rick, you know that whatever you do, it won't bring Lauren back... and what about us? What happened to all that talk of living our lives? Killing Simpson would be nothing more than revenge… and then what? You spend the rest of your days behind bars? How sweet would that be?"

Fuller's temper was subsiding.

"That's what the guy said yesterday."

"Who?"

Rick shook his head.

"Nothing, it's nothing, just an old man's ramblings."

Rose held Rick's face in both palms.

"I love you, Richard. I want us to be together. My divorce is almost done. Think about this, eh?"

"I think of nothing else," he said.

***

Jack Shenton sat behind his desk at the team's Piccadilly offices. It had once been Lauren North's seat, a position of power in some ways. These days, it was more of an apprentices' chair. Sitting opposite him was a rather large young woman. She sported a plain round face and had both heavily tattooed, ham-like arms crossed under her huge bosom. Some of the ink work had been done professionally, but most by someone with a shaky, illiterate hand.

"Where's the boss then?" she snapped, in a thick Mancunian accent.

"Mr Fuller is away in London on business," said Jack calmly.

"And what about the other fella I heard about, the Jock?"

"Mr Cogan is Scottish, and is walking his dog," offered Jack, a hint of weariness in his Liverpool tone. "What is it you need, exactly Mrs…?"

"It's Miss, actually," said the woman nodding at the sodden grubby pushchair to her left that contained a toddler of an age Jack couldn't determine. "His Dad weren't the marrying kind, eh?"

"Right," was all Shenton could think to say.

The woman sniffed loudly and wiped her nose with the back of her hand.

"Well, I heard that you lot here can help folk with stuff. Y'know, stuff that the coppers can't deal with like." She eyed the young Scouser suspiciously. "But I don't reckon you'd be right fer the job. Yer not much more than a kid yer self are yer?"

The 'private investigation' agency that Fuller and Cogan had set up after the Russian job had quickly turned into more of a public service. The team were already perceived as some kind of Robin Hood style group, helping the poorer people of the city with issues that were immensely important to them, things that appeared almost impossible for the authorities to resolve. Difficult neighbours, violent boyfriends, bullies and petty criminals had all been brought to bear. The team charged a nominal daily rate, but regularly recovered their fee from the wrongdoer rather than the wronged. However, the biggest issue Shenton and the team now faced, was their ever increasing workload. They were now forced to choose their battles wisely, based on a person's need. That, and how much fun it would be to do the job in the first place.

Jack managed a brief smile. "Looks can be deceiving, Miss…?"

"Greenwood, Stacey Greenwood," offered the woman, leaning over to check on her sleeping child.

"Well, Miss Greenwood, we can sometimes help, yes, but it depends on the problem," said Jack patiently.

The woman sat back in her seat, unfolded her arms and sniffed again. "I've been cuckooed ain't I?" she announced. "Right set o' twats they are n'all. Even got plants growin' in't baby's room."

"Sounds shockin'" said Jack. "And the Bizzies? What are they doin' like?"

The woman pulled her face, turning her countenance from simply plain to butt ugly.

"How can I go to the cops? Don't be soft, these bastards would have 'grass' sprayed on me door same day and break me legs soon as look at me."

"I see," nodded Jack. "Then you do have a problem."

"I reckon I should wait until the Jock… I mean the Scottish bloke gets back from his walk," she said, lifting her considerable bulk from the chair. "This is a job fer a man, not a boy."

"Sit down, Stacey," said Jack firmly. "Like I said, looks can be deceiving."

The woman gave Shenton a stern look but did as he asked and sat. "I'm listening."

"How many plants?" asked Jack. "And how long before they're ready?"

Stacey screwed up her face again. Shenton decided that someone should tell her not to do it so often as it may frighten her kid.

"Do I look like a weed grower to you?" she snapped.

"Okay, how long have this crew been in your house?"

The woman began to play with her fingers. There was a mixture of embarrassment and nervousness there. "Close on six months," she said finally.

Jack was incredulous. "Six months! What the hell are they growing?"

"This is their second crop," mumbled Stacey, still finding something interesting under her nails.

Jack narrowed his eyes. He knew all about cuckooing. They'd been doing it in Croxteth for years, but it was rare that any gorilla grower would stay longer than one crop. If the players were staying put, that meant they were using at least one of the residents as a runner to move product or cash or both across County Lines.

"What did you do to bring this on?" he asked sternly. "Or who, and what do you owe?"

Stacey swallowed. That twisted up unappealing face gone, replaced by one of genuine hurt and sadness.

"It ain't me, It's our Billy ain't it," she began. "He ain't the sharpest, y'see. He's a bit thick, if y'know what I'm sayin'? School says he's on the spectrum. This crew picked on him cos he's that way, slow like, gave him some weed, a few E's then before he knew it, he was moving stuff out of town, on his own bless him. On the train most nights he is, up to Blackpool and that."

"I take it he has their phone? One they gave him to use?"

"Aye, it never stops bleepin' and ringin' all hours of the day and night."

Jack nodded. He knew the script well.

"Then I suppose they came knocking to use your flat to grow a crop?"

"Somethin' like that. Look, erm…"

"Jack."

"Yeah, right, Jack. Maybe you could have a chat with me sister, Leanne. She's real close to our Billy. He tells her everythin'. I just need these bastards out of me flat and off our Billy's back. Like I said, they're a right set of nasty swines. Everyone's shit scared of 'em round our way."

Shenton picked up a pen. "And where is your way, exactly."

"Stockport. Lanky Hill. Pendlebury Towers, number 97."

"Don't know it."

"You don't want to kid, believe me."

Jack stopped scribbling down the address and looked up at Stacey

"I lived in Crocky all my life, love," he raised his brows. "When I wasn't in the nick, like. I'm used to shitholes, believe me."

At that, in walked Cogan with a very wet and lively Bruce the collie.

"Aye aye," he chirped. "Great weather fer ducks out there hen, hope ye got something te cover yer wain."

Stacey looked over at her ageing pushchair.

"I've a blanket for him."

"But it's chucking it down doll," said Des peering into the pram at the kid.

"Poor bugger will be soaked before you make it te the tram stop."

"I'll run yous home," said Jack, standing and pulling on his tracksuit top. "Like you said, I need to have a word with your Leanne anyway, now is as good a time as any if she's gonna be home."

"She's home," nodded Stacey. "And thanks, that's very kind of yer."

"De ye need another pair of hands, son?" asked Des.

"Nah, thanks, Mr Cogan," said Jack. "I'm only havin' a recce, like."

Rick had unusually taken the train. First to Leeds to visit Lauren's grave, and then on to London to meet with Rosemary Longthorn Grey, therefore Jack had use of his shiny Range Rover.

"We've no child seats," he said, as he lifted the empty buggy into the boot. "So best you hold him in yer arms and sit in the back."

Stacey clambered into the prestige car and rubbed at the sumptuous leather seats as she sat.

"Must be good money in this private investigation game," she said as Jack fired up the engine.

Shenton smiled.

This was an event in itself. Even one so dour as Stacey Greenwood couldn't help but notice. When the lad broke into a grin, the whole space around him lit up.

"This is Mr Fuller's car, love. He bought this before we started up the agency. I suppose you could say, he's not short of a few quid like."

"I can see," muttered Stacey, taking in her plush surroundings.

"What's yer postcode," asked Jack, finger poised over the sat nav.

"SK57RN," offered Stacey. "And look, when we get there, I'll go up first and if any of those toe rags are about, I'll bell yer and you get off."

Jack finished inputting the code into the machine, then turned and looked over his shoulder into Stacey's face. That beaming smile, that youthful, happy expression, those sparkling eyes had gone. All that was left, all that remained, was the boxer, the powerful young man standing in the centre of the ring eyeing his opponent for the first time. Unblinking, unnerving, unshakable.

"We'll be goin' up together, love," he said. "No danger."

The drive took almost half an hour. Heavy traffic clogged the usual fastest route, so the Range Rover's navigation system took the pair via Ardwick, Longsight, Levenshulme, and Burnage.

Much to Jack's surprise, the area described by Stacey as Lanky Hill,

Stockport, was actually called Lancashire Hill.

"Should've guessed," he muttered to himself.

He edged the hundred grand car along Penny Lane, towards two huge green and white clad blocks of flats, Hanover Towers, and its mirror image, his destination, Pendlebury Towers.

Jack was instantly dragged back to his youth, to the days when he genuinely didn't know where his next meal was coming from. Fighting the Strand Crew on streets of Croxteth, fighting his mother's latest violent trick, rolling tourists for their wallets in the city centre, doing doughnuts in stolen cars down on the docks. Was Jack a bad lad back then, or a lost soul just doing what he had to do to survive? Who was to say? But one thing was for sure, since meeting Rick Fuller, and particularly Des Cogan, he really didn't care for the past. He'd escaped, and that was all that mattered.

Shenton stepped from the car and opened the tailgate. Stacey dropped her child into the pram and fastened him in.

"You don't need to do this y'know. If any of them lads are in our flat, there'll be trouble, deffo. One of 'em carries a knife too. So I hope you're tooled up."

Jack zipped up his top to the neck and shrugged his broad shoulders.

Before his incarceration for killing a local drug dealer in a fist fight, he had boxed at light welterweight. That had risen to full welter whilst inside the notorious HMP Altcourse, and now, as he approached his twentieth birthday, his trainer had told him to think of himself as more of a middleweight. He would fight his next bout at an immensely fit, twelve stone.

He lifted his fists towards Stacey.

"I've got these, if that's any help."

The woman just shook her head.

"Let's get out of the rain, eh lad?"

Mercifully, the lifts in the twenty two storey tower block were operational. They worked, they were filthy and stinking, but they worked.

"Just like home," muttered Jack as he read some of the graffiti sprayed on the stainless steel wall next to him.

As the elevator approached the ninth floor, the pair could already smell the crop of cannabis that was growing in Stacey's flat. Of course, any of the residents of the building could have called the cops, used Crimestoppers or whatever other anonymous service GMP were operating, but why would they? Would you trust the cops if you lived in Pendlebury Towers?

Which is exactly why, despite the sickly stench, the crop kept on growing and the growers were freely using Stacey's electricity to do so.

The pair arrived at flat 97 and Stacey wriggled her key into the lock.

"Only me, love," she called out as she shoved the heavy reinforced door open.

Other than the overwhelming odour of skunk, the flat appeared clean and tidy.

Jack quietly stepped into the long narrow hall behind Stacey. Instantly, a younger woman, who he presumed to be Leanne Greenwood, appeared from the lounge with a worried look etched on her face.

"I thought you'd got lost, Sis," she said, grabbing at Stacy's sodden push-chair. "You've been ages."

Jack instantly decided that two sisters couldn't be less alike. Stacey was truly obese, had a love of tattoos, piercings and blue hair dye, where Leanne was slim, fresh faced, extraordinarily pretty and naturally blonde.

Jack was about to give Leanne his best beaming smile, when he saw a tall, well muscled guy appear behind her. He was dressed head to foot in black. Black Air Max, black trackies and, even though the flat was ridiculously warm from all the grow lamps hanging everywhere, a thick black hoodie, pulled over his number one crew. Shenton put him at a similar age to himself. The face pushed Leanne roughly out of the way almost knocking Stacey's child from his buggy.

"Who the fuck is this?" he growled striding towards Jack.

Now, Leanne had no way of knowing who her visitor was, but she was bright and streetwise enough to be able to think quickly.

Before the guy could reach Shenton, Leanne answered his question.

"It's me new fella. He's come to pick me up. Leave him be why don't yer."

The guy turned back to face Leanne, face contorted with anger.

"What did I tell you about fucking visitors?" he bawled, grabbing at her top with his heavily tattooed hands, his stubbled face inches from hers.

"Hey, soft lad," shouted Jack. "Take yer hands off."

The guy instantly released Leanne and lurched towards Jack.

Stacey found herself trapped between two angry young men. Her unwanted visitor, and her invited guest.

She held up her hands and used her considerable bulk to try and stop the former's progress down the hall.

"Come on Lenny," she soothed. "He's just our Lee's fella, that's all. He don't mean nothin.'"

"Yes, I fuckin' do," snapped Jack.

ROBERT WHITE

The face easily barged by Stacey, who, seeing her chance, ran to her son and pushed him into the lounge, out of harm's way. Lenny stopped a few feet away from Shenton, sensibly just out of punching range. He eyeballed Jack, head back, a sneer on his face. And that's when the young Scouser saw it. Lenny may have had his best hard man look on, but there was still that whiff of doubt in his eyes, that hint of hesitation. The nearly man, the almost there. Shenton had seen it dozens of times. It was normally in the ring, just after he'd landed his first few clean shots, hurting his opponent, sending him the mental and physical message as to how the contest would undoubtedly end. That said, it was clear to Jack that this guy was used to coming out on top in a physical challenge and wouldn't lie down easily. He'd met many a lad just like him, faces who always got their own way, just by flexing the odd muscle, just by being who they were, their rep as a bad boy carrying the weight, instilling the fear.

But not today.

Lenny cricked his neck, slipped off his hood, bared his teeth.

"So what's a fuckin scum bag Scouser like you, gonna do now then?"

It was the swiftest of movements. Stacey missed it completely, too worried about her child. Leanne just saw Jack's right shoulder dip slightly. She hadn't noticed the bend of the knees, or the subsequent upward movement where he used all his biggest muscle groups to deliver the right amount of kinetic energy and all his upper bodyweight to that single uppercut to his opponent's solar plexus.

Jack's trainer loved the shot. He always told him to imagine that his fist would punch straight through his foe and burst out of his back.

Lenny, the man in black, made a horrible groaning sound before he folded in half at the midriff. To be fair, he did his best to stay on his feet, taking two or three shuffling steps backwards, vainly attempting to retain his balance, but it was no use. He went down with a thud, gasping, unable to breathe. He felt like his throat had been cut. Bright stars formed in his vision as rivers of pain spread from his gut down to his balls.

Jack considered lifting him up and finishing the job with a right cross to his temple but decided that he may need Lenny conscious.

He watched, curious, calm, head to one side, as the face gulped in what air he could manage, doubled up on the floor, knees almost to his chin.

Shenton casually stepped over him and tapped an open mouthed Stacey on the shoulder.

Robert White

"I'd get a bucket if I was yous love. He's gonna be sick any second."

Moments later, Lenny proved Jack correct and threw his KFC into Stacey's washing up bowl.

Jack waited patiently until he'd finished retching.

"Now, listen to me soft lad," said Shenton, bending down and grabbing the face by his hoodie. "One chance, and one chance only. Your crew's business is done here, pack up and fuck off, d'ya hear me?"

"You're…fuckin'…dead," panted Lenny.

Jack shook his head ruefully and looked up into Leanne's pretty face.

"They never learn, this kind, eh?"

Leanne gave him a half smile. Half happy to see Lenny meet his match, the other half worried about the rest of the gang and what they may do to her and her family.

"Suppose not," she said quietly.

Jack shrugged.

"Do yer windows open up here?" he asked.

"Why?" said Leanne nervously.

Jack gestured towards the still gagging Lenny.

"Cos, I'm gonna dump him. Chuck him out."

Leanne went pale.

"What?"

Lenny, on hearing of his possible fate, was doing his best to get to his feet. Jack slapped him across his cheek so hard, both Stacey and Leanne winced. The would be gangster fell onto his back holding his face, checking his nose for blood and muttering threats.

Apparently, his pals knew where Jack lived and were going to kill him and his family several times over.

"Do they open wide like? Yer windows?" asked Jack again, unconcerned by Lenny's attempted intimidation. "Enough for me to just shove the prick out, like?"

Leanne was about to answer, but Lenny was now wide eyed and consumed by his own fear. He began to rummage in his pocket for his phone, found it, hit a speed dial contact and put the set to his ear. Jack stamped on the phone and Lenny's hand in one powerful move. There was a nasty cracking sound as both suffered shocking damage. Lenny screamed, gripping his ruined right with his good left.

"You fucker! You fucking Scouse cunt, you've bust me hand."

Jack hunkered down, got in close.

"Did yer think yous could fly with two good hands then? Was that it eh, soft lad? We're up nine floors. What d'ya reckon that is mate? A hundred feet? One twenty? I'd say closer to one twenty. No one could survive that eh? Not one twenty. You'd bust everythin' wouldn't yer? Yer neck, yer back, yer legs, yer skull."

Jack lifted his head and looked at Stacey and Leanne in turn.

"Go open yer biggest window, girls."

Lenny managed to sit up. He cradled his fractured hand and tried to move his fingers, then looked up into Jack's face, lip curled.

"You won't throw me out," he snorted. "That'd be murder."

"Not me first time, pal," said Jack grabbing Lenny by the scruff of the neck and dragging him along the hall towards the lounge. "You get used to it after the first couple."

At that, Lenny went into a panic mode. Any thoughts of besting his foe, long gone. He did his best to twist from Jack's grasp, but Shenton was way too strong, far too determined.

"No, no, please, no," Lenny whined as he was dragged along the floor. "Listen… mate. I'm sorry about yer bird and that. I didn't mean nothing by it. I just look after the plants and that eh? I've nothing to do with anythin' else. The others sort the kid's runs. Look, I could do you a deal eh? A few free ounce to sweeten all this."

Jack kicked over a table full of cannabis plants so he could reach the lounge window.

"Do I look poor to yous, soft lad. Do I look like I need charity?"

"He's got a brand new Range Rover outside," chirped Stacey, who now seemed to be enjoying watching Lenny squirm. "He's loaded. And don't fuckin' lie, yer twat. You send Billy out every night doing your dirty work. He's only fuckin' fourteen yer sad bastard."

Lenny gave Stacey a dark sideways glance.

"You'll get yours," he spat. "Our kid will see to you, yer slag."

"Enough of yer trash talk pal," said Jack lifting Lenny to his feet. "Yer going for a ride in the sky."

In that moment all the would be gangster's fear, all his pain, was suddenly washed away in a wave of self-preservation. He had to take his chance, had to fight back. He began by swinging his good left hand towards Jack's chin. Shenton simply rolled backwards, and the punch sailed harmlessly by. Lenny followed that with an attempted head butt, but that only served to put him completely off balance.

Jack had lost all patience and caught his opponent with a chopping left as he staggered forwards.

Lenny hit the deck with a slap, bleeding, semi-conscious and groaning.

As Shenton bent down to pick Lenny up again, he felt a gentle hand on his shoulder. It was Leanne.

"I think he's had enough, Mr... erm..."

"Oh, yeah sorry... Shenton," said Jack, slightly taken aback. "But I'd rather you called me, Jack."

"Jack it is then," smiled Leanne. "But..."

"Yes?"

"I'd rather you didn't kill Lenny. I mean, I agree that he's a repulsive nasty person and he's been really horrible to us, especially my brother, Billy, but he doesn't deserve to die, does he?"

Jack shrugged.

He'd never actually intended to throw the rancid waste of space out of the window, but he had planned to find out exactly where his pals were by frightening the living daylights out of him.

"Suppose not, but if he doesn't tell me what I need to know, I've no option, love."

Leanne knelt next to the moaning Lenny.

"Did you hear that, Lenny. I tried to save you."

The villain rolled on his back. He bled from a cut above his right eye, the left side of his face was red and swollen.

"Thanks for nothin'," he groaned. "And I thought he was yer fella. How come you didn't know his fuckin' name?"

"So," offered Leanne quietly, ignoring Lenny's question. "Never mind all that. Why don't you tell Jack here what he needs to know, then maybe you can go?"

"What about my weed?" croaked Lenny.

"That's mine. In lieu of my fee," said Jack. "Call it a special gift from you to me, like."

Lenny screwed up his face.

"You'll never get away with this, our kid will..."

"Kill me, yeah you said. So, I take it your brother runs the crew?" asked Jack.

"Yeah... and, so what?" said Lenny.

"Name?"

"Matty."

Jack looked at Leanne who nodded her agreement.

"And where is your Matty now, pal?"

Lenny rolled his eyes. Snorted a small laugh.

"You're makin' a big mistake."

"As you keep sayin'. So, tell me where I can find him, or I'm gonna upset this pretty lady and dump yer out the fuckin' window anyways."

"He'll be at the Edge," said Lenny quickly.

Jack looked at Leanne who had raised her eyebrows at his compliment.

"He means The Egerton Arms in town. He won't be on his own though, Matty I mean, there'll be at least another two with him." Leanne pulled a worried face. "He carries a knife too."

Jack nodded, eased his phone from his pocket and dialled.

"Hey, Jacko," said Des answering on the second ring. "How are ye getting on with our Magpie problem?"

"Cuckoo," corrected Jack.

"Aye that."

"Apparently, the main man behind the issue is called Matty, and he's currently drinking in a boozer called The Edgerton Arms in Stockport. He likes to carry a blade and he's a couple of faces with him, so it sounds like I might need that extra pair of hands you mentioned."

"Is that right?" said Des. "Well, funny you should mention it, but our glorious leader, Richard Edward Fuller has just walked in the door, piss wet through and all angry lookin'. Erm… just a mo. son."

Jack heard Rick in the background, asking Des about the job.

The Scot came back on the line.

"He wants a word, son."

FOUR

Galbally Security base, County Tyrone 16th February 1992

The patrol were flown from Hereford to Galbally in a civilian liveried Augusta Westland AW109. Although the aircraft looked inconspicuous enough, it was actually flown by 8 Flight ACC, the Joint Flight Special Forces Aviation Wing. The chopper was dual crewed, with both pilot and co-pilot wearing night vision goggles to allow the aircraft to cross the Province and drop its human cargo at the base in total blackout.

This tactic was of course designed to keep Fuller and his team safe, but it also meant that none of the four man patrol could see a thing once the chopper had crossed the Irish sea.

Bouncing around at a tad over one hundred and seventy miles an hour and at five hundred feet in pitch black was not a nice way to travel.

"I fucking hate those things," moaned Butch as he hopped from the craft. "I'd rather jump from a Herc any day of the week."

"And me," shouted Jimmy over the noise of the rotas.

"Come on ladies," bawled Rick. "If you get a shake on, we might have time for a brew before we set off."

The four men were instantly escorted to a small wooden cabin within the compound of the base, away from the general population, out of sight, out of harm's way. As they walked they drew the odd glance from some of the other squaddies prepping their vehicles for patrol, but if you worked in places like Galbally, you quickly learned not to ask too many questions, especially of four men dressed in jeans and leather jackets, armed to the teeth and carrying Bergens full of equipment.

The cabin itself looked like something left over from World War Two. Basic was an understatement, but it was warm and kept the team out of the wet weather. Security was everything in places like Galbally. After all, this was a UDR run base, and you never quite knew who was who. Spies were everywhere, even wearing UDR uniform.

Rick organised his patrol.

"Okay lads, lay all the kit out on these tables here. The last thing we'll need is a stoppage on this job, so, one final check of each weapon, load and tape all the spare 5.56 mags and check over the comms. There are extra batteries for all of you. Des, make sure the med pouches are as they should be, again there's one each, and I don't want any excuses on the body armour either. We all wear it, it's non-negotiable. I'll get a brew organised and find out where our transport is."

Des, Butch and Jimmy simply nodded. There were no questions to be asked. The job was on, and the adrenaline was already building. They knew why Rick was carping on about the armour too. With the ceramic plates front and back, it was heavy and cumbersome even on a short tab. Add to that, the fact was, unless you got shot chest or back dead centre, against a 7.62 round, it was about as much use as a chocolate fireguard. So, quite often, it got left behind.

But not on Rick's watch.

Twenty minutes later, Fuller was back with a pack of shitty vending machine plastic cups and a kettle full of water.

"Beggars and choosers," he said, ripping open the pack. Then, "Aww, fuck."

"What?" asked Des.

"They've given me veg soup," said Rick, shaking his head. "Probably some dickhead's idea of a joke."

"Warm and wet," offered Jimmy. "All that matters when it's pissing down."

And it was. The Irish weather had not disappointed. Lashing rain and a bitterly cold February wind battered the small cabin. Once the patrol had their ducks in a row and hit the road, it was going to be a long, cold, few hours.

Rick found a plug socket and got the kettle going. Minutes later the four men sat around a small wood burning stove sipping shockingly bad soup.

"I hear this crew are getting the chop," offered Des, frowning whilst poking the top of his soup with a finger.

Galbally was run by 6UDR, a battalion of the Ulster Defence Regiment. Approximately twenty of those soldiers manned the base and patrolled the area using FV603 Saracen armoured personnel carriers, but the word was, the politically divisive regiment was to be amalgamated with The Royal

Irish Rangers. There had been just too much criticism of the religious mix of volunteers and cadre troops over the years, allegations of sectarian killings, infiltration by the Provos, the list went on and on. Hence the need for the patrol's separation.

"Damned shame if you ask me," said Butch, securing his sidearm in his shoulder holster. "Lost a lot of good blokes this lot."

At that the portacabin door flew open and in stepped RSM Billy Loughran. He was a tall well built guy with a shock of curly red hair and rugged face that had, 'don't mess with me,' written all over it.

"Lads," he said, nodding at the patrol. "Who's in charge?"

Rick stood and acknowledged the man.

"Sar' Major."

Loughran held out a calloused hand.

"Good to have you on board, lads," he said in his thick Belfast brogue. "Your transport will be here at eight on the nose. You'll be split into two pairs and driven to your FOP in separate Q cars. Now, your drivers, the boys from 14 Int, are awfully jumpy at the moment, there's a shitload of actions going on and any new faces on the manor are getting the full once over from the Provos. Any car with three up draws too much attention round here, and we can't fuck this one up, so they'll want one of yees to lie across the back seat out of sight, with the other as the front passenger... okay?"

Rick nodded.

Loughran took a deep breath.

"Right, I'm sorry to have to do this te yees boys, but I have my orders from on high. De yees all have yer yellow cards?"

All members of the British Armed Forces carried a number of small information cards to assist in the execution of their duties in Northern Ireland. These were generally referred to by their colour. The most important of these was the Yellow Card, which contained the rules of engagement, the guidelines for opening fire on your enemy.

Loughran could tell from the four blank looks that the patrol did not. He fished in his uniform pocket and dropped four on the table.

"There yees go lads," he said.

Butch picked one up.

"I had one of these when I first came to this shithole. I wiped my arse with it."

"And I have a Lieutenant Colonel who gives me my orders, big lad," snapped Loughran. "And he said to give yees all a card. And now yees have one. Some of the upstairs bods are shitting bricks, see. With all these changes coming, all these enquiries, they think that these ops may come back and bite them in the arse further down the line, so… just take the fucking card and do as yees please with it, son. I've done my bit… okay."

"Fair enough, Sar' Major," said Rick, stepping in. "We've already had the hard word from our CO. We know the score."

"Aye, I'm sure," said Loughran quietly. "I feel a prick, so I do, but it's how it is right now. Times are changing."

"Aye, fer some they are," said Des, pushing his Browning into his belt. "It's fine fe the Provos te shoot our lads in the back, blow up his wife and kids, but we have to play the game because some Rupert is worried about his fucking knighthood. And I don't reckon the Tyrone Brigade will be shouting a warning to the poor bastards in Drum Manor tonight either, eh?"

Butch stood, opened the door of the wood burner and threw all four yellow cards into the flames. He turned and eyeballed Loughran.

"And neither will I," he snarled.

The RSM held Butch's gaze a while. He showed no fear.

"Get home safe, Trooper," he said and turned for the door.

Once the patrol were alone again, Rick sidled alongside Butch Stanley.

"No need for the theatrics," he hissed. "Next time, smile sweetly and say, yes sir, okay?"

As promised, at exactly 20.00hrs there was a knock on the portacabin door, and two scruffy looking blokes shuffled in. Both had long straggly hair and droopy moustaches, and much to Rick's annoyance, the darker one of the two was smoking.

They were dressed in what appeared to be the regulation jeans and leather bomber jackets and both were wearing shoulder holsters with Browning High Power handguns slipped inside.

"Alright lads," said the fairer guy in a thick Lancashire accent. "I'm Jerry, this is Mark. He's a Jock but don't let that put you off."

"Where ye fe?" asked Des instantly.

"Drumchapel," offered Mark taking a drag. "Yersel?"

"Other side of the river," said Des, feeling for his pipe after smelling the Det man's cigarette.

"Do you smoke in the car?" snarled Rick at the Scot.

Mark took a look at his fag, then eyed Fuller.

"If you're worried about your health, mate, you're in the wrong job."

Rick glared.

"If you smoke in the car, it's you who should be worried."

"Now, children," offered Des, standing and filling the bowl of his own pipe. "Live and let live, eh?" He turned to his fellow Scot. "Why don't we lepers take our filthy habit out into the rain?"

Once both men had stepped into the shocking weather, Rick turned his attention to the blond haired Det operative.

"I'll still be riding with you," he said. "Can't stand the smell of fags."

Jerry shrugged.

"Whatever you want mate," he said. "Let's get your kit stowed then."

The Det, or 14th Intelligence Detachment was a British Army special forces unit, established during the Troubles, which carried out surveillance operations in Northern Ireland.

The training of a Det operative covered all the competences required of an undercover operator.

Advanced high speed driving, surveillance, photography, planting eavesdropping devices, lock-picking and key-copying were all part of their daily routine.

The operators were of course trained to avoid direct contact with the enemy, however, should the worst happen, each man was highly skilled in close quarter combat and knew their way around a plethora of weaponry.

These boys were some of the bravest and craziest men on the island of Ireland and were not to be messed with.

The vehicles they used were known as Q Cars. These often battered motors may have looked like old, knackered Sierras and Cavaliers but they had covert radios, engine cut-off switches to prevent hijacking, anti-tamper devices and covert Kevlar armour plating.

Fuller stood in the rain and viewed the pale blue Cavalier that Jerry stood next to with some suspicion.

"That will get us there, I hope?"

"This girl is mechanically perfect mate," said the Det man, tapping the bonnet. "She may be a little rough around the edges, but she's saved my bacon a time or two."

Rick dropped all his and Des' kit into the boot.

"Let's get the Smoky Joes and fuck off then," he said.

With Rick and Des safely in his Cavalier, Jerry set off on the perilous journey to Granville. Butch and Jimmy were with Mark, just a couple of hundred yards behind.

Both the Det operatives were using covert comms and stayed in touch the whole time giving each other a constant running commentary, noting every vehicle and pedestrian they came across. The sheer depth of the local knowledge the guys possessed was staggering. That wisdom, that experience, kept them alive. After all, you did not want to be caught spying on the IRA, not if you liked your kneecaps.

Thirty minutes later, the four man patrol were all successfully dropped at their forward operating point, a quiet country lane just a little over two kilometres from St Jude's, the place where they would ambush the men of the East Tyrone Brigade.

They clambered a low fence and jogged a few yards away from the road in their civvies until darkness engulfed them. The ground was soddened and slippery underfoot and the wind swirled and howled around them splattering their faces with ice cold rain.

Once safely away from any ambient light, the team dropped their Bergens and began kitting up, helping each other pull on body armour and black waterproof coveralls, before sorting their weapons ammunition and medical pouches. Each man then checked his buddy over. No loose straps, no open zips, no chance of anything falling off or out. Finally they pulled on balaclavas and gloves, and they were ready to move.

"Okay listen up," said Rick, struggling to make himself heard against the shocking weather. "The Bergens stay here with our civvies. Obviously, the plan is for us all to leave the plot together, but if we get separated, this will be our RV. Once we have sight of St Jude's, I'll find a suitable spot to dig in… right, comms checks please."

Each man depressed their pressels and listened for the relevant clicks. There were thumbs up all round.

"Right, I'll take point," said Fuller. "Let's get this done and fuck off… On me, now."

At that, he turned and tabbed out into the darkness with his patrol behind him.

It was a short march, but the wet ground and shocking weather slowed the unit and by the time they had eyes on the car park of St Jude's, it was 2117hrs.

Rick hunkered down behind an old stone trough some two hundred yards from the car park. It gave him and his team some modicum of shelter from the incessant wind and rain and kept them out of sight should the getaway cars pull in and swing their headlights across the field any time soon.

"Okay," he barked. "Des, I need you to tab around those trees to our left and get yourself over to the cemetery and tucked in. We're expecting the two single crewed getaway cars to be first here. Unless we get pinged by either of them, we let them be and wait for the rest of the crew to arrive. Butch, as soon as we have all the players on the car park, you let go with the flare and light 'em up. I will then shout the challenge…"

"What?" snapped Butch. "You'll be tellin' us to fire single shots next."

The yellow cards that Butch had so dramatically thrown into the fire back at the base, listed a series of rules for the holder. 'No live rounds to be carried in the breech. Working parts kept forward. Fire only aimed shots. Fire no more rounds than is necessary.' The list and rules went on.

"As soon as that flare goes up, them boys will start shooting and you know it, Rick," said Des. "It'll be carnage and we could end up on the back foot."

Jimmy nodded. "It'll be the fuckin' OK, OK Corral."

Rick pointed at each of his men in turn. He didn't like the idea of a challenge any more than the next man, But he had to follow his instructions. It was just the way it was.

"And we have our orders," he snapped. "We give them their opportunity to surrender. If they choose not to take it, then it's on them."

Fuller could see that no one was happy with the decision, but it wasn't theirs to make, it was his.

"Go on, Des," he said. "Get yourself in position and give me a comms check once you're bedded in."

The Scot sloped silently off, head down into the darkness.

"Right lads," said Fuller. "We're late to the party, get in your positions. Stay sharp, and like I said, you wait for my challenge or the first contact."

Butch made a show of racking his M16, dropping a round into the breech and checking his safety.

Rick ignored his defiance and made a beeline for a clump of mature trees that bordered the car park.

From now on, it was a waiting game.

Just before ten, the two getaway drivers rolled in. One drove a white VW Golf, the other a dark coloured Saab. The pair seemed extremely relaxed, stepping outside of their cars and huddling together under the canopy of the church's entrance for a smoke or two.

The intel stated that the attack on the RUC base at Drum Manor would take place at 22.00hrs, therefore the East Tyrone Brigade should arrive back at St Jude's by 22.30 at the latest.

Fuller checked his watch.

They were late.

Just as he was feeling a sense of unease, Rick heard them. In fact the whole village must have been able to hear their approach. Whoever was on the top of the lorry was still firing the DSHK into the air whilst his mates were cheering him on. The fact that those falling rounds could easily kill some poor bastard walking home from the pub, didn't appear to have entered these guys' heads.

Moments later a brown Escort screeched into the car park, closely followed by an eighteen ton tipper lorry. Rick could just about make out two men standing in the tip box at the back of the cab. One gripping the heavy machine gun that was mounted on the roof, the other fervently waving the Tri Colour in one hand and gripping an AKM rifle in the other.

Butch opened his mic.

"They think it's a fuckin' party."

"Standby," hissed Rick.

The driver of the lorry dropped from his cab, then clambered upwards into the tipper's rear box to help the other two to unbolt the DSHK from the roof. Rick watched as three other men exited the Escort. Even in the poor light, he could see that all were carrying automatic weapons.

The weirdest thing was none appeared to be in any rush. The three boys from the Escort ambled over to the two getaway drivers, seemingly oblivious to any danger, or the shocking weather for that matter. They did some congratulatory back slapping whilst calmly waiting for the three on the wagon to disassemble the heavy gun.

"Standby, standby, standby... light them up," announced Rick, bringing his own M16 up into the aim.

Butch pointed the Very pistol upwards and pulled the trigger sending the twelve gauge white flare high into the rain filled sky. He pushed the gun back into his coveralls, brought up his weapon and clicked off the safety.

In an instant the carpark and all its occupants were lit up like the proverbial Christmas tree, and the Provos went from calm and casual to full on headless chicken. One heavy set guy began barking orders at the three men lifting the machine gun from the roof of the wagon.

Fuller stayed in cover but bawled "Army... Stop or I fire."

The guy that had been waving the flag, instantly turned towards Rick's position and opened up with his AKM on fully auto. Fuller threw himself to the ground as rounds cut through the undergrowth and slammed into the mature trees that surrounded him.

The remainder of the SAS patrol didn't need any further orders.

From his position in the graveyard, Des had a perfect sight picture of the flag waver on the wagon and cut him down with a single shot. His two pals instantly dropped down, out of sight, protected by the high sided tipper box, before popping up with their weapons in the aim and firing short bursts into the tree line.

Butch went for the three men from the Escort who had hunkered down behind the old car. He'd selected semi auto mode and began peppering their positions with short bursts.

Jimmy Two Times turned his attention to the getaway cars. Small arms fire had been coming from inside the Saab, but the driver's aim was wayward, and his rounds had flown harmlessly above Smith's head.

Ignoring the Yellow Card's orders, Jimmy set his weapon to fully automatic and instantly turned the Swedish saloon into something that resembled a cheese grater. Moments later, the driver lolled from his shattered window, blood pouring from a headwound, pistol still dangling from his trigger finger.

The two remaining players on the truck were having some success. Being in good solid cover and able to pop up from any angle, they were keeping Des and Rick busy. That was until one decided to turn and fire towards Butch. The rash move put him side on to Fuller, his silhouette caught in the dying embers of the flare.

Rick couldn't miss.

He caught the guy around the temple, the round exiting his skull, splattering blood and bone into the air. The player's legs buckled, and he disappeared into the box of the tipper.

For some inexplicable reason, the third guy in the wagon then decided to go for broke. He stood up in plain sight, face contorted in rage, raking the graveyard and trees, his AKM spewing white hot 7.62 in all directions. Des fired another single round, and the shooter met his fate.

Rick got on comms.

"Butch, what we got left?"

With the flare's artificial light all but gone, it was getting harder to spot the enemy by the second. Rick considered ordering Butch to send up a second round, but with the advantage of surprise gone, all that would do would light up his own patrol as well as the Provos.

"Deffo two behind the Escort, and I think we still have the Golf driver somewhere," shouted Butch over the racket of the Irish fire.

Rick kept low and began to edge closer to Butch's position. He knew he needed to get eyes on the men in cover behind the Ford to finish this thing. Seconds later, he was almost within touching distance of Dave Stanley. Butch nodded to his patrol leader, then pointed towards the Escort.

With the flare now completely burnt out, and nothing more than the dim streetlamps dotted around the church for light, it was a big ask to spot their prey until they fired.

One positive was that the boys had kept on doing just that, and that gave Fuller and Butch a chance. Using the Provo's muzzle flashes to note their positions, Fuller dropped into the kneel and formed his sight picture. He waited as Jimmy and Butch began laying down so many rounds, the boys huddled behind the car couldn't get their heads up. Rick could just see the shapes of the men cowered in the dark, trying their best to stay alive. He squeezed the trigger, took four single aimed shots and all movement behind the car stopped.

Rick got on comms. "Anyone see anything?"

"Looks clear," said Butch.

"What about the Golf driver?" asked Des

"Think he's down," offered Butch.

Fuller was just about to stand, when he heard a long burst from an AK off to his right.

His comms crackled.

"I'm hit, I'm hit," shouted Jimmy.

Butch, being the closest to his wounded comrade sprinted over to his position. He opened his mic as he ran.

"Man down," he shouted as he reached the scene. "Repeat... we have a man down."

Butch fell to his knees and ripped open Jimmy's med pack. Smith was lying on his back in the mud. Blood poured from a wound just above his collarbone. Most bullets would have done minimal damage, but the hi velocity round fired from the AKM had caused considerable trauma on exit. Jimmy was bleeding badly. Butch found a battle dressing and applied pressure to both sides of the wound. He looked over his shoulder and peered back towards the car park.

"Where is that fucker?" he hissed to himself.

The shooter, the man in question, was up and running. He burst through the trees just to Fuller's right and raced off into the fields, throwing his AKM to the floor as he did so. He then sprinted off exactly the same way the patrol had tabbed in. Rick swung his M16 around his back, drew his Sig and set off after the boy.

The bitterly cold rain drove into Fuller's face, peppering his eyes, making it almost impossible to see. Worse still, the ground underfoot was lethal. Fuller made ten yards before losing his footing and falling heavily. He cracked his left knee on something hard as he fell, sending jolts of pain up his leg. Pulling himself to his feet, Rick set off again, hobbling for the first few yards. He couldn't see his prey, but despite the wind and rain, was sure he could hear him up ahead.

Seconds later, his gut feeling was confirmed. The Provo had obviously suffered a similar fate to himself and fallen in the slippery conditions. Rick heard him grunt and curse. He must have been just yards in front, but Fuller still couldn't see him.

Rick dug in, powering himself forwards with all he had. Despite the cold, he was sweating inside his balaclava, and he felt beads running down the back of his neck. He peered into the murk and was sure he could just make out the man's outline as he too ploughed on through the mud.

Rick was gaining, less that ten yards from his man, but he fell again. This time he tripped, and his forward momentum slammed him into the ground face first, cracking his head close to his temple. Stars flickered in his peripheral vision and blood poured from a cut above his right eye. Fuller wiped it away, roared with rage and frustration and bawled at the man ahead.

"Army... stop or I'll shoot."

But the man didn't stop, he just put more distance between them.

Rick set off again, but the ground was getting worse. Deeper, water filled channels and divots made progress slow, and he found himself on his backside almost as often as he was on his feet. Yet Fuller would not give up. He was drenched and covered in mud, his right eye was closing, and his hands and feet were numb with cold, but he powered on.

Moments later, he could just make out the dim lights from the lane where the Det boys had dropped the patrol off. He was very close to the team's chosen RV.

He was also close to his man.

The guy was hobbling towards the road, just yards from Fuller. Rick finally had eyes on his target, but the Gods were once again against him. The wind picked up again, and the rain turned from heavy to torrential in a matter of seconds. It came in sheets, the sheer volume of water once again cloaking his enemy.

"Stop," he bawled. "Stop or I'll shoot."

But shoot at what?

Rick's legs ached, his boots were caked in mud, and they weighed twice what they should, yet he drove on, forcing himself forwards, lungs burning. Then, just as he thought he had no more to give, he came upon his foe.

The man was just yards from the lane, bent over, hands on knees, rain dripping from his hair and nose, his hot breath pouring out in plumes of white. He was no more than a silhouette, but it was him.

Fuller stopped, steadied himself and pointed his weapon.

"British army," he shouted. "You are under arrest."

The guy slowly straightened himself and looked up, eyes locked on his foe.

He smiled.

"Fuck you," he spat, and pushed his hand inside his jacket.

Rick fired twice, a double tap to the man's chest. The Irishman fell backwards, legs twitching.

Fuller hobbled over, keeping the man covered, but there was no need.

The Provo was dead.

Fuller grabbed at the Irishman's right hand which was still inside his jacket and pulled it free. He expected to find a sidearm, a revolver, an SLP, but there was none. Instead, he found a photograph, a small square picture. He pulled it free from the man's palm and turned it towards the dim light that emanated from the nearby lane. Rick wiped his eyes, then the picture and felt his stomach lurch. It showed a woman, a dark haired pretty young thing, a woman… and a child, a girl, maybe five or six years old.

Rick gritted his teeth, grabbed the dead man by his jacket and shook him.

"Why?" he screamed. "You fucking fool… why?"

Fuller released the man, stood and pulled off his balaclava. His whole body shaking.

"Trooper!"

A man was clambering over the small fence that separated the road from the field.

"Rick squinted into the half-light; rain dripping from his nose and chin. He raised his weapon.

"Identify yourself."

The guy raised his hands but kept walking.

"It's me, Jerry."

It was the Det guy who had driven Rick and Des to the FOP. He looked down at the dead Provo, then into Fuller's face."

"He went to pull something from his jacket," shouted Rick against the howling wind. "I gave him the challenge."

Jerry turned down the corners of his mouth.

"He's no weapon then?"

Rick shook his head.

"He shot Jimmy then ran. I figured that…"

Jerry turned and jogged back to his car. He rummaged in the boot a moment then returned holding a plastic carrier. The Det guy then knelt by the Provo, removed a pistol from the bag and placed it in the dead man's hand.

Jerry stood and gave Fuller a look he couldn't read.

"All's fair in love and war, pal," he said.

Des and Butch got Jimmy back to the RV, and he was airlifted to hospital. He'd lost a lot of blood, but the prognosis was good. He'd actually been shot twice but the ceramic plate in his body armour had prevented a direct hit to his chest. Luck and Fuller's insistence saving his life.

The remaining three members of the patrol were back in Hereford exactly as their CO had said, in time for breakfast next morning, but Fuller couldn't bring himself to eat.

The debrief was completed that afternoon. Eight Irishmen were dead, and no one questioned any actions from the patrol. Lt Col Holmes was delighted.

Fuller never talked about the man with the photograph. Jerry, if that was even his real name, remained in the Province to continue his tour with the Det.

He was never even interviewed.

ROBERT WHITE

FIVE

Manchester, Piccadilly

Des had done his best to keep a careful yet troubled eye on his longest and dearest friend of late. After Lauren's murder, he'd once again seen Rick in his darkest moments. It had been Cathy all over again. Yet, since his return from Thailand, he had watched Fuller try and rebuild his life, rise from the depths, the only way he knew how. More recently, he'd marvelled at Rick's resilience, astonished at the way he'd thrown himself back into a world they both knew so well, a world of espionage, a world of cloaked figures living in secrecy, figures living on the edge.

And then, of course there had been their wee agency.

Since its inception, Fuller had appeared fine, putting all his time and energy into their little venture, even coaching young Jack along, spending hours over in the lock up, teaching him the intricacies of the many weapons the team had at their disposal. They'd talked tactics, and unusually for Rick, he'd even recounted some old missions, telling his tales of daring, as the young Liverpudlian had listened on in awe.

Much to Cogan's surprise, Rick had even struck up a relationship with Rose. A relationship that appeared, at least on the surface, to be progressing well.

So, in the main, on the surface, Fuller had seemed... okay.

But Des knew better.

Since Rick had learned of Larry Simpson's release, he'd begun to see another far more troubling change in his friend, a shift that worried the Scot, kept him awake at night.

Any man, no matter how strong mentally or physically, has a breaking point, a cliff edge moment. Sometimes, if he is lucky, he can be brought back from that precipice, and learn to live again. Once maybe, but twice? Add into that mix the fact that the person at the centre of his pain was now strolling around the city a free man, well, there was little surprise that Fuller was slowly becoming a ticking timebomb. The gradual drip, drip of revenge filling his gut with hate. And that hatred was beginning to bubble up, to rise to the surface of his daily life. Rick was morphing backwards. Back to the man Des had known in the days when he'd first lost Cathy. Cold, unfeeling, dangerous.

Cogan knew Fuller had been to visit Lauren's grave, and in some ways he was grateful for that. He'd hope he may find some closure, some solace there. But the days in the run up to the anniversary of her murder had been difficult to say the least. Rick had found the bottle again, drinking himself into oblivion most nights, snapping and snarling his way through each day. That, of course was to be expected. But he also knew that during those alcohol fuelled nights, Fuller had begun to seek Larry Simpson out. Rick now knew where the ex-detective lived and where he worked, and Cogan was also aware, that in those last, awful, brutal, nineteen days before his trip to Leeds, Rick had been spending more and more of his time watching Simpson. Watching and ...planning.

Fuller had walked into the office, just as Jack had called to say he needed a helping hand with a little job he'd taken on over in Stockport.

It wasn't a big deal, just a set of teenage drug dealers who needed to know where they stood. A frighteners job. Read the little angels their horoscope, tax some of their ill gotten gains and Bob was your Auntie's brother.

But because Jack had taken Rick's Range Rover, the big fella had been forced to walk from Piccadilly station and had been caught in the shocking Manchester weather. His suit jacket was soaked, and his dander was well and truly up.

He'd grabbed the phone from Des and asked Jack about CCTV on the pub car park, as well as the internal layout of the gaff. He was sharp and angry. Angry in a way that Des hadn't seen since those days in oh six when Fuller had worked as Joel Davis' enforcer. One of Manchester's biggest drug dealers, Davis was an evil, vicious bastard who drew everyone in his echelon down to his level, including Rick. Des had hoped those days were long gone, but no, Fuller's heart was darkening with every passing day and Cogan felt powerless to do anything about it.

He had insisted they swing by the lock up, where Rick had changed out of his wet clothes, dumping his new Savile Row number and pulling on jeans, sweatshirt and his trusty leather.

Of more concern to Cogan, was that in addition to collecting Des' Discovery, he'd also pulled three Sig P229's from his gun cabinet. Des knew Rick had seen his armourer lately and he'd had each of the weapons re-chambered to take the more powerful .40 Smith and Wesson cartridge. The same rimless round used by the FBI.

Rick had pushed one of the SLP's into his belt and dropped a second in the Scot's lap as he'd driven his Land Rover towards the plot, a town centre boozer in Stockport, The Edgerton Arms. The third Sig, he'd kept in a black cloth sack, alongside a few other trinkets Des hadn't seen him pack.

"About time these fuckers learned a lesson," he'd growled. Eyes wild, teeth clenched.

As Des parked the Land Rover across the road from the boozer, he saw Jack sheltering from the rain, huddled in the entrance, top zipped to the neck, hands in pockets. Standing with him, was a pretty blonde.

The young boxer clocked the car immediately. He grabbed the girl by the hand and they both ran to the Discovery and jumped into the back seat.

"Thanks for this, Mr Fuller... and yous, Des," said Jack. "This is Leanne, she's Billy's older sister, the lad who this crew have been using to move gear around the last six months."

Rick turned in his seat and eyed the girl.

"And what's your relationship with this lot then?"

Leanne was taken aback slightly.

"I don't have any relationship with them," she said, a hint of resentment in her tone.

Rick wasn't convinced.

"You're telling me you don't know 'em?"

"Of course I know them. Everyone round our way knows them. But it was our Billy they picked on."

"He's special needs," butted Jack. "They've got him running County Lines, and now they've a crop growing in the flat. It's shockin'. There's a baby in the gaff. They're fuckin' animals."

"And they're inside the pub, now?" asked Rick flatly.

Leanne nodded.

"Matty, he runs the crew. He's wearing a black Nike baseball cap."

"There's a surprise," snapped Fuller. "And who's he with?"

"A lad called Mikey, real nasty bastard he is, fair hair, big guy, likes the gym, and another lad, tall, wiry. I don't know his name, he's new on me, but they're all together. They're playing pool in the back room."

Rick nodded, pulled the final Sig P229 from the cloth sack and tossed it to Jack. The Scouser caught it, checked it over, and pushed it in the back of his waistband.

Leanne was wide eyed.

"Jesus Christ, you're not going to shoot them, are you? I mean, they're bad lads, but…"

Rick turned again, eyes flat, fish-like. All in the car could feel his anger. All in the car could see his rage, but only Cogan knew what was really hurting him, what was tearing him apart inside.

Fuller pulled his face into a sneer.

"What do you expect us to do, love? Ask them nicely not to bother you anymore? Ask their mother to ground them? Take their fuckin' X Box away for a week? You couldn't or wouldn't go to the cops, so you came to us. When you did that, you knew what you were getting, so… you want us to help, or not?"

Leanne looked across to Jack for some kind of support, but Shenton was stony faced. He shrugged.

"Mr Fuller's the boss. He knows how best to handle these things."

Leanne turned again.

"I just want our Billy safe and away from these animals. And yes, of course we want them out of our lives. But not dead. That's not what any of us want."

Rick nodded.

"I'll see what I can do… You sure there's no CCTV in the carpark, Jacko?"

"Deffo Mr Fuller. The bar's camera'd up, but nothin' past the entrance door."

Rick gave Cogan a nudge.

"Come on Desmond, swing this heap into the car park. It's showtime."

He turned back to Leanne, eyes as dark as wet black marbles. "You stay in here and don't get out, no matter what, okay?"

"Okay," she said, lips trembling.

The three men stepped from the car and walked towards the rear of the pub away from prying eyes. Rick striding out in front.

Des caught up with him in a vain attempt to calm the situation.

"Bit heavy handed this, eh pal?"

Rick didn't even turn or break stride.

"If you're getting squeamish in your old age, you can stay in the car. All girls together," he spat.

Jack shot Des a glance. The Scot gave him a reassuring wink.

Once they were behind the building, safely out of sight of passing pedestrians, Rick opened the black sack again and pulled out three balaclavas, three pairs of leather gloves and three sets of cable ties.

"Right," he said handing out the goodies. "Which one carries the knife?"

"Matty," offered Jack. "But that don't mean…"

"I say we presume they're all carrying," said Des.

"Exactly," said Fuller, "But it's good to know anyway. Right, we take all three down at gunpoint, get them secured against a wall and shitting it, then let me do the talking. This is a two minute operation. Maximum aggression."

He peered around the edge of the building a moment holding up a hand to indicate the team to wait.

Rick lingered, scanning the area again until a couple of guys that had just left the pub jogged across the road towards a kebab shop. They didn't turn or even notice the team.

"Come on," said Fuller. "No time like the present."

Matty and Mikey were playing pool. The third face, the one Leanne described as wiry, a lad called Pete was leaning against the bar watching proceedings. Pete was new to the crew. He'd just done a two stretch for armed robbery and was still finding his feet with Matty and the boys. That said, he liked his new job, enjoyed taxing the runners, seeing the kids squirm. It was just his cup of tea. They'd been in the pub for almost three hours and had the tap room to themselves as none of the regulars wanted to be in there. Not with Matty and his crew on the piss.

Too volatile, too treacherous.

Pete turned and waved his pint pot towards a flustered barmaid. She was working alone and was doing her best to serve in the main bar and keep Matty and his minions happy in the smaller back room.

"Fuck's sake," shouted Pete. "What's it take to get a fuckin' drink in this shithole."

"I'm just serving this gent," countered the young woman. "And I'll be with you."

Mikey, lay down his cue and joined Pete. He was a big unit, hitting the gym hard each day, a permanently furious, belligerent lad, full to the brim with testosterone that he injected before each training session.

"Fuck him, you stupid cow," he bawled, leaning over the bar. "We want serving. The old cunt can wait."

The elderly customer gave Mikey a withering look from a safe distance, then turned his attention to the barmaid.

"Best you serve him first, love. I'm in no rush."

As it turned out, there would be no more beer of any kind served in The Edgerton Arms that evening.

Fuller, Cogan and Shenton barrelled into the pub through the front door, weapons in the aim, cable ties looped around their left wrists, hands and faces covered.

"Down on the floor," bawled Rick at the smattering of customers as he strode through the main bar. "Don't look at me, look away. Do it now."

The dozen or so regulars didn't need telling twice. They either remained glued to their seats with fear or began to lie face down on the ever so sticky carpet. Either way, they all found something of interest to cast their eyes on, other than the three armed men striding towards the back bar.

Fuller was first into the tap room. He went straight for Matty, the boy in the black cap. The face saw Fuller coming for him and instinctively raised his pool cue in a vain attempt to defend himself. Rick simply batted it away and pistol whipped the boy across his cheek. Rick followed that with a boot to the boy's knee and Matty went down.

Jack made a beeline for Mikey, whose bravado had instantly left him. He pressed himself against the bar, hands raised faster than a Highbury linesman. Jack cuffed him with a sharp left hook. Mikey wobbled as Shenton grabbed him by the back of his neck and pushed him to his knees, SLP rammed into his temple.

"Hands behind your back. Do it dick head. Do it now or you're dead," shouted the Scouser.

Des simply pushed his Sig under Pete's chin and glared at him through the slit in his balaclava.

"Get on your knees son. And dinnea even think about being a brave boy. It's not yer day."

Within fifteen seconds the team had Matty, Mikey and Pete cuffed and in a kneeling stress position, facing the tap room wall.

Jack did a quick pat down of the boys and recovered a blade each from Matty and Mikey and two wallets with ID's including addresses. He threw them onto the pool table and stepped away.

This was Fuller's arena.

Rick got in close to Matty, his mouth almost touching the gangster's ear.

"97 Pendlebury Towers… know it?" he hissed.

"Fuck you," snapped Matty, doing his best to keep his cred in front of his crew.

Rick made a tutting sound, casually pushed his Sig into his jeans, picked up the white ball from the table, pulled back Matty's head and slammed it into his face. The first blow destroyed the boy's nose, the second caught his right eye socket and the third his top lip. The wall in front of the kid was instantly splattered with claret. Matty keeled over backwards, his nose ruined, top lip split open, front tooth missing. He was lying awkwardly on his back, spitting blood and groaning. Rick calmly lifted him back into his stress position, the boy barely managing to stay upright, rocking from side to side.

"You fall over again, and I'll put a bullet in your head," said Rick casually.

Next came Mikey.

Rick slowly wiped the blood from the pool ball onto the boy's tracksuit top.

"Now, I'll ask again… 97 Pendlebury Towers," he said.

Mikey was nodding rapidly, he didn't fancy the same treatment.

"Yeah… yeah I know it."

Rick sniffed, walked to the new boy, Pete.

"What about you son?"

Pete's eyes were wild. He shook violently, his lips trembled.

"Ye…yeah."

Fuller turned his attention back to Matty.

"So, just to get this straight in my head, you know fuck all then? You've never even been to 97 Pendlebury Towers, never preyed on a decent family, never forced a fourteen year old special needs kid to move your shit? And of course, you know fuck all about growing a crop of weed in a baby's bedroom.

Cogan leaned into Matty's other ear.

"Fuck me, pal," he snarled. "If you dinnea shoot this lying fucker, I will."

"Okay, okay, fuck's sake," said Matty, lips swelling by the second. "What about it? What d'ya want?"

Fuller grabbed Matty's collar, lip curled under his mask.

"Simple, I want you to find your own place to do your dirty work. I want you leave the good people of number 97 alone, sonny. Leave them be, or terrible things will happen to you and yours." He gestured towards Matty's wallet lying on the pool table next to his knife. "Looks like we even have your address. How fucking convenient."

"What about me weed?" whined Matty.

Jack stepped in, pushed his Sig into Matty's neck and pulled back the hammer.

"I've taxed it, soft lad. You got a problem with that?"

Matty shook his head.

"What? Eh, erm no, suppose not, fuck's sake, no."

Two minutes and eleven seconds after entering the pub, Des was behind the wheel of his Discovery, pipe dangling from the corner of his mouth. Rick was in a taxi with his black sack full of goodies, and Jack and Leanne were ordering kebabs, directly across the road from the Edgerton.

Once they had their food, they stood together under the shop canopy and watched events unfold. Within minutes, all the customers, including the three faces, had exited the pub. It was almost comical to watch the three dealers running away, hands still tied behind their backs, Matty so disorientated, that he zig zagged along, bumping into his pals every few yards.

The barmaid stood defiantly in the doorway, and shouted abuse at the three as they staggered away, pale and shaken.

It was a full fifteen minutes before the cops arrived.

Bizarrely, no one had seen a thing.

Leanne bit into her kebab and looked up into Shenton's face.

"Is it over?"

"I reckon," he said.

"I'm glad you didn't shoot them."

"We just shit 'em up a bit, is all."

"Right," said Leanne. "What about all that weed, can we chuck it?"

"An old mate of mine from Crocky will collect it all tonight. He'll take everything, the crop, the lamps, the trays, the pumps, the lot."

"I don't know how to thank you, Jack."

Shenton smiled.

"Oh I can think of a few ways," he said.

ROBERT WHITE

SIX

Des had returned home without incident. He'd showered and changed and was ready for some refreshment. With that in mind, he'd called Rick… three times. On each occasion, his phone had gone straight to voicemail.

"Suit yersel," muttered the Scot, dropping his phone onto his kitchen worktop. "I'll go fer a pint on my own then."

He walked into his lounge and looked across to Bruce, his young collie. The dog had clambered onto Cogan's favourite armchair and was watching him intently, head cocked, one comical lopsided ear at a jaunty angle.

"I dinnea suppose ye'd like te come then?" said Cogan.

Bruce jumped down, tail wagging furiously. He trotted over, nuzzled Cogan's hand and gave his fingers a lick.

"I'll take that as a yes then," said Des. "I'll get yer lead, son."

Cogan had recently bought the three bedroom apartment in Little Bollington Mill, Dunham Massey. The renovated buildings offered executive living, good parking and it was an easy commute into the team's offices. It had cost him a pretty penny, but he liked the peace and quiet and the fact that it was surrounded by acres of National Trust parkland. He'd figured that he may as well put some roots down in Manchester, after all, there was nothing to keep him north of the border these days. Grace seemed happy with her new man, and Kaya was doing just fine. That, and as they say, you can't take it with you.

Within walking distance of the old mill, was The Swan with Two Nicks, a lovely country pub that welcomed dogs as much as their human counterparts. The landlord knew how to keep his beer, the food was excellent, and the locals always made a fuss of Bruce. What more could a man want?

Des pulled on his Barbour coat and a thin woollen hat. Although the rain had stopped, the sky still threatened more, and he'd been wet enough times in his life.

"Come on, son," he said to an ecstatic Bruce as the pair headed off for some much needed solace.

The Swan with Two Nicks, was a beautiful old building with roaring fires, and as he and Bruce strolled into the car park, Cogan was already looking forward to sitting close to one of them with a pint or two of Guinness.

As the Scot approached the front door, he noticed a woman standing next to a classic BMW 2002, hands on hips, shaking her head.

As Des got closer, he considered that the woman was just as attractive as the powder blue car, and around the same age.

"Everything okay there, hen?" he asked.

The woman turned and confirmed Cogan's appraisal of her. She was indeed remarkably handsome. He put her in her mid to late forties, petite all round with a shock of auburn hair that framed a pale, pretty face.

She eyed Cogan with a little suspicion, then appeared to decide he wasn't dangerous and gave him a weak smile.

"Oh, I'm a damned fool," she said. "These old cars, it's so easy to do."

"Do what?" asked Cogan.

"I've locked my keys inside," she said, pulling her phone from her bag. "I can ring my son, I suppose. He'll bring down the spares."

Des cocked his head.

"Is he close by? I mean, if no, then I could probably get into it for ye."

She raised her brows.

"Really? What, without any damage? I mean, I don't wish to be ungrateful or anything, but I am rather fond of the old car, and I've just spent a small fortune on the paintwork. I'd happily ask William, my son, but he is all the way over in Salford Quays, and it would be a real pain for him to drive here this time of evening."

"Ne bother," said Des. "I willnea even make a mark, I promise. So if ye just hold Bruce here a second, I'll need to nip inside and get a wee something first."

"Erm, oh, okay," said the woman taking the collie's lead and giving his ear a scratch.

Des strolled to the bar and asked the landlord for a length of packing tape from his bins. The guy gave Des a puzzled look but returned moments later with a length of the thin plastic binding.

ROBERT WHITE

"Cheers, Gus," smiled Des. "I'll be back in a jiffy fer a pint or three."

Moments later, Des had returned to the stricken beauty. The woman watched inquisitively as he bent the tape in two then pushed it between the old German car's door pillar and door seal. With a quick giggle, the Scot had the tape over the car's locking button and seconds later, the door was open.

"Ta Da!" Des said.

"Oh wow, thank you so much," said the woman. She gave the Scot a sideways glance. "I'll not ask how you knew how to do that."

Cogan smiled.

"A mixture of a misspent youth and the British Army, hen," he said.

She handed Bruce back and opened her bag.

"You must let me give you something."

"You will not," said Cogan sharply. "And I'd be offended if ye tried."

"Oh, well, if you insist."

Des clocked her left hand. No rings.

"Ye could buy me a pint though," he asked hopefully.

The woman pulled a face.

"Aww, I'm sorry. With all this key nonsense, I'm running late for my class. I have to be at the village hall in ten minutes."

"Ne bother," said Des, slightly deflated.

The woman was about to drop into the driver's seat, but stopped and turned to the Scot.

"But if you're staying for a while?"

"Aye?"

She gave him a smile.

"Well, I could come back… say an hour or so."

Des caught the woman's eye.

"That would be grand," he said.

"Yes… grand," she mimicked, sliding into her seat.

As Des turned to go inside, the woman wound down her window.

"It's Shona, by the way. "Shona Mackintosh."

"Cogan," said Des. "Des Cogan."

"See you later Des Cogan," she said starting the car.

The Scot gripped Bruce's lead and led him into the bar. He gave the collie a stroke.

"No bad, eh? No bad at all."

***

Fuller sat hunched down in the driver's seat of his Range Rover. The weather had once again turned bleak, and heavy rain ran in streams down the windows. He was cold, his back ached and his left foot was going numb. All this watching and waiting was taking its toll on his ageing bones.

Waiting for him… Larry Simpson, to leave his house and… well, Fuller wasn't quite sure what else.

He'd never been a great fan of surveillance. That had always been Des' forte. He was the patient one, the guy who didn't mind lying in a freezing ditch for days on end. Whereas Fuller was a get it done kind of guy.

Maybe that's just what he should do.

Get it done.

He'd spent many hours mulling over exactly how that should happen. Hours focusing his anger, directing his hatred towards one individual. Feeding the flames of his yearning for reprisal.

Because it wasn't exactly revenge he craved. No matter what Rose may think, or the old boy at the cemetery. No, it was justice. An eye for an eye, tooth for a tooth.

But he had to consider that Simpson was smart, forensically savvy. He'd seen to the demise of many a villain in his time, knew all the tricks of the trade, but more importantly, he knew Rick… very well. DCI Larry Simpson had been desperate to get at Fuller for years, ever since he'd worked for Joel Davies. The bad old days. Before Lauren. He'd even tried to use *her* to get to him. So this would not be easy. Simpson would smell a rat a thousand yards away and slip any trap with the smallest of holes.

Yet somehow, Rick would have his day. All it would take was the right plan, Simpson would die, Fuller could walk away clean, and then just let them prove it was him, just let them.

But what could that plan be? A sniper's bullet?

No, that was too remote, too neat, too sanitised. Any sniper worth his salt will tell you that he is the only soldier in the British Army that truly sees his kill up close, sees the whites of his enemies eyes, sees the damage his round causes. But looking through a scope from hundreds of yards away just wouldn't cut it for Fuller.

In recent days, Rick had even considered taking Simpson on the street, binding him, gagging him, throwing him into a stinking van, then dealing with him at his leisure in some God forsaken backwoods hovel, before dumping his corpse in a hole where he'd never be found.

But Fuller wanted him found. Wanted it known that justice had been served at last. Wanted everyone to know he had taken his retribution.

So that plan just didn't hack it either. Just like the long range sniper's bullet.

It didn't work because this had to be hands on, had to be face to face.

You see he wanted, no needed, Simpson to suffer. Of that, he had no doubt. He had to know who and why, and quick and clean was just too good for him.

Hence the watching and the waiting. Waiting for some kind of sign. Something Simpson did that set off the light bulb, somewhere he went, someone he saw.

The ex Detective Chief Inspector lived in a three bed semi close to Heaton Park, and still drank in The Ostrich pub, the place where he and Lauren had once met during the Todd Blackman investigation. The time when he'd been suspended, the time he'd begun to have his 'so called' psychological issues.

Since his incarceration, he'd obviously lost his job as a DCI, but that hadn't stopped him seeing some of his old CID chums. Oh no, Fuller had watched him, sitting in The Ostrich beer garden, laughing, drinking, living life.

He was thinner and paler, but he still had that smug look about him. That look Fuller couldn't wait to wipe from his face.

Des had rung earlier, but he'd nipped the calls. He didn't feel like socialising and had no intention of involving the Scot, or young Jack in any of his plans. They would have no part in the execution of Simpson.

Larry would die at Fuller's hands and his hands alone.

Finally, just before nine, Larry appeared. He was wrapped up against the bad weather in a heavy parka, hood up, but it was him. Fuller would know him anywhere, the way he moved, held himself. He stood just outside his gate, on the footpath, looking up and down the road. Rick's car was a good fifty yards away, but he slid a little further down in his seat, just in case.

Moments later a taxi pulled into the street, stopped at Simpson's gate and he jumped inside.

Fuller watched as the car pulled away.

"Where are you going tonight, sunshine?" he muttered, as he started the Range Rover and fell in behind.

***

Des sat with his back to the fire, pint in hand, dog lying sleepily at his feet. The pub was beginning to quieten off, the midweek diners eating early, mindful of a day's work ahead in the morning.

Just after nine, Shona Mackintosh walked in.

Des waved, she saw him, smiled and edged her way over.

"Am I late?" she asked. "Things went a little over."

Des shook his head.

"Not at all hen, here, let me get ye a drink. What will ye have?"

"Oh, no, Des. I'll get these. It's only fair. You did me a good turn there."

She looked at his half full glass.

"Guinness, is it?"

"Aye, go on then," he smiled.

Minutes later, Shona was back with the drinks. She placed Des' pint in front of him and took a sip of her own wine before shrugging off her coat and sitting opposite.

"I haven't seen you in here before," she said, leaning down to stroke Bruce. "I take it you're new to the area."

"New to this part of town, so. But I've lived in Manchester on and off a few years now."

"But you're from Scotland originally."

"Glasgow, aye. But I left when I was a wee boy... sixteen"

"Ah, yes, the army, I remember you said," she smiled, took another drink. "That and a misspent youth."

"Aww, I wasnea too bad, Shona. Just a kid with no money in his pocket. They tend te find mischief, if ye know what I mean. But what about yersel? Was ye born and bred here?"

"Heavens no. I'm a Geordie. I know I don't sound much like one, but I lived in Newcastle 'till I left college. Then I moved to Bath for Uni. I met my husband there and we stayed in and around the city until he was offered a wonderful job up here. That was ten, no, eleven years ago."

"So yer married then?"

Des thought he saw a tinge of sadness in her eyes.

"No... divorced." She managed a thin smile. "I'm afraid hubby's wonderful job came with an equally wonderful secretary."

Des caught her looking at his own wedding ring. He touched it.

"Oh, aye this... I'm widowed... actually that's not exactly true. We were divorced a while before she died, but, well… let's just say, we made our peace."

Shona looked like she didn't quite know what to say. Des figured he would lighten the mood.

"But I'm happily single the now, love it 'round here, and I haven't got a secretary, wonderful or no."

"That's a relief," she smiled.

"So what was this class ye went te then?" asked Des, taking a drink of his new pint.

Shona coloured slightly. Des thought her even more attractive for it.

"Oh it's a bit silly really," she said. "I just felt I needed to try something different and meet some new people. You know what it's like living alone, you can end up just rattling around in the house talking to yourself."

"I talk te Bruce here," smiled Des. He leaned forwards, got closer to her.

"So ye dinnea want te disclose yer secret class then?"

Shona hid her face in her hands and shook her head. Des couldn't hide his smile at her bashfulness.

"Okay… it's a pottery class."

Des raised his glass.

"Ah, hoping te meet that Patrick Swayze then I reckon."

"Hardly. It's all women, and I think I'm the youngest by ten years at least. Anyway… what about you, Des, what do you do for a living… to relax?"

"Me, Aww I have a share in a wee business. We provide security fer folks that need it, de a bit of problem solving for people, ye know, them that can't get help fe the authorities like. People with bad neighbours, stalkers, that kind of thing. The cops haven't the time, so they come to us."

"Sounds fascinating… and a little dangerous."

Des wrinkled his nose.

"Nah. Most folks are reasonable once ye explain the error of their ways."

"And in your spare time?"

Des gestured towards Bruce.

"I like the outdoors, always have. He keeps me active, and I do a fair bit of running."

Shona smiled. Des thought her extremely attractive with welcoming green eyes. They held each other's gaze a moment, until the pub door opened. Des looked up, Shona turned too, but quickly spun around, head down.

"Ye okay there, hen?" asked Des. "Ye look as if ye have seen a wee ghost there."

She kept her face away from the entrance, her complexion turning from blushed to pale.

"Oh, just someone I don't really want to see," hissed Shona. "The tall bald guy, black suit. I dated him a while ago. It didn't work out, he doesn't like to take no for an answer."

"Doesn't he now," said Des, giving the guy a quick once over.

He was indeed a tall boy. Of similar age to the Scot, maybe a tad younger. Broad shouldered, well dressed. The suit was like something Rick would wear, complemented with a white open necked shirt showing off a thick gold neck chain.

Cogan gestured towards Shona's half empty glass. "You want another?"

She pulled a pained face and risked a glance over towards black suit.

"I really think I should be going, I…"

"Hey," soothed Des. "Dinnea be letting baldie there spoil our chat."

Shona was already looking for her bag on the floor.

"I'm sorry, Des. You don't understand, he can be…"

Before she could finish, the guy was over at the table, beer in hand, big self-righteous smile on his face.

"Well if it isn't the lovely Shona," he said. "This is a surprise, the village virgin drinking wine on a school night?"

He shot Des an icy look.

"Must be a special occasion. This the new man, is it?"

Shona swallowed what looked to Des like a large lump of discomfort.

"This is Mr Cogan," she managed. "He helped me with my car and…"

"Aye, son, I am," interrupted Des, eyeballing the guy. "I'm the new man alright. That's not an issue te ye is it?"

Black suit put on a massive fake smile.

"Not at all, Jock."

"My name's not Jock," offered the Scot, eyes icy cold. "And I personally find that term offensive. Yer no meaning te be offensive are ye son?"

The smile faded.

"I was just being friendly," sneered black suit, resting a hand on Shona's shoulder. "This lovely lady and I have some previous, don't we doll?"

Shona almost jumped out of her seat at his touch.

"Michael, please," she began. "That's ancient history and I'd rather you left us to our drinks."

"You heard the lady," glared Des. "Why don't you take yer shiny suit and yer baldie heed and leave us in peace."

Michael looked furious.

"I think you need a lesson in manners… Jock."

Gus, the landlord had been watching proceedings like a hawk from the bar. The Swan was not used to any form of aggression on the premises, and he had no intention of allowing it this night. He knew Michael Stewart well. He was a regular. A brash, confident, wealthy man with a tendency to lose his temper a little too quickly. He didn't know much about the wiry Scot, he was a new customer by comparison, but he looked a handful.

"Now then gents," shouted Gus from behind his counter. "Keep it friendly please."

At that, Bruce lifted himself from his comfortable position and turned towards Michael Stewart, his hackles up, teeth bared, a low growl rumbling in his throat.

"See," smiled Des. "It's no just Shona here that disnea like ye. And Bruce is an excellent judge of character."

Michael stepped back from the snarling collie. He pointed at Cogan.

"I'll see you again, Jock," he said. "When you haven't got your mutt with you."

"That's as maybe," smiled Des. "I'll look forward te it."

The guy turned and walked back to the bar to join his pal. There was a fair bit of glaring and pointing, but they both steered clear.

"Sorry," said Shona, obviously embarrassed. "We all make the odd mistake."

Des smiled and made a show of leaning across the table and taking her hand.

"We've all made a few, hen. But don't let that bully spoil our night. I can handle him. I promise you."

Shona looked at Cogan. He was confident and calm, his weathered skin, the scars around his eyes, the natural hardness of his body, his calloused hands, all told a story, a story of a man who had seen and done things only a few others had, and she believed every word he said.

"I will have that second wine after all," she said.

***

The taxi didn't go far. Fuller had followed at a discreet distance thinking it may go into town, but Simpson had obviously decided upon it due to the nasty weather rather than the mileage.

It pulled up, two wheels on the pavement, outside the Royal British Legion on Bury New Road, engine rattling like a train, just less than two miles from Larry's house. However, Simpson didn't go into the club.

He paid the driver, zipped up his parka and walked straight past the entrance. He then strode along the pavement, head down, to the far side of the terrace, pausing briefly to look at the front door of the premises on the opposite corner, before disappearing around the back of it.

Fuller parked his Range Rover, slipped quietly out of the driver's seat, turned up his collar against the cold and rain, then carefully followed in Simpson's footsteps.

Rick had a feeling about this night. A gut feeling that he considered a breakthrough. He had no idea why, but as he followed his prey, there was a spring in his step.

Rick took a good look at the door Simpson had been so interested in, but there was nothing out of the ordinary there, just a plain white plastic affair with little to separate it from its neighbours. If anything, it appeared unused.

It was only as Rick edged his way around the rear of the property that things began to make more sense. There he found a small car park that held three high end marques, a nice RS4, and a pair of big Merc saloons. Rick scanned the area before he moved any closer. He knew Simpson would be surveillance conscious and the last thing he needed to do was walk straight into him. He waited and watched for a full five minutes until he was convinced that the only place Larry could have gone, was inside the building that the carpark served. Rick crept around the RS4 then stood at the bottom of four concrete steps that led to the rear entrance, a shiny fire engine red painted door with a brass plaque to its right which read, 'Sadie's Kink Society.'

"Now we know why the front door doesn't get much use," said Fuller to himself.

He clocked a small CCTV dome just above the lintel. With the name on the plaque suggesting the clientele may value their privacy, he doubted it was recording the faces of its visitors, more likely it was there for the benefit of whoever was sitting behind the very glossy red door, deciding who to let in… or not.

He walked up the steps and pressed the intercom.

"In for a penny," he said.

No sooner had he released the button, when the speaker crackled into life and a deep, gruff Eastern European voice said, "This is a private club, Sir. Do you have an appointment?"

Fuller went for broke.

"I'm a friend of Mr Simpson's," he said. "I believe he's here already. He recommended this establishment."

Of course Rick had no way of knowing if the voice would simply seek out Larry, ask him the question and blow Fuller's story out of the water, but he had the feeling it was worth a try.

Seconds later, Rick heard the electronic lock click open and he stepped out of the cold and rain.

Once inside, he edged his way along a white walled corridor where a large ornate desk was planted at the far end. His feet sank into thick carpet, the same shade as the entrance door. Somewhere, classical music played, Vivaldi, Gloria in D.

"Dramatic for a whore house," muttered Rick.

The place was oppressively warm, and he undid his coat as he strode towards the desk and the mountain of a man that sat behind it.

Rick considered that the guy was huge in every way, from his cannon ball shaved head to his ham sized hands.

"Take a seat, Sir," growled the guy. "As you are a friend of Mr Simpson, I'm sure he will have informed you that you must be a member to take advantage of the services here." He slid a single sheet of A4 across the desk, along with a blue Biro. "Fill this in please Mr...?"

"Colletti," said Rick peering at the form.

"Mr Colletti," nodded the guy. "Complete it, please. The Membership fee is three hundred and ninety nine pounds, will that be cash or card?"

Rick raised his brows.

"Cash," he said. "And the cost of the services?"

"That is between you and the girl, Mr Colletti. And as I am sure your friend has explained, as the services on offer here at Sadie's are somewhat of the exotic variety, some cost far more than others."

Rick pushed the completed form across the desk and counted out eight fifties.

"I don't have change," smiled man mountain.

"There is a surprise," said Rick.

The guy shrugged.

"What is a pound to a man who wears Paul Smith, Sir?"

Fair enough, thought Fuller.

Man mountain slipped the cash into a drawer and turned his rather dated computer monitor around so Rick could see the screen. There, displayed in less than hi resolution clarity were six pictures of skimpily clad young women; each had a colourful name emblazoned across each shot.

"Here are the girls we have in the house tonight, Sir. Girls two and five are currently with clients. You may choose any of the others. Are you looking for a submissive or a dominatrix, Mr Colletti? Or maybe a two girl service?"

That caught Rick on the hop.

"Erm, no, one is fine… a submissive," he managed.

The guy leaned in and lowered his voice, even though no one else was around.

"The best subs are number two and three. But as your friend, Mr Simpson is currently entertaining, number two, may I suggest… Keri. Just twenty years old, size eight, nice titties, eh? And don't let the skinny look put you off, she can take the punishment, believe me. She loves it."

Rick did his best not to look the way he felt inside. It may well have been the oldest profession in the world, but it still stank.

Finally he managed.

"Okay, I'll take your word for it. Keri it is then."

The guy sat back in his chair, picked up a phone and dialled. "You have a client," he snapped. "Be ready." He then turned to Fuller and gave him a knowing look. "Room three, top of the stairs," he said.

"Okay," said Rick, pushing back his chair.

Before he made it to his feet, the guy grabbed Fuller by the wrist and squeezed. He was immensely strong.

"And don't kill the bitch, eh? That comes very expensive."

Rick trod the stairs. They were covered in the same deep pile red carpet as the corridor making the whole place feel expensive yet tacky at the same time. He noted the small Bose speaker on the landing that had been responsible for the quiet background music. The piano of Mozart had replaced Vivaldi. Symphony No 41 in C Major, or The Jupiter Symphony, known for its good humour and exuberant energy. However, even Wolfgang at his greatest couldn't manage to drown out the slaps and groans coming from the other rooms.

Rick stood and examined the long corridor ahead of him. Inside one of those rooms, of course, was his enemy, Lawrence Simpson. The sheer proximity of the man sent his pulse rate into overdrive.

Finally Rick stood at the door of room three. It sat directly opposite number two.

He'd selected girl three, Simpson, girl two, did that mean that Simpson was in there? Just feet away? Is that the way it worked?

He could feel the blood in his temples, the rage in his heart.

He turned and walked across the landing, considered getting even closer, putting his ear to the door, but he was stopped in his tracks. There was the turn of a lock behind him and door three opened.

"Hello, Sir, I'm Keri."

Keri, if of course that was her name, was prettier than her photograph and was dressed in the skimpiest of black lingerie. Some would have called her slim. To Fuller, she was skinny, too skinny. And for some ungodly reason, she had decided to have breast enhancements. They looked out of place on her tiny frame, unbecoming, indecorous to the point of grotesque. Rick's first thought was what kind of surgeon would have agreed to such a thing, then he pushed the idea away. The girl, like man mountain downstairs, was from Eastern Europe. Bulgaria? Romania? The Balkans? If you had the money, you could buy yourself anything there.

"Hello," he replied. "I'm Stephen."

The girl allowed her head to fall to one side and smiled, letting her long dark hair fall over her narrow bare shoulder. Rick thought it well practised.

"Well, come in, Stephen," she said. "We are going to have so much fun tonight."

Rick stepped into the room, and it wasn't what he'd expected. For some reason, after the deep pile crimson carpet in the hall, he'd had the idea that he'd be walking into some king of faux dungeon, whips, chains, the whole nine yards. Instead, he noted that the furnishings, bedding, drapes, towels, indeed everything in the room, was of decent quality and spotlessly clean.

Keri saw him looking around.

"Your first time at Sadie's?"

"Yes," he managed, feeling ever so slightly on edge.

"She runs a tight ship. That's what they say in England, no?"

"Something like that."

"Everything here is nice," she gave him another smile that showed off her perfect veneers. "Just like me."

"I expected something else," he said.

Keri stepped in close to him and stroked his cheek with a tiny hand.

"You can have anything you want, Stephen. I have all the toys you may ever desire to use on me. Restraints, floggers, hooks, electro." She pushed her body into him. "You can do anything you want to me, Stephen. Anything at all."

"Is that so?"

Keri stepped back, leaving her right palm on his chest. Again a well-rehearsed move.

"For two hundred, of course... anything."

Fuller slipped off his coat and sat heavily on the end of the super king sized bed. He pulled three hundred pounds from his pocket and handed it to the girl.

"I want something special," he said.

Keri snatched the cash greedily.

"Your heart's desire," she purred.

"An acquaintance told me about this place," he said. "Maybe you know him? Maybe he has taken advantage of your services before?"

Keri sat next to Fuller and began to stroke his hair.

"We don't talk about other clients, Stephen," she said. "Sadie doesn't like it. It isn't professional you see."

"Lawrence Simpson," said Rick, ignoring the girl's practised speech. "He's here now, across the landing. He chose girl two."

Keri went pale. Fuller saw genuine fear in her eyes. She shook her head. "I...I've never heard of him. And like I said..."

Fuller stood, his mellow mood changing in a split second. He towered over the girl, fists clenched, teeth bared.

"I know what you fucking said, but you're lying. I know you're lying. I can see it in your face, your eyes."

Keri wriggled herself off the bed and stood.

"Look, if you want to whip me, beat me, slap me, fuck me, then get on with it. You've paid for the privilege, but..."

"But what?"

"But I can't...won't, talk about Larry."

"Larry? I didn't call him Larry, did I?" Fuller took hold of the girl by the shoulders, looked into her pretty face.

"I'm not here to hurt you, or to have sex with you. I couldn't whip you if my life depended on it. I'm here to find out about Larry Simpson. Take the three hundred, tell me what you know, and I'll be gone."

"You a cop?"

Fuller shook his head. Locked eyes with her again. No point in beating about the bush.

"He murdered my girl."

Keri closed her eyes, took a breath, twisted from his grasp and sat back on the end of the bed, hands clasped, staring at the floor.

"Look, Stephen. There is something you should know. Sadie specialises in clients who are into BDSM. Doms and Subs. It's how she's made her money and believe me she's made a fortune. These guys, her customers, will pay anything to inflict pain or receive punishment. More often than not, they don't even want sex. It's all about power and dominance or its polar opposite. I've been here for over a year and Larry has been a client all that time. He's here once, sometimes twice a week. I'd been here maybe a month maybe when… when he chose me."

Keri looked up into Fuller's face.

"He's crazy. I thought he was going to kill me. If it hadn't been for Oliver, the guy downstairs, I think he would have done. He's into breath control, strangulation, suffocation, but, well, I kind of suppose you know that."

"Go on," said Rick quietly.

"He fractured my larynx. The cartilage was damaged, and air was escaping back into my chest. I was in hospital for ten days."

"Yet Sadie let him back in here?"

Keri gave Rick a wry smile.

"Sadie has seen it all. Done it all. I've heard rumours about girls dying during a visit. Beaten to death, strangled. Clients dying too. Heart attacks, strokes, you name it. But she's an expert at keeping the lid on things. Men who are into this scene tend to be powerful, rich, politicians, policemen. And she knows where all the bodies are buried. She's protected. And anyway Larry paid Sadie off… and me. These days, she only allows him to visit Naomi, the number two girl. She's the only one who can handle him."

Fuller was incredulous.

"But you came back."

Keri nodded.

"Stephen. I make a grand a day and maybe have sex with a client once a month. Sadie needs girls that look like me. Young, skinny. It attracts the Doms. She looks after me, I look after her. Another two years and I'm out of the game for good."

Fuller's mind was working overtime.

"Do you know where Naomi lives?" he said.

SEVEN

"And what are you looking so smug about?"

Fuller was making coffee in the team's Piccadilly offices and was eyeing Des as he did so.

Cogan was sitting at his desk, petting Bruce. He had a smile on his face and a twinkle in his eye.

"Is a man not allowed to look pleased with himself once in a while?" he replied. "Or do we all have te have a coupon like yer good self. Like a boy who's lost a pound and found a penny."

"You do look very happy, Mr Cogan," chipped in Jack who was counting a wad of cash on his own desk.

"Well, maybe I've a right te be," said Des. "Maybe, I met a very nice lady last night, and we are going out fer a wee spot of dinner tonight."

Rick stopped his coffee duties and narrowed his eyes.

"Where? If she's so nice to have you smiling like a Cheshire cat, you can't take her for a bloody curry. That's your usual opening gambit."

Des looked a little sheepish.

"I know, I know, but ye know me and food. I cannea be doin' with all that fancy stuff when ye get a wee mouthful o' salad and flowers stuck in the middle of a great big plate."

"So? Where?" asked Rick again.

"Well, ye know that handsome fella off the tele, that boy fe Yorkshire who cooks with all the butter and that…"

"James Martin?" offered Jack.

"Aye, that's the one," nodded Des. "Well he's just opened a place here in town… in 235 Casino. It says it's traditional British, so I reckon that will do me."

"I reckon it will do yer pocket too, Mr Cogan," said Jack, wrapping another bundle of notes with an elastic band.

"Looks like I can afford it," said the Scot, gesturing towards the considerable amount of cash on display.

Rick began to pour three cups.

"Yes, what is that exactly, Jacko?"

"Erm, this is our fee for the job we did in Stockport yesterday."

Fuller walked over to Jack's desk, dropped a cup in front of him and picked up a bundle of notes.

"Must be five grand there," he said.

"Seven," said Jack.

Des stopped petting his collie.

"Now forgive me here, son, but I dinnea reckon them lassies fe Stockport had that kinda cash, and neither did the wee boys fe the boozer."

"Course not," said Shenton, screwing up his face. "This is from the weed those faces was growin'. It was all but ready to chop and dry see. Well, not just the weed, the lamps, pumps trays, the whole shootin' match. An old mate of mine bought the lot. And cleaned Leanne's flat for her too."

Fuller darkened.

"You sold drugs?"

Jack looked worried.

"Well, not exactly. I mean the girls wanted the gear gone like, and y'know, it just seemed a win-win situation…"

Rick stood over the young Liverpudlian, face like thunder.

"Who gave you permission to make that decision?" he snapped.

"Erm, well it was just like, erm, I just did it on the hoof like. Y'know, it seemed the best solution. Yous and Mr Cogan were busy with erm, well whatever yous were doin' so… and I never even touched the gear, honest. It was safer than me chucking it in the skip, eh? I'm sorry, Mr Fuller, really I am."

"Cut the kid some slack," said Des. "He did what he thought was right. And come on Rick, people in glass houses. Remember you and Joel Davies?"

Rick stepped away and collected his and Cogan's coffee. He dropped Des' on his desk a little too hard.

"Maybe I'm getting touchy in my old age," he muttered.

"And maybe ye have too much on yer mind, eh?" said Des knowingly.

Rick sniffed, turned to Shenton.

"Take a grand each for our trouble and give the rest to the Salvation Army."

Jack raised his brows.

"Wha'?"

"You skint?" snapped Fuller.

"Well no, but I…"

"Then do as I tell you, son."

Shenton coloured and nodded.

"Soz again, Mr Fuller."

With that, the door to the office was pushed open, and two men stepped inside. Bruce was instantly up and barking but wagged his tail at the same time indicating he considered all was well. Des recognised the first of the pair immediately. He was tall, maybe six two, but scrawny, no more than eleven stones, with long thin arms and legs. His hair was cut short, parted perfectly to one side and he wore a very well cut navy suit, pure white shirt and what just had to be some kind of club tie.

"Makes a change not te see ye covered in mud Warren," offered Des, standing and holding out a hand.

"Very nice to see you too, Mr Cogan," said Warren Casey. "Splendid in fact, and yes, I'm delighted to say that the streets of Manchester are far less slippery than around your lovely cottage north of the border. However, I fear I am still allergic to your furry friend."

"Ne bother," said Des. "Jacko, can ye put the boy out in the yard a spell?"

Shenton did as he was asked, and Des turned his attention to Casey's companion. This guy was a whole different ballgame. He'd be about the same height, lithe rather than muscular, double the young man's age but without doubt, a proper handful. The skin around his eyes was heavily lined, yet his gaze was sharp and intense. Despite his shaved head, Des considered the man had once been blond, due only to the colour of his eighties style droopy moustache.

"This is Jerry Commons," offered Casey.

"I know who he is," said Fuller, sipping his coffee and eyeing the man closely. "We've met… in another life."

Jerry nodded at Fuller, stepped silently across the room and the pair shook.

"The Granville ambush, if I recall," said the Lancastrian. "We were never properly introduced. Probably for the best at the time."

"Probably," said Rick. "Either way, I'm Fuller. You may recall Des Cogan here from the same op. He rode in the other Q car with your pal… sorry I don't recall his name."

"Mark," said Jerry. "It was Mark. Sadly, he's no longer with us."

"Sorry to hear that," said Rick, then pointed over to Jack, who had just returned from the back yard. "This young whipper is Shenton. We call him Jacko. A bit green, but a good lad."

Jerry nodded in Jack's direction, then gave Warren Casey a knowing look, an indication that the formalities were well and truly over.

"Ah, yes," said Casey, flushing slightly. "Well gentlemen, I was wondering if we could take a moment of your time?"

"I dinnea see why no," said Des. "We can nip in the back room there, it's more private… Jack, lock the door son." He waved his now empty coffee cup. "And get us all a brew on, eh?"

Jack pursed his lips and nodded. He was feeling ever so slightly like the office skivvy, but then he considered his faux pas with the cannabis crop and figured it best he keep his mouth firmly shut.

"No problem there, Mr Cogan," he said, forcing a smile. "Coffee okay for everyone?"

There were nods all round as the four men shuffled into the smaller back office and found seats.

"And how is your sister there, Warren… young Harriet?" asked Des.

Harriet Casey had worked with the team on a previous operation and had been badly wounded. After leaving hospital, she'd decided to set aside her covert operational duties with MI6. The last the team had heard she had taken up a far safer role alongside her brother at GCHQ.

"Erm… pregnant, is the best way to describe her," smiled Casey. "And happy, of course. She and hubby have opened a small café on the south coast. She's out of the game completely."

"She was well fit," chirped Jack as he pushed open the door carrying a tray of drinks.

"He's twenty," offered Rick by way of an apology. "He thinks of nothing else."

"I were the same at his age," said Jerry, taking his cup from Jack's tray. "Like a dog with two dicks, I was."

Rick raised his brows, took a sip of his brew and got straight to the point.

"So, Warren, as I recall you were an analyst at GCHQ. Languages, wasn't it?"

Casey wriggled in his seat, took a drink, found a place to rest his cup and touched his tie nervously.

"Well, yes, that *was* the case."

"Was?" asked Des. "So not the now then?"

"Erm, no. Not exactly, Mr Cogan, I have changed my position, so to speak."

"Changed to what exactly?" said Rick with a frown.

Casey gave Fuller a weak smile.

"Well, I now work out of Vauxhall Cross."

"The SIS building?" asked Des.

"Well, actually, I sort of flit between there, Thames House and most recently, Stormont House."

"The new Northern Ireland Office," said Rick, darkening with every sip of his coffee.

Casey nodded.

"Yes, Fuller, the Northern Ireland Office. You see, just like Harriet, I was always close to my great uncle. I suppose you could say that he helped me with my education in matters of national security."

"So you're a spy," snapped Rick, getting to his feet. "I knew I smelled a rat. Drink your coffee, son. This conversation is over. I made it perfectly clear after the Russian job that we are officially retired from the game. So, as this is obviously not a social call, I appreciate the effort you have made in coming here... and Jerry, it was good to see you again, But..."

"I'm your new handler, Fuller," said Casey with more than a hint of sharpness in his tone. "And you are still a public servant."

"Was," barked Rick.

"Are," snapped Casey. "Her Majesty's Government decide when and how to retire its special employees." He waved a hand around the small office. "And this is so not you, Richard."

"I have enough money," sneered Rick.

"I'm well aware of how much money you have netted, Fuller, and I know exactly to the penny what is in your bank accounts. You earn, but you spend too. I believe you have the new Aston Martin Vantage S on order. A snip at a hundred and seventy grand, and that you have recently placed a substantial deposit on a 172 square metre penthouse apartment here on Deansgate, priced at a cool one point two million. You have expensive tastes Richard, and your savings won't last you long at that rate."

"I'll manage."

"Aye, and so will I," said Des. "We have a nice wee business here that keeps us busy, the rent paid, food on the table."

"Come on Desmond," said Casey. "Really? This so-called private detective agency of yours is nothing but a leg breaking shop. You spend all your time running around the enchanting social housing of the borough, putting the frighteners on local ne'er-do-wells. Now, as much as I admire your sense of societal responsibility, how long do you think it will be before the cops come knocking? Or worse still, one of Manchester's fine set of gangsters?"

"We'll deal with that if and when it comes on top," said Rick.

Casey sat back in his seat, closed his eyes and nipped the bridge of his nose between thumb and finger.

"Jerry," he said quietly. "Show them."

The older man pulled his phone from his leather jacket and began to play a video. He held it out for all to see. It was footage from the previous day, probably hacked from an outside camera mounted on one of the shops across the road from the Edgerton Arms. It showed Des's Discovery pulling into the pub car park, then Fuller, Cogan and Shenton, stepping out and disappearing behind the building. Seconds later, all three came back into shot wearing balaclavas and carrying handguns.

"Careless," said Jerry, pushing the handset back into his pocket.

"You're a funny guy, Jerry," said Rick. "I'll bet you didn't get that footage by asking the owners." He turned to Casey. "So…how long have you had us under surveillance?"

"I'm a spy," said Warren smugly. "It's more a question of what is a man to do with such damning evidence."

It was Jack's turn. The young boxer stood and walked over to Jerry.

"Giza look at that again, pal," he said.

Jerry obliged and handed Jack the set. The Scouser viewed the video again.

"Yous would never get that by a defence lawyer mate. Can't make out the reg plate, can't make out faces. And in any case, no one in that pub would ever give a statement, they're not divvies. Especially them three dealers…. You got nothin.'"

Des smiled at Casey.

"No as daft as he looks, eh?"

Casey was unperturbed.

"Would you really want the hassle though Desmond? Cops crawling all over this place. Any other premises you may have? Bank accounts seized until the investigation is over. I could go on."

"What I want to know," said Jack. "Is why the threats? If yous are so desperate to have us back working fer yer, why not just ask us, tell us the job and we can say yes or no?"

"Because the answer is no," snapped Fuller. He pointed at Casey "I've been saying no for years and he knows that his great Uncle was the only reason me n' Des kept going back in. Now Cartwright has gone. That's it, there's no leverage anymore, no connection."

"But there is a connection," said Commons flatly. "A connection you know well. And only you guys have the experience."

"Meaning?" asked Fuller.

Jerry shot Casey a glance.

Casey nodded his assent, and the ex Det man began to speak.

"Rick...look, you, me, Des, we're part of a dying breed. Most of the faces that were around when we worked together in '92 are in the ground or finding solace in the bottom of a bottle. This new variety of operator, well...they've never even set foot in Belfast, except on a stag do. Yes, they know the way the Islamic fundamentalists work, the groomers, the suicide bombers, but they've no idea what they are dealing with when it comes to the Provos... you two do."

"Provos?" growled Rick. "There are no fuckin' Provos anymore."

Jerry looked across at Casey and waited.

Warren took a deep breath and began.

"Okay, look, chaps, here is the deal. We all know that the Real IRA called a ceasefire after the outrage of the Omagh bomb, but that armistice didn't last. For the last fifteen years we've tried to stamp out various splinter groups, but without success. One goes, another appears. And last year we learned that a small Republican cluster calling themselves, Republican Action, together with a few disgruntled old boys, and I mean proper Provos, merged with a few hot headed dissidents and once again, another form of the IRA has reared its head. It may be in a slightly different form, they may use 'New' or 'Real' or 'Continuity', but either way, they are back."

Rick shook his head.

"Are you trying to teach us to suck eggs here, son? Did you not read your beloved Great Uncle Cartwright's files? What about Patrick O'Donnell, Kristy McDonald, Ewan Findley, Dougie McGinnis? What about the trail of bodies we left at their farm? Obviously, Cartwright neglected to mention them, and what we did to destroy the New IRA."

ROBERT WHITE

Casey blew air down his nose.

"However, like I said, another faction still lives and breathes. The Continuity IRA, New IRA, whatever the handle." Casey was becoming frustrated. "The fact is chaps, it doesn't matter what these groups are called, or what their make up is. It's of little concern that NIRA were no more than gangsters cloaking themselves as paramilitaries. What matters, what is worrying our guys at GCHQ, is the chatter about this latest bunch making a big splash over here. And this latest alliance now includes some serious players. An East Tyrone group that we believe were responsible for killing a Roman Catholic police officer, and a Belfast group who badly wounded another. Yes, this latest version of PIRA are raw, volatile, unstable even, but they are not going away, they are growing and gaining political ground too. They are like the cockroach you stamp on, only to see its babies run out from under your foot. We believe this, this… Continuity group, are planning a huge atrocity over here in England, and soon."

"So arrest them for preparing," said Rick flatly. "You have the legislation now, use it."

"Not so simple," said Commons. "Just like your young lad here said, even video evidence doesn't mean a conviction. And the locals are just as scared as they ever were, maybe more so. No one in East Tyrone, Belfast or Cork for that matter, would speak out against this shower. They have history on their side, hundreds of bloody years of it. Even the drug dealers are scared of these fuckers. Continuity have learned from NIRA and their mistakes. They still tax the gangs to buy weapons and explosives, yes. Beatings are commonplace, yes. But they are winning hearts and minds too. They can smell a united Ireland and they feel they can achieve it with the gun. It's like going back in time, Rick. The only way to deal with these people is to eliminate them. You should know that… only too well."

Rick sat back in his seat, a wry smile on his face. He'd never given Jerry Commons or that night in that rain soaked field a second thought in over twenty years. It was ancient history.

He gave Casey the hard stare and nodded towards Commons.

"Where'd you find this guy?" he asked. "And what has he told you?"

"He was on Uncle Damien's staff, before he got sick," said Casey smugly. "And I have no idea what you are talking about."

"I've worked for Cartwright since 2002," said Jerry. "I'm not the talkative type, Fuller. This isn't a witch hunt."

Rick turned down his mouth.

"Well Cartwright never mentioned you."

"You either," said the Det man, eyes cold. "Funny that eh? But I did some of the prep work for jobs that had your name written all over them. I can mingle with the worst of them, Fuller. My Belfast accent is as good as any local. Eleven years working undercover alongside the meanest sons of bitches Ireland ever produced. The fact of the matter is this, if you want to stay home and play Robin Hood, knock yourself out. This new crew need slotting, and I don't want to work with anyone who's half hearted." Jerry cocked his head. "Or maybe you've just lost your bottle."

Des thought Rick was about to explode.

"Maybe you want to step out into the yard and find out, son," he hissed.

"Now, now, children," said Casey, holding up a hand. "Fighting between ourselves is not going to solve anything. Look, Fuller, I know all about O'Donnell and his thugs, and I know the sacrifices your team made in Belfast and Cork. I simply believed that you chaps would have enjoyed the opportunity to finish what you started. That, and make a great deal of money."

Fuller was still glaring at Jerry, too angry to concentrate on proceedings. It was Jack who broke the silence.

"How much are we talking, mate? Exactly, like?" he asked.

Casey gave the young Liverpudlian a thin smile.

"I'll deal with the organ grinders, if I may, Shenton."

Jack was not amused.

Des did his best to stop him, but he had youth and momentum on his side. His left arm shot out with the speed of a striking snake. At first, Cogan thought the lad intended to punch Casey, but instead he grabbed at his tie, pulling him from his seat. The spy had no choice but to haul himself to his feet, coffee cup clattering to the floor. The instant Casey was standing, Jack slammed his right palm into his shoulder, spinning him around to face Jerry Commons. Before anyone could blink, Shenton had Casey in the choke.

Jerry made a move to stand. Jack took a step back, dragging Casey with him.

"Don't be a soft lad," he snapped. "In five seconds your boss will be unconscious, another five, a cabbage, and five more, you'll be buyin' a coffin for the posh twat, so sit the fuck down." He gave Casey a squeeze. "Are yous ready to talk to the monkey yet, pal?"

Warren couldn't breathe let alone talk. He nodded as best he could. Jack released him and he fell to his knees.

"Don't underestimate people," pointed out Shenton. "I'd have thought someone with your education would have known that. Now, just because you went to Eton or Oxford or whatever, don't give yous the right to talk to me like that eh? So... I'll ask again... how much?"

Casey, stayed on his knees, holding his throat and coughing. Finally he managed to raise his head and look Shenton in the eye.

"Well, let's put it this way. If all four targets are eliminated, you'll *all* be able to buy a new Aston."

"Four targets?" asked Rick, slowly coming down from his rage.

Casey was getting his breath back.

"Usual IRA active service unit, Fuller. Three men one woman. Intel suggests that they will leave Belfast for the UK tomorrow."

"So soon," said Des. "Not a lot of time to plan."

Warren hid a smile at that. He knew the bait had been taken, he just hadn't planned on being choked to death in the process. Lifting himself to his feet, he wiped the knees of his trousers, gave Shenton a withering look, then ran a hand through his gelled hair.

"No time like the present then, is there, Mr Cogan?"

"We'll need expenses and a full brief," said Rick. "Oh, and one other thing I want to know."

"Go on, Fuller," said Casey, finding his seat again whilst eyeing Shenton warily.

"What does Rose know about this?"

Warren shook his head.

"Out of the loop, old boy. Probably not the best way for you to discover this, Richard, but there's a reshuffle on the cards. Ms Longthorn Grey is due a sideways move and her security clearance has been... downgraded, so to speak. This brief comes from the SIS office, that is all you need to know."

"I need to know who's signing my cheque," snarled Rick.

"I noticed that you still have your Cayman Islands account, Fuller. Twenty percent of your fee will be in there before midnight tonight. The rest when the job is done. Where its origins lie is beyond your pay grade." Casey shot Jack another sour look. "Divide it as you see fit."

The spy stood and gestured towards his companion. "Jerry will fill you in on the details. We understand that the team will be in Manchester before lunchtime tomorrow. I expect them neutralised by the end of the week." He pointed at Fuller. "And no big splashes. This is not a street war."

Des sat back in his seat and made a pyramid with his fingers. He had a knowing look on his face.

"Ye've come a long way since the last I saw ye, Warren. That nervous, cap in hand style ye came in with te get us te help yer wee sister has all but gone. Seems te me that yer very good at putting on a show fer the boys."

Casey could barely disguise his mirth now.

"I get the job done, Mr Cogan. That is my remit, that's what keeps our country safe."

Des felt for his pipe and makings and slowly began to fill the bowl. He looked up at Casey occasionally as he completed his task.

"Well, let me say this te ye, Warren. As Rick here has alluded te, we've been retired more times than Red Rum, so I'm kinda weary of the play acting, the… will-we-won't-we jobbie. Me? I don't give a fuck. If the money's right, count me in." The Scot leaned forwards, elbows on his desk, eyes flashing. "But what I tell ye is this, son. Whoever's left standing in this team after these fuckers get what's comin' te 'em, well, they get *all* of the cash, shared equal, no excuses, grinders or monkeys, they get the whole shooting match. And should things pan out, and ye come knocking on our door in the future with yer posh suit and yer bad attitude, ye learn some manners and treat folks with respect. Ye may have degrees comin' out of yer arse, but young Jack here made sure that your *remit*, as ye call it, went according to plan the last time. In fact, in dropping that Russian fella, he probably ensured yer promotion. So think on, son, eh?"

Casey once again brushed some unseen debris from his trousers and straightened his already perfect tie.

He sniffed.

"Nice speech, Cogan, but if it's all the same to you, I'll bid you good day. As I said, Mr Commons here will brief you. He has access to any kit you may be short of. As for the money, I'll ensure all of it is paid into Fuller's bank account." He gave a fake thin smile. "So best you keep him breathing, then he can divi it up when this is done eh?"

Casey looked at each man in turn as if waiting for a fond farewell. Not one of the team moved. He snorted his derision at the lack of respect and began to turn, thought better of it, and once again faced the room, thin shoulders squared defiantly.

"Without men like my Great Uncle," he announced. "Without men like me, men who work in the shadows, men who play the players, many more innocent people would die. You should all know that."

And with that, he turned and was gone.

"Wanker," said Jack.

Fuller waited for the outer door to close and Casey to leave the building before he stood and walked over to Jerry.

He held out a hand.

"We go too far back to be fighting between ourselves, pal," he said.

Jerry Commons shook.

"I think we have the makings of a good team," he said, then nodded towards Jack. "Even the monkey here."

"What a fucking dick he was," muttered Shenton.

Des stood and slapped the young Scouser on the back.

"Hey, calm down son. Ye'll meet many a man like him in yer time, especially in this game. Now, why don't ye run out and get Rick's motor and we can all have a wee shwally in the Thirsty Scholar whilst Jerry here fills us in on the fine print?"

Jack snatched the keys from Rick's desk and turned, eyes still full of aggression.

"Don't leave me parked outside too long," he snapped. "I don't want another ticket."

The three older men listened as Jack petulantly slammed the outer door as he left.

"He's getting a handful," said Rick.

Des grunted.

"And who de ye think he reminds me of?"

"I was never like that," countered Fuller. "Not that bad. I was always the quiet one."

"No?" smiled Des. "D'ye recall hanging that boy Danny Norris out the NAAFI widow cos he'd eaten the last of the trifle."

"He was a fat twat," said Rick.

"That's why ye nearly dropped him."

"Bastard had me put on a charge," scowled Fuller. "I mean, if he couldn't take a joke, he should never have joined up."

"You ate NAAFI trifle?" asked Commons.

"Why no?" said Des. "If I recall, it was one of the more edible dishes."

There was the sound of a horn blaring outside, and the three men all stood in unison.

"Better not keep Mr Touchy waiting," said Jerry.

***

ROBERT WHITE

The Thirsty Scholar, or, as the locals sometimes called it, The Dirty Squalor, was a popular haunt with the team. A stone's throw from their lock up, it boasted a varied clientele, a recently acquired vegan menu and a wide range of beers from around the globe. Being situated under the railway arches on Oxford Road, it was cool in summer, toasty in winter and quiet enough during the afternoon to afford the crew sufficient privacy should they need it. Martin the Mod was the friendly yet wary landlord who also doubled as a DJ on some nights, playing his priceless selection of soul classics. However on this afternoon, he seemed more than a little stressed.

"The kitchen is closed," he barked the second the team sauntered in.

"So that will be two pints of Red Stripe, one Guinness and a Coke then," smiled Des. "And ye have no idea how gutted I am no te be able te sample yer latest plant based delicacies, Martin."

"Very funny," grumbled The Mod. "I suppose you've already taken great pleasure in murdering some poor unfortunate animals in order to quench your thirst for blood today."

"Aye a good part of a pig and two unborn chickens so far, pal," said Des. "But dinnea let that bother ye, Martin. I'll try te be a better person when I go fer my dinner tonight."

The landlord dropped two lagers and Jack's Coke in front of Des. "I'll bring your Guinness over once it's settled," he said.

Des nodded, smiled and left a good tip. He secretly liked Martin even if it was purely down to his quirkiness.

The four then found themselves a table away from the only other imbiber in the bar. Jerry pulled a laptop from a case, inserted a memory stick into it and waited for the data to load.

"Right lads," he began. "I don't see the point in showing you all the texts and emails, playing you any of the phone calls, or showing you the surveillance videos we've acquired over the last few months. Right now, I just want to give you the quick rundown."

"Fair enough," said Rick.

"Right," said Commons, taking a large gulp of his beer. "The four Irish."

He tapped a key and the first image appeared.

"Connor Walsh," he said, pointing. "Handsome fucker, isn't he? Looks a baby, eh? He's twenty seven would you believe? Part of the Belfast leg of this crew. A New Lodge boy, this one. Spent most of his teens in Alexandra Park, the Republican side of the fence of course. He started out throwing stones at the PSNI as it is called these days, then moved on to firebombing

British owned businesses in Derry."

Jerry clicked again.

"George McCaul."

"He looks a geek," offered Jack.

"That's exactly what he is," said Jerry taking another drink. "He's our explosives man. This boy has perfected the pipe bomb."

"Nothing new there," said Des.

"Not in the name, no," said Jerry. "But how many times did we hear of boys blowing themselves up making the things? Not this fella, though. Oh no, our George is a clever lad. He has degrees in Physics and Chemistry and could recite the bursting pressure of common schedule 40 1-inch wrought steel pipe in his sleep. He was recruited from a dissident group, called, Republican Action Against Drugs, whose favourite pastime was chucking the said pipe bombs through weed dealers windows whilst they watched Corrie. RAAD now form part of this NIRA or Continuity IRA, call 'em what you wish."

Jerry tapped the screen.

"And don't let this skinny, four eyes look fool you either. George shot a seventeen year old kid in both kneecaps back in February. His crime? Dealing legal highs on a street corner on the Bogside. He's a vicious little fucker, and not exactly stable."

Jerry moved on.

"Now here we have the real muscle of the crew, Seamus Fennel."

"He's a unit," offered Rick.

"You can say that again, pal," said Jerry. "Six four, eighteen stone. Even his own are scared of the bastard. Not the sharpest, but that isn't his job. He's there to protect the other three, to make sure they get the job done, and to guarantee that whoever is providing the weapons and explosives, doesn't rip them off. Apparently, he's a decent boxer, but his preferred knockout punch is a seven pound lump hammer these days."

"Nice guy," muttered Des.

"So we don't know the armourer then?" asked Rick. "I mean, I take it they'll come across clean and meet the explosives guy once they are here?"

Commons nodded.

"Correct, we're all agreed on that, but who the guy is…. Well that is another question. We have a name, Abbas, and a voice recording, but he's always used a burner and has never been on long enough for us to trace him."

"Syrian?" asked Jack.

"What makes you say that son?" turned Jerry.

Shenton shrugged.

"I spar with a lad called Abbas, he's from Damascus. Got bombed out and walked it all the way here. Tough fucker he is."

Jerry nodded.

"A possibility, Jacko. Worth a look at," he tapped some more. "And then finally, we have... Maria O'Shea."

"Jeezo," said Des. "She's a looker, and no mistake."

Commons snorted.

"Don't be fooled by her looks either, Scotty, she's Judy Buenoano, Myra Hindley and Rosemary West all rolled into one. Pretty as a picture, eh? Body to die for. And believe me, die they do. They don't call her The Black Widow for nothing."

Rick leaned in and enlarged the shot, focusing on the woman's face.

"Where is she from?" he asked.

"East Tyrone," said Jerry. "Bandit country. You know it well."

EIGHT

Maria O'Shea spun her naked body from the bed, leaned forwards and grabbed her t shirt from the bare floorboards. She quickly pulled it over her head to cover herself, stood, and padded to the tiny kitchenette in the corner of the shabby flat.

"Fuck's sake, Maria," snapped Connor. "Have ye no feelings at all so. I've just rolled off of yeez, and yer away to make the tea before my sweat is feckin' dry.

Maria didn't even turn. She simply lifted two stained mugs from tarnished brass hooks and dropped a tea bag in each.

"What d'ya expect there, Connor?" she said to the wall. "A nice kiss and a cuddle while we wait fer Seamus to bring the car?"

Walsh pushed himself upwards and rested his broad back against the headboard.

"Yer a cold fish, so ye are, Maria."

She poured boiling water, stirred, added milk, picked up both mugs and shuffled back to the bed.

She sat on the edge, handed Walsh his tea.

"Here, and stop yer moaning, Ye got yer balls emptied didn't ye?"

"Aye, and I didn't hear any complaints from you either."

Maria shrugged, tucked a wayward, ebony curl around her ear.

"It helped pass the time, so. You know how easily I'm bored."

Connor slowly shook his head.

"Yer all heart, so ye are."

"And your nothin' but a walking erection. So drink yer tea and get dressed. We've a boat to catch."

Connor stretched down to reach for his underwear, spilling his drink on himself in the process.

"Fuck's sake, now look what ye made me do."

Maria sniggered. She liked Connor, liked the way he made her feel. But he wasn't for her. Yes, he was good in bed, and there was no doubt he was committed to the cause. Handsome enough too. But it was the grey matter that he lacked. What was the point in lying next to a man who didn't have anything interesting to say?

"I didn't make you do anything, ye bollocks. Come on, get showered."

Twenty minutes later, the pair were dressed and ready to leave. Connor sat hunched on the end of the unmade bed, reading his ferry ticket. He and Maria were travelling together, Belfast to Liverpool on Stena Lines, the overnight crossing.

"Hope there's a double bed in this cabin," he muttered.

Maria dropped their two dirty mugs in the sink and snorted to herself. Yes, they would share a cabin, but she was certain that there would be no sex involved. She could already feel her anticipation building, a feeling deep in her gut that no man could ever deliver. Only the taking of a life, only striking terror into the enemy could afford such euphoria.

O'Shea considered those first nerves, that first tingle of excitement, a good thing. They gave her an edge, kept her sharp, focused...deadly. So, the last thing she would need was Connor crawling all over her on the ferry ride to England. There were far more important things at stake.

Like dead soldiers.

She was confident that there would be nothing to worry about on the boat, or the customs at Liverpool for that matter. No weapons or explosives would be transported. They were already in Manchester awaiting the team. The handover was already scheduled, the time the place, the fee, it was done and dusted. Of course, all of the ASU would travel clean. Hard lessons had been learned over the years with the old IRA making rash decisions about how to transport their weaponry and cash. Precious lives and equipment had been lost due to poor planning. But not this time. Every bullet, every ounce of explosives and those very special RPG's that would cause such horror, would be in their hands within twenty four hours.

The four would travel separately. Connor and Maria by ferry, Seamus and George by plane, Aer Lingus into Manchester. No one had as much as touched a gun or ammunition in weeks. Their clothes were new, their car, recently purchased from an elderly couple in Leeds was legal and anonymous. Even if every sniffer dog in England inhaled around them, they would walk away shipshape and smiling.

Yes, the journey may be a piece of piss, but it was what was planned in the coming days that would need guts and guile.

Three targets. Two bombs and one RPG attack, all carried out simultaneously.

The first, a bomb strike at 6 Military Intelligence Unit in Rusholme. Then, detonating at exactly the same time, another massive IED planted at 209 Battery 103 Regiment Royal Artillery, on Belle Vue Street. Finally, and definitely the most controversial, an RPG attack on B Detachment, 207 Field Hospital in Bury. This, it had been argued by the high command, was not technically a legitimate target, as B detachment recruited civilian nurses and doctors to perform in war zones across the world, and an attack on the 207 would inevitably mean non-military casualties. But Maria had fought to keep the training facility as part of the plan. To her, anyone who assisted the British Forces in any way, was a justifiable objective.

She turned and watched Connor pulling on his jacket. He looked pale and preoccupied. Deep in thought.

She considered that he too may be feeling the first sting of unease. That, or he was still brooding about her not lying in bed with him whilst he bathed in the glow of their sexual antics. She knew that it must be hard for him. Being in love with someone who just didn't love you back was no fun. And there was no doubt Connor was in love with Maria. He'd told her as much after a few too many in a Belfast bar. Drunk he may have been, but he'd meant every word and she knew it. She'd seen it in his eyes then, and if she was to draw him close this very moment, she would see it again.

Yet despite his doe eyes and undying attentiveness, it wasn't to be and there was no point in giving the guy hope where there wasn't any. Did that make Maria a cold fish? Maybe, but better an icy truth teller than a welcoming liar.

Despite the problem of Connor's unrequited love, Maria knew she could rely on him. When things got hairy, he wouldn't be found wanting. He was a tough boy, dragged up on the streets of New Lodge, fighting his way through his teens, killing for the cause at the ripe old age of twenty. He didn't have the brute strength of Seamus Fennel, or George McCaul's near psychotic levels of viciousness, but he had a calm air about him that Maria knew would be needed if they were to succeed across the water.

Some women would have called him the complete package, and yes, she could do a lot worse than Connor Walsh, but Maria O'Shea was damned certain… she could do an awful lot better too.

She was brought back from her musings by the sound of heavy footsteps climbing the narrow stairs that led to the flat. They stopped at the landing, and the unmistakeable voice of Seamus Fennel boomed from behind the locked door.

"Come on, yer bollocks. Move yourselves," he growled, then banged on the door so hard Maria thought he may punch straight through the timber. "Connor," he shouted. "Put yer dick back in yer pants and move it."

Maria snatched open the door and glared at Seamus, her emerald eyes flashing in anger.

"Keep yer voice down, you oaf," she hissed. "Every nosey bastard in the block can hear yees."

"And who's gonna say a feckin' word around here?" Seamus countered. "I'd rip the head of any man who dared."

He pushed his way into the room sniffing loudly, wiping his nose with the palm of his hand.

Maria grimaced.

"You are just fucking gross, Seamus. Have ye no tissue?"

The giant of a man rubbed his hand down the lapel of his jacket and snorted his derision.

Connor pulled his face.

"Can ye not see ye have snot all down the front of your coat there now, Seamus."

Fennel leaned into Connor's face.

"What I have on me coat, is none of yer business, pretty boy. Now, grab yer cases and let's fuck off."

Connor glowered at the mountain of a man. He had no time for Fennel's antics, his bully boy tactics. It had been the high command, the Brigade, that had insisted on Seamus' inclusion in the team. It was an old fashioned ruling, one that should have been left where it belonged, in the past. The days when every ASU had to have a big brash scrapper as security were long gone. With his thunderous voice and bad attitude, all Fennel did was draw attention to the team. Connor had pleaded with the Brigade not to include him, to take a leaf from the book of the Special Forces. Jobs like these required tough men and women, no doubt. But they also demanded the grey men that the SAS were so proud of. Folks who could walk into a bar, a café, an office and leave again without anyone really noticing them. Average to look at, exceptional in their craft. But no, his plea had fallen on deaf ears. They insisted this job needed a man like Fennel, a man who would literally walk through walls for the cause.

"Aye, I'll get the cases, so I will," snapped Connor. "You just make sure that creep McCaul is sitting up front with yees. The pair of ye deserve each other."

"That's right," chirped Maria. "I don't want the slimy fuck staring at me tits all the way to the ferry. I'll sit in back with Connor."

Fennel grunted.

"You'll sit as ye find. I'm not here to chauffeur yees around like fuckin' royalty." He turned for the door. "Now, come on, look sharp and bring yer cases, ye only have an hour before ye board."

Maria took a step to the side and stood in the path of the huge Irishman. She looked up into his battle scarred face, eyes wide, nostrils flared.

"Now you listen to me, you overblown fool. What you seem to be forgetting here, is that the Brigade put me in charge of this team. Yes, me. Not you Seamus. You're a hired hand, a ten a penny workhorse, a glorified bouncer with a brain the size of yer cock. Now button yer lip and *you* pick those cases up, ye hear? Connor, you walk down with me."

George McCaul was waiting downstairs by the team's car, a silver Peugeot. He'd spent the morning cleaning it and removing the stickers from the rear window. He was a man of details. People wouldn't remember the car. To the general public the 305 saloon was as inconspicuous as you could get, but they'd remember the 'Grandad's Taxi' or the 'Go Green Go Vegan' stickers. He'd checked for contraband too, under the seats, in the glovebox, all the nooks and crannies. Okay, the Brigade had bought the car from an elderly couple, but that didn't mean that their son hadn't used it, dropped a wee spliff down the back of the seats, left the remnants of a bag of charlie in the glovebox.

Details. George was a man of details.

He was also a man with a constant hard on for Maria O'Shea.

As she walked out onto the footpath, all red faced and angry about something, he considered that she was the most beautiful thing he had ever seen.

"Hiya, Maria," he said, smiling to reveal his brown uneven teeth. "Want to sit up front with me?"

O'Shea almost ripped off the car door handle and dropped into the back seat.

"Feck off, George," she spat. "You sit up front with your pal Fennel."

George's thin smile fell from his face.

"I was only being friendly," he muttered, climbing into the front passenger seat.

"Well this isn't a wee jolly, George," said Maria shuffling across to let Connor into the car. "And I'm not here to be friends with any of yees."

George shot Walsh a dark, knowing look.

"Aye, suppose," he said.

Finally, Fennel dumped the contested cases heavily into the boot and slipped into the driver's seat. He looked into the rear view, directly at O'Shea.

"Any last instructions before we set off... Ma'am?" he managed.

"Just drive the fuckin' car, Seamus," said Maria. "And take it steady why don't yer. The dock's only twenty minutes away."

***

As the active service unit made their way to the port of Belfast, a group of quiet men entered the small grubby flat Maria and Connor had just vacated, stripping the bedclothes, bagging the mugs in the sink, dusting for fingerprints, sampling DNA, lifting fibres. All would be methodically collected, and together with the photographs and audio recordings they had taken the last forty eight hours, be used to make a case against the four Irish.

Of course, these men and women were not to know that all their hard work, all their risk taking could be for nothing. Theirs was an insurance policy, nothing more.

The real work, the toil of covert assassination, the politics of murder, was about to begin in earnest across the Irish Sea, in England, and Rick Fuller would be its prime minister.

NINE

"What is it, Casey?" snapped Jerry Commons into his phone as he walked along Wilmslow Road in the heart of Rusholme's curry mile.

"Are they all on board?" asked the spy.

"Of course."

"I sensed some hostility."

"Come on, what did you expect from Fuller? A cake and candles to welcome you into his fold. He barely tolerated your Uncle Cartwright, and if you hadn't noticed, right now he has a lot on his plate."

"Mmm," mused Casey. "Maybe we should help him out with that. Allow him to concentrate on the matters at hand."

"Not exactly in The Firm's remit, is it? Slotting ex coppers, I mean. Especially ones who have technically served their time."

"Technically, yes. But Ms North was 'technically' one of ours. I'm sure it could be made to happen."

"You know what I think, Casey?"

"I'm sure you are going to educate me, like it or not."

"I think, if you took that opportunity away from him, he'd be no use to any of us."

"Where is he now?"

"Sitting in his motor outside some brass' flat in Hulme. She works at that knocking shop Simpson is so fond of. Uses the name Naomi."

"He's distracted. I don't like it."

"Too late now, Casey. You wanted the best. He's the best."

"Still?"

"Still."

"And have you told him?"

"About?"

"About O'Shea, of course. Who she is."

"What's the point."

"Good man, least said, soonest mended."

"Look, Casey, unless you have anything important to say, may I suggest that you leave me in peace to find a good curry house."

"You are such a Philistine, Jerry. I'm surprised Cogan's not with you. He's another who likes to take his life in his hands with every dish."

"He's got a date, Casey. I'll call with a sit rep when we're on plot tomorrow."

At that, Jerry closed the call, peered into the window of the Al Madina workers café, spied an empty table and pushed open the door. As of midnight, MI6's surveillance teams would be pulled off the four Irish and, just as importantly, Fuller, Cogan and Shenton. Once that was done, The Firm would be blind and Jerry would be their only point of contact. It's how they worked, how they wanted it, heaven forbid they actually witnessed any of the wrongdoings they paid their black ops people to undertake. It was fine to spy on their private lives, especially on the run up to a big op, but once the action started, they didn't want to know the details. Perish the thought. Careers could be ended, knighthoods lost.

Jerry found a seat and ordered lamb Balti, 'Apna style' meaning 'our way', cooked slightly longer, with more spices than usual, alongside, gol-gappa semolina fritters, potato and chickpea chaat and a tangy tamarind 'khatta pani' sauce.

Killing, even planning a killing, made Jerry Commons hungry.

***

Fuller watched the girl arrive at her flat. At least he presumed it to be Naomi. He'd only ever caught a glimpse of her half naked picture when the huge Eastern European guy had turned his computer towards him during his visit to Sadie's Kink Society. In that shot, of course, she was made up, big lashes, plumped red lips, poker straight blonde hair. Whereas this girl was pale, devoid of powder and paint. Her hair was tied up in a knot at the top of her head and it appeared darker. And she wore skinny jeans topped by a long oversized parka coat that hid her figure.

That said, she had opened the door with a key and let herself inside, so he figured he had a fighting chance of being on the money.

He'd taken a full hour to decide upon his clothing for this meeting. After all, how did one decide what shade of suit to wear to take a common prostitute to a good dinner?

As he and Lauren had become closer, he had noticed that his obsession with clothes, shoes and the good things in life had waned. They had become less important to him, his compulsions diminished.

However, in recent times, in these darker days, they had returned with a vengeance, alongside his ever shortening temper and lack of sufferance of fools.

So after much deliberation, he'd decided on a black Hugo Boss two piece, black Thomas Pink shirt and tie, and black patent leather brogues by Alfred Dunhill. Of course, if his chosen wardrobe and offer of a good dinner didn't move his plan along, there was always the suitcases full of money sitting in a wardrobe in the Palace Hotel.

So, it was time to get this party started.

Rick pulled a North Face parka over his suit jacket and strode towards the downstairs flat.

He took a breath, knocked and waited. Finally he heard feet padding down the hall and whoever those feet belonged to slip on the security chain.

The door opened a few inches and the same girl he'd seen enter moments earlier peered out, eyes full of suspicion.

"What d'ya want?" she said.

"Naomi?" asked Rick quietly.

"Wrong house," spat the girl and slammed the door shut.

Now completely certain he had the right address, and girl, Rick stayed put and knocked a second time, this time with more urgency and vigour.

Seconds later the girl wrenched at the door, again, the chain still firmly in place.

"Look, if you don't fuck off mate, I'm calling the coppers," she shouted.

"You mean the police, as in Larry Simpson?" asked Rick, keeping his cool.

The girl's jaw dropped slightly as she glared at Fuller.

"How do you know Larry?"

"We have the same tastes in women," he said. "Except, I have deeper pockets."

Naomi stood on her tip toes in an attempt to look behind Fuller.

"Is he here? Larry, I mean?"

Rick shook his head.

"I'm alone."

That defiant look re-appeared.

"How'd you find me. How'd you get my address?"

"Guess it's those deep pockets again," he said. "They tend to loosen lips."

"I'm sure," said the girl. "But I only do business with regulars out of here. You'll have to come to the club another night."

Rick pushed his hand into his trousers and pulled out a roll of notes.

"How about we start with five hundred to get you dressed and ready to go to dinner? Then another five to get you to my hotel?"

Fuller counted off ten fifties and pushed them through the gap between door and frame.

"I'll wait in the car," he said, dropping the cash on the mat before turning to leave.

"Erm, hey, wait, I mean, I'm not sure about this pal. Hey…" shouted Naomi, grabbing at the notes at her feet. "Erm, well if I come, I mean erm… how posh? What should I wear like?"

Rick stopped at the gate and turned.

"I don't do cheap," he said. "So try your best not to look it."

He sat in his Range Rover, engine burbling and checked his Rolex. Forty minutes had gone by. He was beginning to think his ploy hadn't done the trick. Maybe the girl had decided that five hundred was a nice little earner just to stay home and watch Eastenders. Maybe the fear of walking out into the night with a man who had simply knocked on her door had got the better of her.

He doubted the latter. After all, she was the only escort at Sadie's who was willing to take on Simpson and his perversions. The working girls must have talked together, she would know the dangers involved. No, she had either decided to take the five and fob him off, or…

Naomi stood at the passenger door shivering, her arms wrapped around her slim frame. Gone was the mousy top knot. She had opted for a shoulder length brunette wig, and the lashes were back, the bright red lips too. She wore a figure hugging black dress that was cut off one shoulder. It stopped just below the knee but was slit up the left thigh to reveal a little more of her slender legs. Rick felt his stomach lurch, his head spin. He had seen a dress just like it before. It was a Reiss Bella and Lauren had bought one from Selfridges on Exchange Square just before she was murdered.

Naomi rapped on the window.

"Are you gonna let me in, it's Baltic out here."

Fuller snapped out of his malaise and hit the remote locking.

"Jesus," she snapped as she slid into the seat. "I were freezing my tits off out there. You okay? You look like you've seen a ghost."

Rick turned and eyed her.

"Where'd you get the dress?"

She had to think.

"Erm, charity shop if you must know. I have a run out on the tram to Altringham once a month. Posh over there, see. You can get all sorts of good stuff, especially if you're size eight like me. Designer this y'know." She looked herself up and down. "It's alright init?"

"I do know," he said, shifting the car into drive. "And yes, it is alright."

As Rick pulled away, Naomi examined him. She was finally able to get a good look at the man who had knocked on her door and thrown five hundred pounds on her mat, for… well that was the question, for what exactly? Well, under normal circumstances, she would say, sex of course, what else? But somehow this guy seemed just that little too handsome, that bit too confident for that. He was the type that could pull just about any woman he chose. That said, Naomi knew the world didn't turn like that, some blokes, no matter how attractive, just got off on paying for it, found the thrill of being able to act out any fantasy they could imagine too much of a pull. Look at Larry Simpson. He was gorgeous, and what a fuckin' weirdo he was. So good looks alone didn't mean that this guy wasn't just a regular punter, or a nutter for that matter.

That aside, unlike most of her regular customers, and Larry for that matter, this bloke had a very nice car, good suit and a Rolex watch. That could have been a copy, there were a good few of those around Manchester for sure, but she didn't think so. No, this guy had cash and lots of it, which meant he could pull any manner of women, or buy the highest class call girls the city could offer. So, if she was being honest with herself, and Naomi was always that, what did this guy really want with her?

"What's yer name?" she asked.

"Stephen," said Rick. "Stephen Colletti."

"Italian?"

"Grandfather's side."

"You look a bit Italian."

"Is that a compliment?"

She smiled.

"Suppose. You are good looking, even with the scar."

Rick touched the star shaped wound on his cheek with a manicured finger.

"Car accident."

"Yeah right," scoffed Naomi, opening her bag.

"You can't smoke," snapped Rick. "Not in the car, not outside, not at all."

Naomi frowned.

"Hey, don't get frosty, man, or I'm out of here. I don't fuckin' smoke. Fags, weed, nothin'. I were lookin' for me gloss." She twisted in her seat and leaned across to be closer to him, revealing just a little cleavage. She was working him. He knew it, she knew he knew it.

"I bet you like shiny red lips don't yer?"

Rick put his hand into his inside jacket pocket and removed a cotton handkerchief. He handed it to her.

"Wipe it off," he said. "All of it, the gloss and the lipstick."

She narrowed her eyes.

"Are you a psycho or summat? I mean, if you're a serial killer, I'm tellin' you now, I'm tougher than I look me."

Rick turned his head and their eyes met.

"I'm not here to hurt you, Naomi. I just want to take you to dinner."

"Dinner?"

"Yes."

"And then a hotel?"

"Yes."

"To fuck, right?"

"To talk."

"Talk? What? Talk naked, talk dirty?"

He turned the car into a side street.

"We're here," he said. "And once you're inside, you'll understand about the lipstick."

"You're sayin' I look cheap after all that? I did my best y'know. To look classy like"

Rick undid his seatbelt and turned to her.

"The hair is fine. The lash extensions are a little over the top, but at your age, still okay. The dress is great, your shoes… well there is nothing we can do about those now."

She looked at her feet.

"What's wrong with me shoes. These cost me ninety quid."

Rick wrinkled his nose.

"They are a copy of a pair of Saint Laurent Cassandra Monogram Sandals, that would set you back close on a grand. I can see they're snide from here, hopefully no one else will notice. But the whole restaurant would certainly spot the lips."

"I like my lips red."

"So do I, but not in that dress… come on let's eat."

Naomi teetered after him as he strode from the car. She watched the way he moved, the way he held himself. Was he a copper? No, she thought, not a copper, a soldier maybe?

And a very sexy soldier at that.

TNQ was one of a raft of new eateries that had emerged in the Northern Quarter in recent times. The classic restaurant and bar was stylish but relaxed with exposed wooden floors and grand windows. Classic it was, but it wasn't frighteningly fine dining, so Rick considered it suitable.

They were shown to a window table where their waiter took an overly long time seating Naomi. Rick wasn't surprised. She was a very attractive young woman.

She sat and bit her lip.

"D'ya think he noticed me shoes?"

Rick smiled.

"I think he noticed just about everything else. Relax. Now, what do you like to eat?"

Naomi wrinkled her nose.

"I could go a drink first to be honest. Settle me nerves like."

Rick caught the waiter's eye and ordered an espresso martini for her, and an Evian for him.

"Don't you drink?" she asked.

"Not when I'm doing business."

"And that's what this is then, business?"

Rick swerved that one.

"Tell me about yourself, Naomi. If that is your real name?"

She took a deep breath before exhaling down her nose, leaned forwards, elbows on the table, the candlelight accentuating her obvious beauty.

"Look, Stephen, if that is *your* real name, the one thing I won't do for money, is tell you my life story. So if you were hoping to get off on listening to me carp on about how I got into the oldest profession in the world, what I've done with this guy or that guy, if I come when I'm with a punter, all that shite, you're going to be disappointed."

Rick nodded and stayed silent as the drinks were delivered. Once the waiter was out of earshot, he sat back in his seat, narrowed his eyes.

"We all have baggage," he said. "All have some history that we'd rather not recall. But I don't want to hear that. What I want to know is… what you want to do next?"

Naomi gave him a knowing look.

"Go to your hotel?"

Rick took a sip of his water then lay the glass carefully on the table. He sniffed and rubbed his face with his palms. When he looked up again, Naomi noticed his eyes had changed. There was a darkness in there that she hadn't seen before. A brooding malevolence.

"Stop working me," he spat, accentuating each word in turn.

Naomi wasn't sure what to do, how to handle the man in front of her. Should she stand up and walk away, take the five hundred and cut her losses? She knew she should, but…

"Look," she said. "I'm here because you paid me to be here, Stephen. This isn't fuckin' blind date you know? Why don't you just tell me what it is you want?"

"I asked, what do you want to do next?" he pushed. "You can't be a whore all your life."

Naomi coloured and looked around her to see if any nearby diners had heard his comment.

She pinched her lips. He thought he detected the merest hint of a tear.

"If…" she stumbled over her words. "If you want to use my body for your own enjoyment, inflict pain for your pleasure, then your money will more than cover that."

He could see her anger rising, the earlier flush of embarrassment transforming into a reddening rage.

"But," she pointed a shaky finger. "Don't you try and hurt me with your words. Don't insult me and certainly don't ever fucking patronise me."

This time a woman on a nearby table did look across, eyebrows raised by the colourful language.

"It wasn't meant to be an insult," said Rick flatly "Or patronising just a straightforward question. In my limited experience, women in your profession usually have a plan to get out of it."

"Limited experience?" snorted Naomi finishing her cocktail rather too quickly. "So how many girls have you paid for in your lifetime?"

"For sex?"

"For sex, yeah."

"None."

She ran a finger under her right eye to dry it, lifted her empty glass and waved it at the waiter.

"This night gets more interesting by the minute," she muttered. "Okay, Stephen fuckin' holier than thou Colletti. So, you want to pay me a thousand pounds to find out what I want to be when I grow up?"

"Yes. You could put it like that."

She leaned in, skin shining, lips parted. This time she wasn't working him.

"I want what everyone wants, Stephen. Health wealth and happiness."

Her drink arrived, and she took an overly large gulp of it.

"Two of those, you can't buy," she said. "But as for wealth, I'm the biggest earner in Sadie's. You know why?"

He shrugged.

She lifted her hand, palm flat down and held it above the flame of the candle that sat on the table between them. Rick knew what it felt like. He'd played the drinking game where you did just that. Within five seconds your flesh began to blister. Naomi eyeballed him and kept her palm steady.

"My pain threshold," she said. "I can take an extraordinarily large amount of it."

Rick could smell her burning skin. He grabbed her wrist and pulled her hand away.

"Stop that. I believe you," he said.

Naomi looked at him from under those heavy lashes. She was smiling, breathing heavily. She'd obviously enjoyed her party trick.

"I was always the weird kid. I liked to fight the bigger boys in school, loved to take their punches, loved the soreness of my knuckles from throwing my own."

"Maybe you could have taken up boxing," he offered.

She smiled at that.

"It didn't pay well enough."

"Fair one."

She looked into his face again.

"So, Mr Stephen Colletti, how come you are so rich?"

"I'll tell you later, at The Palace Hotel," he said. "Right now, let's eat."

Just before midnight, Rick slipped the card key into his hotel room door, and the pair stepped inside.

"Nice," said Naomi, feeling just a little giddy from the cocktails. "Very posh. Four poster. Good for tying me up."

"Why? Were you thinking of running away?" asked Rick.

"You're funny," she slurred. "A bit fuckin' scary, but funny."

Rick wandered over to a large ornate wardrobe, opened it and removed two metal briefcases.

"Ah," giggled Naomi. "You brought your own whips." She stepped in close to him. "Best unzip me if it's going to get crazy."

Rick gave her a sideways look.

"You can keep your clothes on. I want to talk business."

She pouted, flounced over to the bed and sat heavily. "I think I should at least take off the cheap sandals, eh?"

"No arguments there," he said.

Naomi began to undo the first shoe.

"Anyway, in the restaurant you said that you would tell me the secret of your wealth. How you make your money."

Rick dropped both cases on the bed next to the girl, slipped off his suit jacket, folded it and lay that next to the cases. Next, he casually pulled a silver revolver from the small of his back released the cylinder and unloaded it dropping the six rounds into his left palm.

He held up the empty weapon in his right.

"I kill people," he said.

Naomi was wide eyed and instantly sober.

"Is that thing fucking real?"

Rick showed her the empty chambers, clipped the barrel back into place and tossed the weapon to her.

"Kimber K6S, the world's lightest magnum .357 revolver. 3 inch barrel and an internal hammer that makes it ideal for a concealed carry."

She caught the gun and rolled it around in her hands.

"And you had this in your pants all the way through the meal?"

Rick nodded.

Naomi rubbed the gun with an index finger.

"Now that is fuckin' horny." She looked up at him. "When you say, you kill people. Is that for pleasure, or for money?"

Rick lifted one of the metal cases lay it flat and undid the two clasps. He then slowly lifted the lid, to reveal its contents.

"Mary mother of God," hissed Naomi, scrabbling across the bed to take a closer look. "How much is in there."

"Fifty grand," said Fuller.

She dropped the gun on the bed, grabbed a bundle and flicked through each note admiringly.

"Fifty fucking grand, wow."

Then the light came on. She looked at the case, then the revolver, then up at Rick.

"Oh, erm… just a minute now, pal. Y' don't think for one second that I'm going to…"

Rick picked up the handgun and began to slowly reload it, one round at a time. That black look, that glassy, shark like gaze had returned.

"A few moments ago, you asked me if I killed for money or pleasure."

"And?"

"And the answer is… it's complicated."

"I'm fucking sure it is."

Rick tossed the loaded handgun back to Naomi. This time she almost dropped it with nerves.

"Feels different now, doesn't it?" he asked.

"Heavier."

"Not just heavier."

"No," she said quietly, staring at the weapon in her hand. "More, more lethal."

"Lethal is the word. One shot is all it would take, and you could walk out of here with all that money, and whatever is in the other case."

Naomi shook her head and lay the revolver on the bed.

"Nah, not me. That isn't who I am."

"No… it's who I am," said Rick.

She stood and walked to him. She was so close she could feel his breath on her cheek. She gently stroked his face, looked up into those dark eyes.

"What made you this way, Stephen?"

He backed away, putting space between them. There was something about this girl that attracted him, something he couldn't fathom. But that would be crazy and let's face it, his life was complicated enough.

"If I was a shrink," he began. "I'd say, it was losing my dad before I was ten, my mother before I was a teen, the army, the murder of my wife by the IRA, and then… and then my own obsessions."

She closed the gap again, this time he didn't move away.

She wrapped her arms around his waist and rested her cheek on his chest.

"And I'm the textbook whore. No dad to speak of, mum on the game to make ends meet. Jesus, what a good Catholic girl she was... first sold me when I was thirteen. What about that for a story uh? And now? Well now there's no going back. No such thing as a normal life for me. It's this or..."

"Or what?"

She looked up at him.

"Or that fifty, I suppose."

"Actually," he said. "It's a hundred," and planted his mouth on hers.

***

Cogan sat in his lounge sipping a single shot of Jamesons. Bruce was at his feet, stretched out on his back between his master and the roaring log burner.

If Des had been truthful with himself, he'd hoped for some company this night. Company in the shape of the very lovely Shona Mackintosh. But things hadn't quite worked out the way he'd expected.

Their evening had started well, with cocktails at The Alchemist on New York Street. Shona had been chatty enough to ensure that there had been no awkward silences, and he had found her to be good company throughout the excellent meal at James Martin, Manchester. Indeed, he was delighted with the way their first date had progressed.

Des had decided to drive, so unlike Shona, had taken just two drinks all evening. He knew taxis from town to the suburbs could be difficult to obtain at night, and therefore he'd decided to take his car to avoid any awkward moments. Everyone knows that standing in the cold, waiting for a cab, surrounded by tipsy revellers was never a great idea on a first encounter. So the pair had walked, comfortably to Des' car, still chatting away.

However, it was as Cogan manoeuvred his Discovery out of the city centre that Shona had begun to look increasingly uncomfortable.

He'd suggested a night cap at The Swan with Two Nicks, which Shona had turned down a little too sharply, and whole thing grew colder from there on in.

It had been as if she couldn't wait to get out of the car to avoid any physical contact. Now, Des was no expert on females, indeed he would probably rate himself a total amateur, but it seemed to him that something, or someone had knocked the lady's confidence recently. Shona had been fine whist in public, but in private, as the time grew close for even the slightest intimacy, a peck on the cheek, a goodnight kiss, she'd fallen to pieces.

On a positive note, she had agreed to see him again, and had seemed to enjoy their evening.

Des sipped his Irish whiskey and gave Bruce a rub with his foot.

"I can pick 'em, eh son?" he said.

TEN

It had been an early start. Rick, Des, Jack and Jerry sat at an outside table at the Oven Door, transport café, just off the East Lancs Road at Haydock. They had two vehicles parked nearby that Jerry had commandeered. A black Mitsubishi Shogun and a silver Isuzu Trooper.

Despite Fuller's promise of a quiet conclusion to the operation, the crew were taking no chances and both cars were packed with kit, some taken from the Manchester lock up, some that Jerry had requisitioned.

Loaded in the 4x4's were four assault rifles in the form of the Israeli made ACE31's, a relatively new weapon that Jerry had managed to prise out of the hands of the secret service armourer. It fired the standard Soviet designed 7.62 round and weighed in at just 6.6lbs. The ACE featured a six-position telescopic stock, fitted with the optional cheek-piece. The weapon usually came with iron sights as standard, but Commons had managed to acquire each rifle specially fitted with the Trijicon ACOG 4x32 optical sighting system. The state of the art sight had been specially modified to fit the ACE and was widely used by the US special forces for day and night operations.

Rick had donated some CQC (Close Quarter Combat) kit, in the form of four PDW's (Personal Defence Weapons.) These were his favoured and near silent HK MP7A1's. All fitted with suppressors, extended magazines and Elcan reflex sights.

Not as quiet as the armour piercing PDW's, and far less lethal, were a box of M84 stun and half a dozen L83A1 smoke grenades. Then there was Cogan's bomb disposal kit, covert comms sets, listening devices, four sets of body armour, first aid kits, boots, gloves, hoods and coveralls, not to mention each man's personal handguns and enough ammunition to start a small war.

For now, Fuller had every intention of doing the job Casey's way, but if things went tits up, it was best to be the boy scout.

All, except Rick, were tucking onto their full English breakfasts.

Rick was feeling a trifle delicate as it had been a little after five in the morning when the surprisingly funny, charming and intelligent, Naomi had left his room carrying the first of her silver cases. His plan for Larry was moving on, but he also knew that patience was essential. Right now he must stay focused on the job at hand.

Simpson would just have to wait a few days to meet his sticky end.

He pushed a poached egg around his plate, took a sip of black coffee and lay down his cutlery.

"I must say, pal" smiled Des. "Ye look like ye had a rare old night last night."

"It was you that was on the date," countered Rick. "Shona, wasn't it?"

"Aye," said the Scot, shovelling a lump of black pudding into his mouth. "And very nice it was too. But I reckon she'll be a slow burner, if ye get ma drift."

"He means, he didn't get his leg over," chipped Jerry.

Des pointed a fork full of sausage.

"Yer only jealous there, Mr Commons. At least I had mysel some female company."

"And me," said Jack, shaking his head. "But I don't reckon I'll be seein' her again, like."

"Leanne?" asked Des. "Why no? She seemed a nice kid. Bonny too."

Shenton took a drink of his orange.

"Bit too keen, if you know what I'm sayin, Mr Cogan."

"So many women and so little time, eh son," quipped Jerry.

Jack reddened slightly.

"Somthin' like tha' yeah."

"None of which explains why our glorious leader here looks like a limp rag this morning," said Des.

"Something I ate," snapped Rick, giving Des a look to ensure the conversation stopped where it was. "I'll be fine once we get moving... So, Jerry, you've been on the blower to the big house, what do we know now? Any updates?"

Jerry shoved his plate away and took a gulp of tea.

"Pretty much as we expected, Boss. O'Shea and Walsh made the ferry crossing into Liverpool and have taken up a rented flat in Aigburth."

"Classy," muttered Jack. "Proper shithole that is. I used to go on the rob round Sefton Park... shockin'."

"Maybe they're on a budget," offered Jerry. "The terrible twins, Seamus Fennel and Gorgeous George McCaul, landed into Manchester and they've a rented flat too, nothing sparkling either, out of town... Bury of all places."

"Funny one," offered Rick. "I can understand them travelling separately, but I don't get this two centre holiday they seem to be on."

Jerry shrugged.

"Could be they want to keep one place forensically clean? Six say they came over naked. No weapons, no nothin'. Who knows, maybe they're shit scared of an ambush."

All four nodded.

"And still nothing at all on their intended targets?" asked Rick.

Commons shook his head.

"All we can say for sure is that there is more than one, and that they're all military. Our first job is to get into these two flats and get some ears in there. If the boys from Six are correct, this crew intend to make a real splash, so they must be planning to use some big stuff... mortars maybe. But with McCaul on board, I'd bet a pound to a pinch of shit that they'll use IED's at one site, at least."

Rich stretched himself and tapped Jack on the shoulder.

"So, it's me and you Jack," he said, with a sideways glance. "Off to your hometown and the delightful, Ms O'Shea."

"Yes, Mr Fuller," said Shenton sheepishly.

Rick pulled four mobile phones from a bag between his feet.

"Ok lads, here's a burner each. You all know the script. We use these the next few days until this this is done. GPS, Data Roaming, and Wi-Fi are all disabled, then soon as we're done, we dispose of them.

"Not much use without data, is it?" muttered Jack.

"It's a phone, kid," said Jerry. "And don't even think about carrying your own set. This crew are extremely surveillance conscious and may even have a backup team who have access to track and trace data. Even with everything switched off, you still leave a digital footprint of your move-ments with a mobile. So if this all goes pear shaped, a phone's history will help put us all behind bars. That means when we're done, so are these sets. If you get a tug son, the first thing you ditch is this."

Jack grabbed at his set and gave it a disdainful once over.

"Suppose."

"Right," said Rick. "Des, Jerry, keep this tight. If you must have direct contact with any of the targets, make it in a crowded place."

"Seamus likes a drink," offered Jerry. "He'll find the nearest boozer."

"Just keep your heads down," said Rick. "I'm not trying to teach you to suck eggs, Jerry, I know you're the guy with the experience here, but I have a feeling it might be your two players that make contact with the armourer, and he'll be our first target."

Jerry smiled.

"No need to remind me, Rick. I'm as keen to collect my share on this one as any of you. And speaking of targets… any more thoughts on the mechanics of all this? I mean, the noises coming from the top are to do this as quietly as possible, but I just can't see it panning out like that."

Rick nodded and pushed his own burner into his jacket pocket.

"The way I see it is this. They can't do anything until they take delivery of their weapons and explosives. Like you said, we know they came over clean, so that has to be their first move. Okay, we may be lucky and they could start to recce their targets before they get the goodies, but I don't think, so. I say we get our ears in these two flats and wait for them to meet this Abbas guy, then decide on our next move. If it's a straight handover in a pub car park or whatever, maybe we have to take it easy and follow the goods. If it's somewhere quiet, well…"

Jack was looking confused.

"Why don't we just slot the lot of 'em now. Before they get a chance to blow anyone up?"

Des was finding his pipe.

"That's a fair one, son," he said. "And it may have to be that way. But if we can get hold of their explosive kit, timers, detonators etc, before Georgie boy starts to make up his bombs, we could fix it that they go off when we want them to, rather than when he expects them to. Then the headline reads, 'Bombers blow themselves up' instead of 'Secret Service restart Shoot to Kill Policy.'"

"Oh yeah, see what you mean there, Mr Cogan."

Des tapped his temple.

"Up here fe thinkin', son," he smiled.

ELEVEN

Silver Street, Bury, Greater Manchester

Jerry Commons and Des Cogan were parked in their Shogun outside The Clarence, a fairly upmarket gastro-pub close to Bury centre. On the opposite corner were a couple of other pubs, one a Wetherspoons, that, like several other establishments in the town, had taken the name of Bury's famous son, Sir Robert Peel.

They watched as Seamus Fennel and George McCaul pushed open the heavy front door and disappeared inside.

Des checked his watch.

"Well pal, ye said big Seamus liked a drink, but even by Scottish standards, eleven in the mornin' is taking the pish. They havenea even unpacked, son."

Jerry gave Des a wry smile.

"They think they're on their fuckin' holidays, these boys. It will have been cases dropped, and find a pub, no danger. I know these two and their pals better than my own family, Desmond. This job has been running for almost three years. I've been working with Six over the water for the last nine months and only took a step away when we lost Mark."

"The guy fe Drumchapel? The one that took our patrol te the FOP at Dungannon? The St Jude's job?"

Jerry nodded but stayed silent.

"Jeezo," said Des. "The way ye told it back at the office, I'd figured he'd been gone a while, like."

Jerry sniffed.

"We did three more tours together after your ambush. But things were changing, methods shifting. The brass were becoming more and more politically aware and there was the first whiff of peace in the Province. The Good Friday Agreement was still a couple of years away, but even so, me and Mark were dinosaurs, has beens. We knew what was coming. We'd lived and breathed the Troubles for nine years. Everyone knew that there would be splinter groups who would never give up the cause, even if ten American presidents came to call. But that wasn't our problem anymore. We both put our tickets in together, June '97, and that was it, job done, civvy street beckoned. I'm a spark by trade, Mark was a brickie. It was back to normality. Well, so we thought."

"Never as easy as ye think, eh?" said Des knowingly.

Commons shook his head.

"We were both bored shitless. I'm single, so easier for me I reckon, but Mark was married with a couple of kids. He was pulling his hair out. His missus and little ones had become used to their lives without him. They barely knew him, and within twelve months, they'd split, and he was dossing on my sofa. Things were pretty bad to be honest. We were both on the edge. Too much beer, too much anger, too much time to think."

Des nodded. It was the curse of the professional soldier. You got so used to being part of something special. It was like being a member of a very exclusive club, where any of the fellows would lay down their life for yours. That feeling of belonging was hard to replicate, but the excitement, the thrill, the danger, that was near on impossible. And men like Jerry couldn't do without it. Men like Jerry and men like Des Cogan.

Commons shifted his weight in his seat.

"So, we were properly pissed off, the pair of us, couldn't see a way out. Even had a look at some mercenary work in the Middle East. Then, maybe three or four months later, we were up in York on a building job, we'd been rained off see, so me and Mark were doing what we did best, getting pissed in this bar in the Shambles. Anyway, we are five pints deep when in walks this posh bloke with grey hair. He sits at our table, all full of himself, lays his brolly down and orders himself a brandy."

"Cartwright?"

"One and the same, my mate. Anyway, he beats about the bush for a few minutes, telling us all about ourselves and what a mess we were making of our lives."

"Sounds like the old goat."

Jerry smiled.

"Aye, anyway, he offered us a little watching job. Some ultra-right wing fascist groups that MI5 thought were planning a terror campaign. The mission turned out to be a complete balls up, and we missed the guy. Bad it was. He went on to kill three, including a pregnant woman. Some of the injured lost legs. It was horrendous, pal."

"When was this?"

"99."

"The boy Copeland then?"

Jerry nodded.

"Yeah, Cartwright and his mob got a lot of stick for that one. The press found out that the boy had been a member of these other groups… the BNP and the National Socialist Movement. Unfortunately neither of the ones we'd been watching."

"Easy te say after the event."

"True, anyway, that was the beginning of it and Mark and me were finally back doing what we did best."

"And Cartwright gave you this wee job?"

"The beginnings of it. He was ill. We all knew that, but he was determined to catch this crew. One last hurrah. He always said that this splinter group were the most likely to restart the Troubles. Less gangster, more idealist, more partisan. Six had been playing around on the periphery for a while, then finally, when it was becoming more obvious that NIRA's military intentions lay over here, he pulled in me and Mark. We did a fair amount of travelling between the Province and the South, then once Casey took over, we were full time in Belfast. Back home."

"So what happened? How'd Mark get compromised?"

Jerry darkened.

"O'Shea. She clocked him in the Dungloe Bar in Derry centre. No idea why, but she didn't like the look of him. He was wearing covert comms, I was parked a couple of streets away listening in. I heard her asking him where he was from, all the usual fuckin' shite. Which school he went to, y'know the script, Des. Fuck, you're from the Gorbals."

"Aye, I know it only too well, pal."

"Anyway, Mark had never needed to change his accent, the Glasgow twang had always been good enough for the Provo's. All brothers together like. But not this time, O'Shea was like a dog with a bone. Where was he staying? Did he know this guy? That guy? Either way, I'm getting twitchy as fuck by all this, so I leave the car and start walking to the boozer. I'd not got ten yards when, I hear it go off."

Jerry looked at his feet a moment. Took a deep breath. Des could see he was hurting and knew his pain well.

"By the time I'd reached the bar, he'd gone, and so had O'Shea and whoever took him."

He took another breath and released it through pursed lips.

"It was four days before his body turned up. They'd worked him over real good. He was almost unrecognisable. They'd done his knees, fingernails… bastards. But they'd not found the wire. Somehow, Mark had managed to dump that on the pavement outside the bar as they'd bundled him out."

"So they could never be certain he was working fe The Firm?" said Des.

Jerry shook his head.

"You know all about interrogation pal. Do that to a man, he'll admit to anything. He'll tell you black is white. But no, they could never be a hundred percent."

"And here we are," said Des. "I'm no being funny here, Jerry, but I'm surprised The Firm still kept you on this job. Y'know, with all that personal shite goin' on in yer head."

Commons looked the Scot in the eye.

"When you work black, they seem less concerned about your mental stability," he snorted. "I mean look at Rick, if he's not a man on the edge, I don't know who is. And let's face it, we're all deniable after all." He rubbed a hand across his bald head. "Anyway, it was this, or I got on a plane to Belfast, slotted all four and hung their bleeding corpses from the nearest fucking lamp post."

Des gave Jerry a wry smile.

"Fair one, pal. I cannea blame ye. I'd do the same myself."

Cogan stared out of the windscreen and began to think about the ones he'd lost, the way they'd been taken, and by who. There were too many good souls, brave men and women, too many lives ruined, too much blood spilled, often on behalf of people who didn't really care. He watched as two men dressed in suits entered the pub opposite the small event bringing him back to the present, back to the job at hand. Pushing his morbid thoughts to the back of his mind, he sniffed and checked over the surveillance kit he'd packed in a small blue shoulder bag. Finally he tested his comms, pulled his shit together and changed the subject.

"I have te say, these new COV kits are the dogs. No so many wires like there used to be, eh?"

The team had been given the latest deep covert comms sets with tiny flesh coloured wireless earpieces and inductive neck loops with built in microphones, all paired with what appeared to be a BMW style car fob as a PTT (Push to Talk) system.

"Didn't save Mark," muttered Jerry. "I'll do my check soon as I'm in the boozer... You carrying?"

Des pulled his trusty Browning Hi Power from his waistband.

"Never leave home without it."

"The old faithful, eh?" smiled Jerry.

"Aye, go with what ye know, is what I say... Now, I'll get some ears in that flat of theirs and we can get this party started." Des turned in his seat and looked at Jerry. "You're no stayin' in the motor, ye say?"

Jerry nodded towards the Sir John Peel.

"Nah. Three exits on that gaff, and only two visible. Their flat is too close for comfort. I need eyes on both of them. If they drink up and leave, you'd only have a couple of minutes to get your arse out of there."

"Well, you keep yer head down, pal, we need ye on this one."

"This is what I do best, Des."

Cogan pulled out his pipe and opened the car door.

"It's what yer pal Mark did too, Jerry. Like I said, you take care with these boys, eh?"

***

Des sauntered past the Clarence pub and turned left down Bolton Street. He strolled by a row of small shops and then the East Lancashire railway station, until he came to Castlecroft Road on his right. On the corner was what looked to have been a solicitors' offices, but they appeared to have been empty for some time. Next to those, was a rather tired looking brown door which opened directly onto the street. On closer inspection, Cogan could just see that a faded number 84 had once been hand painted on the top.

"Bingo," he said to himself, stowing his pipe and hitching his shoulder bag into a comfier position.

He stepped over the road, pausing on the pathway outside his intended target, then looked about him and knocked. Of course, all the intel told him this was the right place and that the flat would indeed be empty, but if someone had it wrong, and never let it be said otherwise in these matters, it was better to find out now rather than after he'd picked the lock and was standing in some poor bastards front room with a Browning in his fist.

He waited, knocked again.

Content that the flat was unoccupied, he depressed the fake car fob in his pocket.

"I'm going in," he said.

Jerry didn't reply.

Des checked that the small LED on his remote PTT was flashing. It was. He tried again, but still, there was no response from Commons.

Cogan checked the street again, considered wandering back to the Sir John Peel to check on his oppo, then decided against it.

"In and out, son," he muttered to himself. "In and out."

He lifted his lock picking kit from his bag and selected his latest pick gun.

As with most of his Regiment, Des had been schooled in the art of picking locks. However, using jiggler or skeleton keys took time, and in broad daylight standing on the pavement just feet from a busy road, he needed speed. He required a tool that would open a yale lock in seconds, and not leave a trace of damage, and his latest Kronos electric pick gun was just the job. He quickly slipped a tension tool into the bottom on the lock and rested his forefinger on it to prevent it from vibrating out, then inserted the pick needle and fired up the gun. In less than five seconds he was in.

The front door opened directly onto a stairwell. Cogan stood at the bottom, gently elbowed the door closed behind him and looked upwards. Nothing seemed out of order. Plain white walls, stained brown stair carpet, bare lightbulbs hanging from ancient wiring, just a standard cheap rental.

He stowed his pick gun, rummaged in his bag again, and this time removed surgical gloves and shoe covers. Des quickly slipped them on, grabbed his Browning from his belt and edged himself quietly up the stairs, senses tingling. Within seconds he'd reached the landing. It was little more than a metre square with a grubby door either side. Des gently pushed the one to his right and it creaked open to reveal a toilet and shower that hadn't been cleaned since Adam was a lad.

He sniffed and grimaced before turning his attention to the door on his left. Pointing his Browning skyward, gripping it in his right, his left cradling the butt, he gave the second door a gentle nudge with his boot. It opened onto a short, narrow corridor, same paint, same carpet. It sported three further doorways. The one at the far end was completely ajar, allowing Des to see that it led into a tiny empty kitchen. However the other two were firmly closed.

With his Browning now in the aim, he edged ever forwards until he reached the first closed door which turned out to be a bedroom. It boasted two singles, newly made up and two pieces of wheeled hand luggage, both unopened by the side of each bed. The two boys had indeed just dropped their bags and gone drinking.

The final door led him into a lounge which looked over the rear of the property. Des stepped in and swept the room with his weapon. Once he was happy the whole flat was clear, he went about the purpose of his visit

Cogan had four bugs to leave.

Now, modern clandestine listening devices fall into three basic categories. 'Leave and retrieve,' 'hard wired,' or 'plug and play.' After much discussion with Jerry, it had been decided that the plug and play option was best. The leave and retrieve, by its nature required two visits to the plot and only once you had 'retrieved' your unit could you play back the recording, so no real time listening. The hard wired options meant dismantling plug sockets or other household appliances to get them installed, and that took time, so the plug and play won the day. The four units Des would leave were disguised as light bulbs. They looked and worked just like an ordinary bulb, and the tiny internal transmitter ran off the mains, so no batteries to worry about. Add to that, the units could be set to transmit on any given frequency, including the team's own encrypted covert comms sets, so, a no brainer.

Cogan had been in the flat for just four minutes and thirty seconds when his task was complete.

He tried Jerry again.

"JC come in."

There was a crackle, then, "Receiving. Bloody duff battery, pal. You on plot?"

"Roger, that. On my way back to the FOP. Where are our boys?"

"Living the dream mate, three pints deep already."

"Roger," said Cogan. "See you in five."

As Des pushed his SLP into his waistband, he found himself peering out of the lounge window. It looked down onto a funeral director's premises, then, behind that, stood an imposing building that obviously dated back to the Victorian era. He noted the fencing around it had razor wire on the top and that there was a red sign near the gate. Cogan pulled out a set of small binos from his bag and had a better look.

The sign read, 'B Detachment, 207 Field Hospital.'

"Surely no," he muttered. "Not even these fuckers would..."

He was brought back to the moment by the sound of a key in the front door.

He hit his comms.

"I have company," he hissed.

"Both targets still here," countered Jerry quietly.

Des heard the door downstairs swing open.

"Seamus!" shouted a male voice from the bottom of the stairs. "Seamus, George, you there?"

Des stepped silently over to his only hope of escape, the lounge sash window, but that was painted shut.

He grabbed at it, then shook his head. Even if he were able to force it and drop down the fifteen feet or so to the back yard, it would mean the Irish would know the flat had been compromised and the bugs would be rendered useless. In fact, the whole job could be tossed. The four may get cold feet and try again another day.

Cogan edged himself into a corner, facing the lounge door, Browning in the aim. Whoever it was visiting the Irish boys, if he walked into the lounge, it wasn't going to be his day.

Des took in air through his nose, controlling his breathing and heart rate. Even so the room became instantly oppressive, hot and sticky, and he felt a trickle of sweat making its way down the small of his back. Just to make matters worse, he heard footsteps begin to make their way upwards.

The Scot exhaled slowly and clicked off the safety on his pistol.

"Seamus!" the voice shouted from the landing. Then a pause, a turn, and steps downwards. "Fucking piss heads," said the voice as the front door slammed behind him.

Des let out a long breath and hit his comms.

"JC come in."

"Go ahead."

"Get me a feckin' pint in."

***

"So what did this mush sound like then?" asked Jerry, sipping a glass of shandy whilst Des gulped a Guinness.

Cogan eyed their two targets who were at the far end of the pub, getting louder and more raucous by the minute.

"I'd say he was youngish, thirty, deffo under forty. He had a local accent, Lancashire, Manchester, but there was something else mixed in there."

"Asian?"

"Possibly, Arabic maybe? But the way he called these two, 'piss heads' makes me think he was born here or been here a long time."

"Could he have been our Abbas?"

Des shrugged.

"Possible, but I reckon he'll be back sooner rather than later, so we may find out before too long. I take it this pair of comedians haven't had a visitor in here?"

Jerry shook his head.

"No, no phone calls either that I've seen. They've just concentrated on getting royally wankered."

Des felt for his pipe.

"Well, I'm gonna have a wee smoke and give the big fella a call, see what he's up te."

Jerry watched as Fennel and McCaul ordered another round of beers with whiskey chasers.

"Don't think you'll miss much here, pal. While you're on though, ask him what he knows about that Reservist place you mentioned, the one behind the flat. Could be a target that y'know."

"Aye, yer right," said Des and slipped out onto the street.

Once on the pavement, he lit up, took a long deep drag and exhaled a long blue plume into the crisp air.

"Now," he muttered as he stowed his pipe and found his phone. "Let's see how yer man is doin'."

Rick answered on the first ring.

"Afternoon, O' Lord and master," said Des. "How's tricks?"

"Watching Mata Hari and her sidekick eat McDonalds if you must know."

"Riveting… Let's hope that The Firm don't lose her head when this is over."

"What?"

"After Mata Hari was executed by firing squad, her body was donated to medical science. Her head was embalmed and kept in the Museum of Anatomy in Paris, but someone nicked it, and it has never been found."

"How do you know this shit?"

Des put on his best Manuel accent.

"I read it in a book," he said.

"Very funny."

"How's the soft lad?" asked Cogan.

"At the flat dropping the bugs."

"Aye, I've just finished that wee job."

"And Fennel and Co?"

"On the piss and have been since they landed. They'll be no bomb making this aft, I'll tell ye...but hey listen, pal, it may be a coincidence, but the flat this pair are staying in overlooks an Army Reserve Centre, says 207 Field Hospital on the gate."

"Jesus, yeah, I know it. I went there once to pick up a radiologist the head Shed wanted for a job. It's run by Army Medical Services, they recruit Consultants, Surgeons, Nurses, all that kind of stuff. It's a medical training centre for the Territorials. We go to war, they sew your fuckin' leg back on."

"So they'll parade once or twice a week in the evenings then, just like all the reservists."

"I reckon so."

"I'll find out when."

"Good call. Listen, Des, I'm off, these two have finished their Big Macs."

"Keep it dry, pal," said Des, and closed the call.

He walked back into the Sir John Peel to find Jerry finishing his shandy. The two Irish had ordered an all day breakfast each and were shovelling the last of it down their necks in the far corner.

"That should soak up a bit of the alcohol," said Des.

"At least it's keeping them quiet," smiled Jerry. "How's the other two fairing?"

"About the same as us, I reckon. There doesn't seem to be any urgency right now, but at least we have ears in both flats."

Jerry wrinkled his nose.

"They won't keep this up for long, pal. I reckon this is their last blow out."

As if to prove Jerry's point, Fennel and McCaul stood in unison, gave the barman a wave, and began to leave.

"Here we go," said Des. "Game on."

***

O'Shea's and Walsh's rental was situated close to Sefton Park on Irwell Close. It was a third floor two bed affair with easy access and parking. The

Irish had driven to it in a silver Peugeot 305 and had spent a couple of hours inside the premises whilst Rick and Jack irritated each other in their Trooper, by being unable to sit still.

For some reason, the Irish had decided to keep the car parked where it was and a taxi had pulled into the small carpark and took the pair away. Rick had followed them to McDonalds on Aigburth Road leaving Jack to take his turn at lock picking and changing lightbulbs.

Rick watched O'Shea and Walsh demolish their food before they stepped out and into another cab.

"You all done, Jacko?" asked Rick into his comms as he followed his targets, three cars back.

"Roger that," said Jack. "I'm just having a stroll round the block seein' where else I can break into, like."

"Everyone's a comedian today," snapped Fuller. "You stay switched on, son. These clowns are not, repeat not, en route back to the flat, so jump a cab yourself and I'll direct you."

As it happened, O'Shea and Walsh were headed for The Aigburth Arms, a modern pub situated on the busy Victoria Road. The moment Rick saw the gaff, he knew it would be impossible to park anywhere close by without being clocked. He would just have to go inside and get in close.

Not what he was hoping for.

The only plus, was that the pub was large and had enough nooks and crannies to sit in, out of the way of prying eyes.

The moment Fuller stepped inside, he clocked the pair. Connor Walsh was sitting at a table for four that looked out onto the car park. He was indeed a handsome boy, but what hadn't been captured in his photographs was the virulence of him, the anger, that toxic intensity. This was a boy who could bear a grudge until his last breath. It was in his eyes as he peered out of the window, clocking each car as it pulled in. Rick could clearly see Maria O'Shea too. She was off to the left of the long bar paying for a pint of Guinness and a bottle of sparkling water.

Rick put her in her late twenties, five ten, slender and long legged. She was indeed a natural beauty with raven black hair that shone no matter the light, and the greenest eyes he'd ever seen. Yet it wasn't her looks that made a man stare, it was her boldness, her manner, the way she moved, held herself, spoke. She captivated everyone around her. Yet, just like Walsh, there was an edge, a sharpness to her, something that set her apart from

the thousands of other beautiful women he had seen before. She looked…
dangerous.

The moment Rick made it to the bar he was approached by a young,
efficient member of staff. He ordered himself a black coffee, asked for a
menu and deliberately edged himself further away from O'Shea, feigning
his deep interest in the lunchtime specials whilst keeping an ear on his target's conversation.

As he ran a finger down the list of offerings, he could hear that there was
a problem with O'Shea's water. The glass bottle was a screw top, and the
barman was struggling to open it. She grabbed at it sharply.

"Give us it here the now," she barked. "Are ye a man or a mouse?"

The barman coloured and did as he was asked. Yet despite her bravado,
O'Shea couldn't get the top to budge either.

"I'll get you another," offered the young barman.

O'Shea's eyes flashed.

"That's the trouble with you English," she said. "You admit defeat too easily."

Maria did a quick recce of the bar before her gaze rested on Fuller. Rick
had his back to her, menu still in hand. He inwardly cursed as he clocked
her moving towards him in the mirrors behind the optics.

"Hey there, big fella," she said as she sashayed ever closer, bottle in hand.
"You look just the type to help a damsel in distress."

Just what he didn't want, direct contact.

He turned and lay on his best grey man act.

"I'm sorry?"

Maria stopped dead in her tracks, her spectacular eyes locked on his.

She allowed her head to cock slightly.

"And just what could a fine looking man like yourself be sorry for?"

"Figure of speech," said Rick. "We English are over polite."

"Really?" said Maria, narrowing her eyes, examining Fuller closely. "You
don't strike me as the type."

"What, to be polite or English?"

She smiled and held out her bottle.

"Could you?"

Rick was looking over O'Shea's shoulder at Walsh. Connor had risen
from his seat, face like thunder and was impatiently collecting his pint that
Maria had left on the bar.

"Maybe your husband could help you," said Rick nodding in Walsh's direction.

"I'm single," said O'Shea with a forced smile. "We're just here on business."

Rick took the bottle, tapped the screw top on the edge of the wooden bar a couple of times then cracked it open.

"There y'go," he said.

O'Shea held the bottle in her hand but looked at Rick.

"You're not from around here are ye? Not with that accent. Where ye from then? London, I'd wager."

Rick knew this was not going well.

He opened his mouth to speak, just as Jack Shenton strode in.

The Scouser pushed his way between him and O'Shea.

"Alright there, Dad," he said, in his finest Liverpudlian, squeezing Rick on the shoulder. "Have yer ordered or wha'. I'm starvin'. I could eat a scabby donkey me."

O'Shea took a step away.

"This your boy then so?" she asked. "Looks like a soldier to me. You must be proud."

Jack turned.

"Me? In the Army? Are yous off yer head or wha'?"

O'Shea wasn't convinced.

"Really? You look…"

"Listen, love," snapped Jack, oozing youthful confidence whilst unzipping his tracksuit top. "Looks can be deceiving, and, as yer obviously a woolly, take my advice and stop twinkling them lovely green eyes at the old fella here, or me Mam will scratch 'em out for yer, right?"

Rick gave O'Shea a helpless look and shrugged.

"Not my day," he said. "He's the protective type."

"Or mine," said Maria stepping away. She flashed Rick a smile. "Enjoy your food, so."

Fuller watched her walk back to a still furious looking Connor Walsh. The pair exchanged some trite words before they returned to Walsh's chosen table. O'Shea shot Fuller one last sideways glance.

"She's suspicious," hissed Jack.

"She's fishing," said Rick. "But you did well there… what do you want to drink?"

"Coke, and I'll have the cheeseburger please… Dad."

"Don't be too clever."

"I thought that was boss."

"Boss?"

"Y'know, good, funny, cool. And after all, you could easily be my old man. I mean, you must be…"

"That's enough now."

Jack smiled.

"I like this undercover shite. Yous can be anyone you want can't yer?"

"I suppose you can, but I can't see why anyone would want to be my boy."

Jack gave Fuller a look he couldn't quite read.

"And I can't think of a reason why any lad would not, Mr Fuller."

"I don't like the look of either of them," hissed Walsh.

"If you keep eyeballin' them, Connor, you might bite off more than you can chew, so."

"I could take…"

Maria grabbed Walsh's wrist.

"Yes, you probably could, but that isn't why we're in this shithole is it? Fuck me, this town is about as salubrious as Belfast, and that takes some doin.'"

"I was just sayin'"

"And I'm tellin' yer. Calm the fuck down. The young lad's a local for sure."

"The big fella ain't, and that scar on his face…"

"Is a gunshot wound, aye, do I look like I was born yesterday, Connor?"

"Well so. I mean, how'd ye get a wound like that and still be walking around?"

O'Shea shrugged and took a sip of her water.

"Maybe he's just the lucky sort. And there's no tellin' who gave it to him is there? I get the feelin' he's been a bad boy in his day, nothing more."

Connor took a swig of his pint, wiped his mouth with the back of his hand and risked another glance over.

"What did I fuckin' tell yees," spat O'Shea. "Ye look like a hare in the headlights, ye bollocks. Stop with yer fuckin' staring."

"I think we should get a picture," snapped Walsh. "Send it to the Brigade. Maybe one of the old boys will recognise the fucker."

Maria risked a look over of her own. She watched Fuller and Shenton, heads down, tucking into their food order, casual as you like. No signs of nerves, no indication that they felt they'd been compromised. Connor was talking bollocks as usual. He was on edge was all, and anyway, O'Shea figured that if MI6 wanted to put a tail on their team, they wouldn't do it by placing two operatives fifty feet away in plain sight, would they? They'd

TOOTH FOR A TOOTH

have a full crew on the job, telephoto lenses, the works. That said, Connor did have a point, and it was better to be safe than sorry, so it wouldn't do any harm to try and get a shot of the older one. There was something about him. Not just the looks, the clothes, the confidence, but something else, something she couldn't put her finger on. One thing was for certain though, had things been different, he was definitely the kind of man she would have wanted to get to know better.

And that was a rarity.

Maria pulled her phone from her pocket and set the camera. She tried several times to get a clear picture by resting the set on its edge on the table and randomly clicking away, but the results were either way off centre or blurred.

"Here," snapped Connor, grabbing the phone, "Let me have a go."

Maria glared at him at first, but then realised his plan. He walked around the table and draped his arm around her.

"Let's have a nice selfie then," he said with a smile. "Something to remember Liverpool by, eh?"

Walsh held up the phone, and rather than have the camera in selfie mode, kept it firmly pointed at Rick and Jack.

"No pouting now," he joked snapping three shots in quick succession.

He handed O'Shea the set and she scrolled the images.

"Yer not just a pretty face there, Connor," she said quietly. "I'll get these off to Cork, soon as. The old crew there will know him if he's been a player, for sure."

Walsh was feeling pretty pleased with himself, and it showed.

"The dickhead should've switched the flash off," said Jack, digging into the last of his fries.

"Not as sharp as they think they are, son," said Rick, finishing his pasta.

"Will it matter, Mr Fuller?"

Rick shook his head.

"The chances of anyone across the water recognising me are slim... very slim, but the fact that we've had direct contact with our targets changes things completely."

"Meanin'?"

"Meaning, either we swap our team around... me and you take Fennel and McCaul, or we move on the whole crew soon as. Finish the job."

Jack nodded, wiped his mouth with a paper serviette.

"I've always thought we should slot 'em sooner rather than later, Mr Fuller. I mean if we cock up and they manage to blow up any of these places. I don't think I could live with that."

Rick pushed his plate away.

"You'd be surprised what you can live with, son."

TWELVE

Cogan was cold. Directly across from the flat on Castlecroft Road was a small, grassed area with a few mature trees and bushes. He'd managed to get himself tucked in behind one and had a great view of the entrance of number 84.

In essence, this was a belt and braces exercise and unfortunately, Des had drawn the short straw. The bugs were working just fine and any movement, phone calls or visitors would be instantly picked up by Jerry or the Scot simply by monitoring their comms. However, both men liked the idea of getting eyes on any further mysterious visitors before they got inside the flat, so one of them had to be outside freezing their tits off.

Sadly, all Cogan had to report so far, was the constant snoring of their targets.

That was until Rick called.

"Our pair are on the move," he said. "They are in the car they arrived in, a silver Peugeot 305 Echo Charlie Zero Two Bravo November Alpha, now mobile, heading west."

"Okay pal," said Des. "Keep me posted. Sounds like our boys are just waking up too."

Cogan pushed his burner into his jacket and rubbed his hands together against the chill. "JC, come in," said quietly.

"Go," answered Commons from the relative warmth of their Shogun.

"Our two are up and about."

"I can hear, yeah. Must have finally slept it off."

"Could be a coincidence," said Des. "But Rick just called. The Liverpool crew are on the move."

Cogan could hear the two Irish moving around inside the small flat. There was some coughing and snotting and the toilet was flushed twice.

Then the kettle was boiling.

"How the fuck are we gonna find this place in the dark," asked Fennel. "I always said the meet should be simple. A feckin' pub car park, like back in the day."

"Yer nothin' but a big old dinosaur eh Seamus?" said McCaul. "It couldn't be simpler. As soon as yer man gets here with the van, we'll be on our way and meet up with Maria at the marina. Then, I'll put the location of the tower in me phone and it'll take us straight there."

"Maybe the boy with the van knows his way?" said Fennel. "It's his lot we're meeting, eh?"

George was losing his temper.

"He's a fuckin' gopher ye idjit, a fuckin' driver. Ye think Abbas is gonna tell all an' sundry where and when he's doin' his business?"

There was the sound of paper being unfolded.

"Well, fuck yer then," snapped Seamus. "I'll use me map. Look, the tower is here, see, and none of these roads from the marina are made up, so pound to a pinch of shite, yer fancy fuckin' phone will be as much use as tits on a bull so."

"So we'll use yer fuckin' map then," said George, a note of exasperation in his voice. "Let's just get on with the job, eh? I can't wait to get started."

Des had heard enough. He got on his comms.

"Ye get all that, JC?"

"Aye."

"Well, you know the lay of the land better than me. Rick says O'Shea and Walsh are heading west, that would mean towards the docks, eh? So when these bozos say, 'the marina and the tower,' what are ye thinking?"

"I'm thinking we're in the shit, that's what."

"Go on."

"Well, I reckon the marina he's talking about is Crosby, north of Seaforth dock, and the tower they're on about is a mile from there, Seaforth radar tower. It's been derelict for years. They've picked a good spot. Ideal for an exchange, but we'll have no chance of following them once we get off the main roads, it's all single track. We'd be pinged in an instant."

"Standby," said Des and pulled out his phone.

"Go," said Rick sharply.

"Listen up," said Des. "We have a face on his way here with a van. Soon as he arrives, we think this crew are going to RV with your pair at Crosby marina. They've mentioned Abbas by name and a tower. JC reckons that could be a disused radar tower about a mile from their RV, at Seaforth. Apparently it's an ideal spot for a handover, but it's that last mile or so that is the fucking issue. Jerry says we have no chance of following in a vehicle, it's all unmade single track stuff. Perfect for our targets, but we'd be spotted in an instant. We'll need to tab in. Get there ahead of them."

Rick was silent for a moment.

He sniffed.

"O'Shea and Walsh won't move from the RV without Fennel for protection and McCaul to verify the goods are kosha. The driver of your van will be just that, a driver. The real players will be at the drop, at this tower you mentioned. Des, I know this is shit, but somehow, you need to slow your targets up to give you and JC the chance to RV with us. Then we can all tab in and set ourselves. This could be a blessing. We could end all this tonight. If it's ideal for a handover, it's ideal for an ambush. Me and Jack will make our move now. I'll call you with our FOP once we get closer."

It was a big ask, but Cogan knew it was their only hope.

"Roger that," he said. "I'll call you when we're en route. But hey, Rick…"

"Go on."

"If this delaying tactic goes pear shaped, I might have to slot this pair and their driver in the street."

"If so," said Rick. "We'll see to O'Shea and Walsh this end and let Six deal with Abbas. One way or another, I say this ends tonight."

"I hear ye," said Des.

Des got back on comms.

"Jerry, Rick wants us to give our boys a problem, slow them down. he wants us all to RV together near the tower and move on the plot as one team."

"Fuckin' hell, Des. Fennel is a ticking bomb pal, you need to watch yourself with that fucker. You don't think we can just put our foot down and get there before them? Do this another way?"

"Not that I can see, not unless you have a spare Heli in your bag."

"If only," said Jerry. "I'll walk down to the station now. I've got your back, pal."

Des hunkered down back into cover and considered his options. In his mind, he didn't have many, disable the vehicle, or take the driver, who, from what he had heard was the only person who knew where he was going for certain. As he mused, he saw headlights. Ducking even further into the undergrowth, he got on his comms again.

"Standby standby," he hissed. "We have a vehicle approaching."

"Roger that," said Jerry, pushing his SLP into his belt as he walked.

The rogue headlights did indeed belong to a van. Des was instantly back on his radio.

"We have a white VW T5 panel van, Oscar Whiskey zero six November Sierra Alpha," said Des. "I can see a driver, no passenger."

"I'm two minutes from the station," said Jerry.

"Roger that."

Then a moment later.

"Confirming our targets are out of the premises," said Des, craning his neck to try and get a better look at the van's occupant. "Wish me luck."

Fennel and McCaul stood on the pavement directly outside the door of the flat. Both Irishmen were wrapped up against the cold. They wore heavy coats and woollen hats and carried two holdalls each that seemed light or even empty. Both scanned the street, appearing edgy, restless. The pair may have been well and truly on the piss earlier, but they looked alive enough now, and that didn't bode well for Cogan's hastily laid plan.

Des took a deep breath and staggered from the bushes, making a show of doing up his fly. As he did so, the driver's door on the van flew open.

"Target three is out of the van," hissed Des, gripping his PTT fob in his left hand and his trusty pocketknife in his right. "Confirmed IC6 male. I'd guess Moroccan, 25 to 35, 5'8" slim build. Black puffa jacket. The Irish are stowing their bags in the back of the vehicle. Standby, standby…"

Des played the perfect drunk. He staggered across the road and began to sing Flower of Scotland the only way he knew…badly. Fennel gave him a sharp look, whilst McCaul ignored the wiry Scottish piss head and got on with closing the back doors of the van.

Cogan reached the Moroccan player first, grabbing him by the jacket and falling into him.

"Hey pal, eh? Sorry eh, am a wee bit pished so I am. Would ye have a wee ciggie there fer an old soldier."

The boy pushed Des away.

"Fuck off you skank," he sneered.

From the player's accent and tone, Des instantly knew that this was the same boy from the flat earlier.

"Hey, dinnea be like that, pal," he slurred, giving the kid a shove for good measure. "I fought fe ma country, I did."

That did the trick. Seamus just couldn't resist taking on an old foe, besting a British soldier, no matter how petty the reason or circumstances. He'd never been able to control his temper. Even as a kid, his huge size had always ensured that he had the physical capability to beat an opponent. Add to that, his total confidence in his abilities with his fists, well, he was the complete package. The consummate aggressor, the absolute bully.

That said, Fennel knew in his heart that he should just jump in the van and leave this drunk to stagger along to the next poor sod he came across. This was the beginning of a massively important operation and any deviation from the plan was a bad idea. McCaul was desperate for his oppo to do the same. He too knew that his was the most important incursion onto British soil by an active service unit since the Birmingham pub bombings. This was not a night for fighting drunks in the street. All they would need would be a lone cop car to be driving by, just at the wrong moment, see the fracas, and they could all be in the shit. But George knew Seamus Fennel only too well, and nothing and no one was going to stop him from giving this old drunk soldier what for.

Seamus pushed by the Moroccan kid and got into Cogan's face.

"A soldier ye say?"

Des was playing a blinder. He closed one eye and did his best to look wasted.

"You're a big bastard," he managed. "Listen pal, I dinnea want ne trouble like, just a wee fag is all."

"Come on Seamus," barked McCaul from a safe distance. "We need to be getting off, leave the cunt."

Seamus didn't take his eyes from Des.

"Oh, I'll leave the bastard alright, leave him in the gutter."

The massive Irishman drew back a ham of a fist and powered it into Des' face. Cogan knew he'd have to take the shot, but he was wily enough to ride it before falling backwards against the side of the van and sliding down onto his backside.

Fennel was going to go in with the boot, but McCaul was having no more of it. He grabbed at the huge man's arm,

"Leave him, Seamus, fer fuck's sake. Come on, we've bigger fish this night."

Fennel eyeballed Des who was lolling against the van. He took a deep guttural sniff and spat on him.

"Murdering fucker," he shouted, and stepped away.

"Get in," said George. "We've a two hour drive."

As the van pulled away, not one of the occupants had seen the knife buried in the side wall of the rear offside tyre.

The Scot picked himself up and watched as the van screeched onto the main drag, headed towards St Peters Way. Seconds later, Jerry was standing in front of him. He grabbed at Cogan's chin and examined his left eye.

"That will be shiner tomorrow," he said.

Cogan wiped phlegm from his coat.

"How quiet is this place they're going to?" he growled.

"Quiet," said Jerry.

"Rick wants this done tonight," said Des. "I agree. And if I get the chance, that bastard is paying fer that one."

THIRTEEN

Rick drove the silver Trooper as fast as he dare. The route from Sefton Park to Crosby Marina was a little over nine miles but the going was stop start. Luckily, they now had the ASU's RV point, so he'd been able to overtake O'Shea and Walsh's car in order to find his own FOP close to the action. His gut instinct had told him that they wouldn't move to the tower until all four of the crew were at the car park. Just as Fuller was keen to have all his team in place before they made their move, O'Shea would feel the same. He just knew it. Safety in numbers.

That said, there was just one niggle. Just one itch that his brain couldn't scratch.

Why were the other half of the team only just setting off from Bury? It was almost two hours away by road at this hour.

Finally, his curiosity got the better of him and he pulled over.

"What's up?" asked Jack.

"What are they doing?" said Rick, half to himself.

"Wha' the Irish?"

Fuller gave Jack a derisory look.

"Who else?"

"Sorry. But I know what you mean, like. Are our pair early or are the other two late?"

"Exactly."

Jack turned down his mouth.

"Maybe it s cos they're clean, like. Maybe…"

Rick pointed.

"You, son, are a bloody genius. Of course. Who'd go to a meet to buy explosives without money to pay for them and weapons for protection?"

"I wouldn't."

"Me either."

"So they need cash and guns."

"Yes, they do," said Rick, pulling out his phone. "So they are not coming straight here, which means, my friend, we… have fucking lost them."

Jack frowned. "We?"

Rick ignored the kid, dialled and waited. Irritatingly, it rang out for over a minute. Finally, the person on the other end answered sleepily.

"Are you in bed, Simon?" snapped Rick.

"Erm, err… yes Mr Fuller. As a matter of fact, I am… well was."

"It's fucking dark, Simon. It's been daylight, but you've missed it."

"Ah yes, but you see, the old crone is away at my Aunt Mary's this week, meaning I have the full run of our salubrious establishment and therefore there is no strict timetable when it comes to breakfast lunch or tea, et al. Therefore, je suis La Belle au bois dormant."

"It's six in the evening, Simon. And I'd never refer to you as Sleeping Beauty."

"A good point, well made, Mr Fuller."

"Listen, Simon, this is very important."

"It always is when it comes to your line of work, Mr Fuller."

"I need you to find a car for me."

"Can I ask why?"

"No."

"Then finding this said automobile will cost you a bag of sand, Mr Fuller."

"Whatever, look. It was last mobile on the A562 heading towards Queen's Wharf. That was…" Rick checked his Rolex. "Eleven minutes ago."

"You're in Scouse land?"

"Exactly."

Rick heard Simon moving about, then the tapping of computer keys.

"Reg?" asked Simon.

"Echo Charlie zero two Bravo November Alpha."

"A Peugeot 305, previous owner from Leeds. Informed DVLA of the sale, but no current registered keeper."

Rick had lost patience.

"Just find the fucking thing, Simon."

***

Des and Jerry had made excellent progress but had run into stationary traffic on the M62.

"Bollocks," spat Des. "Just what we needed."

They had passed the two Irish and their punctured van, back on St Peter's Way well over an hour ago. Fennel and his cronies had been doing their best to remove the spare from under the van and appeared to be making hard work of the task.

"We'll be there in good time, Desmond," offered Jerry, calmly edging his way further down into his seat. "Don't stress. That lot will struggle with the tyre change for sure. Commercial vans are a bastard for having their wheel nuts overtightened. They'll need an extension bar to get them off for sure."

"And maybe they'll have one," mused Des.

"And maybe they won't, pal. Who knows, the big fella upstairs might be looking down on us and the spare could even be flat."

Des snorted.

"I've said more Hail Mary's than the Pope in my time pal, and the Lord never does me those kinds of favours."

Jerry looked over.

"Yer still batting aren't yer? Still at the crease?"

Des managed a smile.

"Aye, I suppose I am."

At that Cogan's mobile vibrated in his jacket.

"Go on, big man," he said.

"Listen up," said Rick with a definite edge to his tone. "Our pair have done a detour. We pushed on in front of them as planned, but I got a bit jittery, wondering why there was a two hour gap between the two crews' arrival times. Anyway, I got Egghead on the case. He's managed to track them using Liverpool's ANPR systems and they are currently in the Kingsway tunnel, headed for the Wirral."

"Any idea why?" asked Cogan.

"We think they're collecting cash and weapons. I mean, think about it, Des. They came over clean and this will be a big transaction tonight. You're not telling me that they would wire this cash to Abbas. They wouldn't risk the trail. No, I reckon they're meeting their money man and picking up some protection at the same time."

"Makes sense."

"I think so."

"Okay, pal," said Des. "We'll crack on as planned and find us all a good spot to kit up. Keep me posted, eh?"

Rick cut the call and pushed his phone into his jacket. He and Jack had made good progress and were just four cars behind O'Shea. They'd negotiated the tunnel and were stationary thirty yards from the Mersey toll booths waiting to pay for their crossing.

"Taking a big chance this," offered Jack.

"Meaning?" asked Rick.

"Well, back in the day when we was on the rob, we'd never do this crossin'. I mean, look for yerself, Mr Fuller, there's bizzies everywhere."

Rick nodded.

"But this crew need cash and guns, Jacko, and maybe the guy on the other side didn't fancy the trip the other way."

"I wouldn't," said Jack. "The coppers on this job have nothin' better to do than turn yous over."

Rick paid the toll and set off a safe distance back from their targets. As if to prove Jack's point, a marked police patrol car slipped in behind them causing some temporarily jangling nerves, but at the first roundabout, O'Shea and Walsh took a left and the cops sailed straight on towards Wallasey.

Rick followed the Irish at a discreet distance along Gorsey Lane before Maria and Connor turned left onto the dock road. There, the traffic became quieter, forcing Fuller to drop the Trooper further back from his target. Finally, he watched as the pair indicated right and pulled into the Seacombe Ferry car park.

"Get your comms on, Jacko," said Fuller, as he sailed past the entrance and into the first residential street on his left. "And give 'em a quick test whilst you're at it son. I want you tucked in, across the road there, just at the edge of the terminal building."

Jack pushed in his earpiece.

"Test, test," he said, thumbing his PTT fob.

"All good," said Fuller, organising his own set. "Okay, stay out of sight, son. This is a watching brief for now."

Jack pulled his Sig from his belt and checked it over.

"Better to be safe than sorry though eh, Mr Fuller?" he said, and slipped out into the night.

Rick waited until Jack was in position before he made his own move. The houses across from the terminal appeared to have been built in an era when most planners were keen to add small areas of greenery to their schemes, keep mature trees in place, make the place feel at least a little rural. So, as he sauntered to the corner of Birkenhead Road, a convenient low wall and a clump of mature bushes gave him lots of cover yet a clear view of O'Shea's Peugeot. It sat, nose to the river in a disabled bay, both targets inside, lights off but with the engine rattling away.

Rick blew on his hands before pushing them into his jacket pockets.

"Don't get too cold now," he muttered to himself. "Heaven forbid."

He hit his PTT.

"Jacko, you got eyes on?"

"Roger," came the reply.

"Okay, standby," said Fuller.

The minutes dragged by for Rick. He hated to wait, hated lingering.

"Come on," he muttered. "What's the hold up?"

Moments later, his wish was granted.

A Black Audi Avant rolled into the carpark and pulled up alongside the target vehicle. O'Shea was first out. She walked steadily around to the back of her car, opened the Peugeot's hatch and then stood there, back to the open boot, hands on hips, seemingly peering over in Rick's direction. For a split second, Fuller thought that somehow she could see him, but of course that was just his mind playing tricks. Even so, he tucked himself further into the undergrowth and waited for movement from the Audi. The seconds ticked by, but the driver stayed put. Maybe he would just wait for Maria and Connor to transfer whatever was in the boot of his German marque into their own vehicle?

But no, eventually, a pair of black trouser covered legs appeared from the driver's door and a white haired man stole slowly out into the chill of the night. He immediately twisted his frame, ducked back inside the cabin and pulled out a heavy leather coat, before slipping it over his suit jacket and turning up the collar. At that, Walsh too opened his passenger door, and moments later, all three players stood huddled together. There was a handshake for Connor, and a hug for Maria, before White Hair opened his tailgate.

Rick pulled out his Swarovski digital binos and set them to record.

He zoomed in as Connor moved three heavy looking bags from the cavernous boot of the Avant and dropped them into the Peugeot. As he did so, Maria and the Audi driver appeared to be in deep conversation.

White Hair still had his back to Rick, but even at a distance and in poor light, it was obvious that he was giving Maria some news, and, from her body language, none of it was good. O'Shea looked concerned for a moment, deflated even. White Hair rested a sympathetic hand on her shoulder. Finally, she nodded at him and appeared to steel herself.

What had he told her?

Fuller did his best to home in on White Hair's face, but the man had been in the shadows for most of the time, his collar still turned up against the cold night. Despite the poor light, Rick could see he was maybe late fifties or more, with that shock of white-grey hair combed back behind his ears and curled at the collar.

Fuller couldn't take his eyes away from the guy. There was something about him that was familiar, but he couldn't quite put his finger on it. He waited patiently for the face to turn, but he stubbornly refused, he simply walked a couple of paces to the back of the crew's Peugeot and closed the hatch for them.

Finally, he gave Maria another hug and whispered something in her ear, before strolling between the two vehicles and resting his hands on the railed fence that bordered the Mersey. As O'Shea and Walsh dropped back into their car and began to reverse out of their space, the mysterious white haired Audi driver remained in situ, apparently gazing across the water at the city lights on the other side.

"They're moving," said Jack.

"Standby," said Rick. "We know where our two are headed. I want a better look at this guy."

"Roger that," said Shenton and tucked himself back in the shadows.

Finally, with O'Shea and Walsh back on the road, the man turned. He felt in his pockets, pulled out a pack of cigarettes and lighter, pushed a fag in his mouth and lit up.

As the yellow-blue flame flickered, it illuminated the man's face perfectly. This time, Rick couldn't have got a better look.

He got on his comms.

"Go get the car, Jacko," he spat, "Start her up and pull her up behind the Audi."

Rick saw Jack turn and sprint across the road back towards their Trooper.

Fuller strode out of cover and across the road to the car park. The man was still standing in front of his car, still casually gazing across the river, enjoying his smoke, obviously relaxed now he had done his part for the cause. Once again, he rested his hands on the rail, leaning forwards, drinking in the view. He didn't see or hear Fuller approach, and before he had the opportunity to throw his butt into the Mersey, Rick was upon him.

Fuller grabbed the back of the man's collar and pushed his Kimber K6S into his neck.

The man didn't struggle, he simply raised his hands.

"Steady on there, son," he said.

"Well, well, if it isn't Patrick O'Hare," hissed Fuller. He spun the man around to face him, his revolver now pushed in the man's gut, ready to fire. "The man every squaddie in Belfast wanted to slot. Your picture was everywhere back in the day. On every wanted poster, in every nick in the province. I heard you'd ran to the States, after you killed that off duty cop that was."

The guy sneered.

"The Good Friday agreement, son. What a wonderful thing," he managed. "I was pardoned. Part of the deal. A clean slate. I'm a free man these days, Fuller."

Rick widened his eyes.

"Surprised I know yees name are ye?" spat the Irishman. "Don't be. Ye see, after I was cleared, the clever boys at six thought they'd turn me. Thought they'd be clever. Spent hundreds of thousands on me they did. They even gave me a wee job, helping them 'find' a few old Provo stragglers on the other side of the pond. Gave me access to all kinds of information they did. All kinds old files, old photographs. Even gave me the use of the office copier. Smart boys eh? So when Maria sent me her wee snapshot of you, well, it jogged my memory."

"So you gave your pals the good news then?"

O'Hare snorted.

"Enough for the Brigade to mark yer fer future reference. Ye see, yer already too late on this one, son. By the morning, the bombs will be made and planted and by the ten o'clock news, half of Manchester will be on fire."

Rick heard Jack pull up behind him, the nose of the Trooper almost touching the tailgate of the Audi. Shenton killed the lights. Rick shot him a look.

"Rev it," he barked.

Jack did as he was asked, punching the accelerator hard. The Trooper's three litre engine screamed, just as Fuller pulled the trigger of his revolver.

There was a dull thud as the .357 slug from the Kimber tore into the Irishman's gut. He gripped Rick's wrist in shock, holding the gun to his own belly, eyes wide, mouth sagging.

Fuller tore his hand away and stowed the weapon in the small of his back.

"Liverpool's nice this time of year," he hissed into the man's face, grabbing at his crotch. "The water's lovely."

Rick tipped O'Hare over the rail, into the black swirling Mersey. He watched his body float for a moment before the current took it away and dragged it down into the churning depths. Then Fuller turned, ran a hand through his hair, straightened his jacket and slipped into the passenger seat next to Jack.

"Smug fucker," he said.

***

Maria O'Shea was driving too fast.

"Fer fuck's sake, slow down," shouted Connor. "We've a car full o' cash and guns, you'll have the Garda on us before ye know it."

The Peugeot was fast approaching the queue for the return trip through the tunnel, and Walsh was nervous enough without O'Shea's disregard for the speed limit.

"Shut the fuck up, Connor," she snarled. "I've got us this far, haven't I?"

Walsh turned in his seat.

"And what's got under your skin, so? What did Paddy have te say te yees that has ye so hot under the collar?"

"Never you mind. It's my own business."

"And mine, I'd say."

O'Shea took her foot off the gas and allowed the small silver car to roll the last yards up to the stationary traffic. She took a deep breath. Connor was right, he had a right to know at least some of what she had just learned.

"It's the guy from the pub," she blurted. "The one you took the picture of. The one with the scar. Paddy had him in his files. He's SAS… or was."

"Fuck's sake," said Connor, a note of exasperation in his voice. "Then we need to call this off, Maria. I'd bet any money he's working fer Six, and who knows how many more of them there are."

O'Shea turned her head and glared at Walsh. It was the coldest of stares. He'd seen the look before. Seen it the day they'd caught the other Brit, Mark, the one she'd said was a spy, the one in the pub in Derry.

He'd watched her work him over in that cold damp warehouse. Watched her do his knees, pull his teeth and fingernails with pliers. Saw how she ignored his screams, his pleas for mercy. Watched her laugh in his face as he'd begged to be saved so he could see his kids again. And then, just when the guy could take no more, she'd set Fennel to work on him and ate a sandwich as the brute beat the guy to death with a hammer.

There had been no emotion then, no remorse, no empathy, and there was none now, only anger, an inner rage, and a hatred for the British that burned inside her, tore her apart.

"We'll not be callin' anythin' off," she hissed. "We will get this job done the way we planned, and by tomorrow night, the good people of Manchester will be counting their dead, just like we've counted ours for generations."

"But what if…"

"What if nothin', Connor," she spat. "This is not a fuckin' democracy. We go as planned, end of. We collect from Abbas now, then straight to the hotel in Longsite and begin our preparations.

*****

"We've been pinged," said Rick into his phone.

He and Jack had just exited the Mersey tunnel and he'd called Des to update him.

"How?" asked the Scot.

"Sheer bad luck, I'll fill you in later, but they know who I am and that I was in the same bar as them in Aigburth earlier."

"Maybe they'll put it down to coincidence?"

"In your dreams, pal. No, that won't wash."

"You think they'll bail?" asked Des.

"Maybe," said Fuller. "Only one way to find out."

"True. But they still collected?"

"Yeah, looked like small arms and cash, nothing too big."

"And the delivery boy?"

"Went for a swim."

"Really? On such a cold night too."

Rick checked his Rolex.

"Have Fennel and McCaul turned up yet?"

"Nope, must be having a nightmare with that puncture. But… standby… aye, the Peugeot has just driven by and pulled into Crosby marina carpark, so it looks like the job's still on. We're in a small layby about eighty yards further back from them. There are some warehouses opposite us with big murals of the Titanic painted on them, you can't miss 'em. I reckon if we follow the building line from here, it will take us to the path that leads us to the tower but keeps us off the road."

"Anywhere to kit up at the RV?"

"Yeah, no worries, just get yer sorry English backside here sharpish."

"Give me ten," said Rick, and closed the call.

Eight minutes later, Rick and Jack were there.

Fuller stepped out of the Trooper, walked over to Cogan and lowered his voice.

"The delivery driver was an old Provo that ran off to the States to avoid the cops. Turns out he was pardoned by our wonderful government, part of Blair's great agreement. And get this, when he came back to Belfast, six got their teeth into him, thought they'd turn him, even gave him a job. He had access to all kinds of old files apparently, even photographs of military personnel, me included. I knew O'Shea had taken a picture of me back in the pub in Aigburth. She must have sent it to him, and the boy put two and two together."

"Jeezo," said Des. "Talk about bad luck."

"Yeah, well, he's gone now."

"Good riddance," said Cogan.

Rick nodded and turned to the team.

"Right, let's get the bags out. We can kit up in those bushes over there. I'm going to risk my own phone and use the GPS to guide us in. Leave any ID and your personal weapons in the cars."

"Here we go again, in fer a penny," said Des, feeling for his pipe. "I'm havin' a smoke while the going's good."

Jack and Jerry lifted the heavy bags full of kit from their respective vehicles and dropped them over the low wooden post and rail fence that separated the layby from a grassed and lightly wooded area that had obviously been planted to partially hide the rather ugly warehouses. Once all four of the team had clambered over too, they split the load between them and tabbed into cover to kit up.

First, each man tugged on coveralls and boots, quickly followed by body armour and hoods. Rick and Jerry pulled on latex gloves and began loading mags. First the specially designed 4.6×30mm armour-piercing cartridges for the Mp7's then the 7.62 hi velocity rounds for the Israeli made ACE31 assault rifles. Des walked over to Jack and looked into his face. As brave a boy as he was, this was all new to him and it showed.

"Ye alright, son?" he asked quietly.

Shenton nodded.

"Think so, Mr Cogan. I just…"

"Just what, Jacko?"

"Well, I just don't want to let yous down like. I mean, you know, if it all goes off like."

"You'll be fine, son," said Des. "Look, strap the ACE onto your back… so. There's a clip here, see? Undo that and it will release. Grab the strap as the weapon falls and away ye go. Ye have thirty-five in the mag, and a spare… here, but keep this big boy in reserve, it's a noisy bastard and even way out here, it'll attract attention, oh and watch the safety catch, it's stiff as fuck. Now, carry the Mp7 on the sling in front of ye. There's forty rounds in the box mag, and again ye have a spare. This wee fucker is silent and lethal, ye hit a man pretty much anywhere in the torso and he's gone, even if he's wearing Kevlar, eh? Have a quick look through the sights and familiarise yersel with the safety eh. It's a three way, safe, single shot, burst of three and auto, okay?"

Jack did as he was asked and then nodded.

"Okay, Des. I reckon I've got that."

"Good lad, now, leave the smoke, flash bangs and all the other wee tools te me and Rick, keep yer comms on and once we get to the FOP, the big fella will brief ye."

"Cheers Mr Cogan," said Jack quietly.

Des smiled and gave Jack a playful tap on the arm.

"Ye'll be on the kop next week pal, singing Kenny's name with pockets full of money and not a care in the world."

Shenton managed a thin smile, pulled up his half mask over his mouth and nose and his hood over his head.

"Best crack on then," he said.

***

"Are ye lost or what, ye bollocks?"

Maria was pacing the car park, phone to her ear.

"We had a puncture," whined McCaul. "And we couldn't get the fuckin wheel nuts off. We had to call a garage, so."

"And where are yees now?"

"About fifteen minutes away."

"And yer sure that you've no tail? Yer clean?"

"As a whistle Maria. Stop yer worryin' won't ye."

She checked her watch. It was just before eight. The meet was planned for nine. There was one road in and out to the tower and knowing Abbas as she did, he and his team would already be parked somewhere close and ready to move. However, the young driver that was with Fennel and Mc-Caul would only give the signal for his boss to leave his safe position once all the players were in place. Everything depended on timing and trust, and the Syrian was not noted for his faith in human nature.

"Just get yer arses here soon as," she hissed, and closed the call.

She continued to pace, scanning the road up and down, nerves jangling. The marina area was popular with joggers and cyclists in the evenings, so it wasn't as quiet as she'd expected, and for the first time O'Shea was rattled.

"Where are you, Fuller," she muttered to herself. "Where the fuck are you?"

Rick was on point, making steady progress, just a hundred meters or so from the team's agreed FOP. They'd tabbed silently over rough ground, keeping away from the single track road that edged the basin and boating marina. Des, Jerry and Jack were tucked in behind him, all scanning the terrain around them for anything or anyone that may cause them a problem. As he tabbed those last yards, Rick could see the Seaforth tower in the distance, silhouetted against the lights of the P and O passenger terminal further south. The radar installation had been constructed in 1973, after the completion of the new dock, and at 86ft high, the 17ft square octagonal turret with its 47ft wide cantilevered control room gave the impression of a massive concrete mushroom. The building had been derelict for years, and despite local attempts to preserve or improve it, the tower was now due for demolition and surrounded by security fencing in an attempt to keep out trophy hunters and wayward kids.

Fuller held up a hand then tapped the top of his head with his palm, a signal for his team to join him.

They all hunkered down together. Rick pulled his phone from his coveralls and held it out for all to see.

"Okay lads, Google maps shows a massive car storage area directly to the south of the tower...here, see? Now there's thousands of brand new vehicles parked there, all shiny and ready for export. I reckon there has to be some kind of security around there, even if it's only a drive by every few hours, so I don't think any of our targets will risk an approach from that side of the plot, meaning the road that we can see running along the basin will be the way both Abbas and O'Shea will enter and exit. Right... you can see here that there are sea defences made up of large boulders surrounding the west side of the tower, and as the tide is out, I suggest that we find a way around or through the security fencing and onto the beach. Once we get tucked in behind those rocks, that will give us a clear view of this flat area... here, on the north face of the tower. I reckon that's where the exchange will take place. It's the only area big enough to park two or three vehicles.

"Agreed," said Des.

Jack stayed quiet for a moment then asked.

"So what's the plan once they get on plot, Mr Fuller?"

"We slot the fuckers," butted Jerry. "We fire through the fence, and if we need to get in close," he pulled a set of small bolt cutters from his coveralls. "We can cut our way in."

Rick held up a gloved hand.

"Let's hope we can get this done at arm's length, lads. This is an old fashioned ambush. Straightforward. Once the deal is going down, both crews will be distracted. The Irish will want to check the gear is kosha, Abbas will want to see the cash. We use the Mp7's where possible, the ACE31's are our last resort. If we start blasting with those, even deaf Aunty Eileen on the Belfast ferry across the basin will be able to hear us. So we conserve our ammo, aimed shots if possible... are we good?"

There were nods all round.

Rick pushed his phone in his pocket.

"Okay, I reckon the rocks give us a natural curve and plenty of cover. Mc-Caul and O'Shea will be wanting a good look at the explosives for sure. They may even want to test a small amount to make sure it's the real deal. That will leave Fennel and Walsh as lookouts. As we have no idea of the numbers in Abbas' crew it will be a wait and see, but however this pans out, we take the main players first. Keep your comms open and eyes on the prize lads." Rick sniffed, "And one more thing, we slot the lot, every last man Jack, and leave everything as it is for the cops to find. The cash, the gear, the corpses, got it?"

Jerry raised his brows.

"So Casey's idea..."

"Fuck Casey," said Des. "He's tucked up in his club having a brandy with his boss."

"Suits me fine," said Commons.

"Okay lads," said Rick. "Let's do this."

It took the team ten more minutes of steady silent tabbing before they found a way around the fencing. Then, as the sky cleared and the moon found its way out from behind the last of the cloud, lighting up the plot, all four were finally in position, their backs to the sea with a perfect view of the only possible meeting spot. Rick wriggled down into cover and checked over his Mp7 one last time. Then he remembered his phone. He'd taken a chance in using it, now it was time to switch it off. Just as Fuller pulled it from his coveralls it vibrated in his hand.

He had a message.

It read:

Larry wants to meet
me tomorrow night at mine,
Naomi.

FOURTEEN

Cogan saw the headlights before he heard the engines. They danced around in the night sky as the convoy of vehicles slowly bounced along the rutted, potholed track that led them ever closer to their agreed meeting point.

He opened his secure comms.

"Heads up, guys. We have four, repeat four vehicles en route. The silver Peugeot, the white T5, a dark coloured van, transit size, I'd say, and a 4x4. Looks like a Merc. The Irish are up front."

Des was using his night vision binos to get a closer look when he heard another familiar sound in the distance.

"You hear that?" asked Rick.

"Roger," said Cogan. "Dirt bikes. Three, maybe four. Sounds like they're approaching from the east side of the tower. Using the same route in that we took."

"Abbas is taking no chances," said Rick. "Stay in cover, guys. No one makes a move until I give the order."

As was expected, the bikes were the first to arrive, and much to Cogan's concern, there were indeed four, their riders dressed in black leathers with matching full face helmets. All had automatic weapons strapped to their backs.

"They look like M4's," said Jerry.

"Standby," said Rick.

The four riders were of course inside the compound, inside the fence that surrounded the tower, separating them from Fuller and his team. They parked up their bikes then removed their helmets and checked over their weapons.

"These boys look switched on," offered Des. "Standby, they're on the move."

Cogan watched on as one guy, the tallest of the four bikers began to bark orders at the other three. He spoke in Arabic, but it was quite obvious what his job was. They all pulled flashlights from their leathers and switched them on.

"Shit," said Des. "They're going to do a sweep before the troops arrive."

The Scot knew that all any of the four riders would need to do was look through the chain link fence that separated them, then down towards the beach, and the team would be compromised.

"We need to move," snapped Rick. "On me now, quick sharp."

Des, Jack and Jerry scrambled from their positions and jogged over to Fuller. Rick was desperately looking for a place to hide his team.

Finally, he spotted a dilapidated low, narrow building to the south of their position. It appeared to be a disused storage unit, an ideal place to hide, but it too was on the same side of the six foot high chain link fence as the tower.

There was no time to go around to the gap again, or for Jerry's cutters.

He jogged over and wrenched at a loose looking section. Jack rushed to help him, using all his strength to try and dislodge the rusting wires holding the links to the posts. Under the sheer brute force of the two men the wires began to give way, and within seconds they had lifted enough of the fence to enable a man to roll under it.

"Go," Fuller hissed, as first Jerry, Des and then Jack managed to scrabble underneath the corroded fencing.

Moments later, all the men were tucked in behind the old building where piles of old truck tyres and other miscellaneous junk had once been stored for a rainy day, put out of sight and harm's way, then forgotten, never to be used.

"Well that's fucked the job," whispered Jerry.

"Hold yer water," said Des. "Let these boys do their sweep and once the crews arrive maybe we can take another look see. We're inside the compound now. If we can edge our way around the tower, we can get in behind this lot."

Rick wasn't so sure. He had studied the landscape well. He knew it was possible to approach the plot from the south side of the tower, but the land fell sharply away just after the base. Of course if they made it that far, they would have height on their side, but once the shooting started, anyone firing from that ridge would be in full view of their enemies and those dirt bikers carried M4 carbines and there would be little cover. That meant any approach would have to be noiseless, and his team's attack, merciless.

The four men sat in silence and listened to the events unfolding across the compound from their position. They could hear the convoy of vehicles trundling into the cut at the foot of the tower. Doors opened and closed and there were muffled voices.

Des tapped Rick on the arm.

"I reckon I'll take a quick look, pal."

Fuller nodded.

"Don't take any chances though Des. Nice and easy, eh?"

Cogan edged himself out of cover and around the old storage shed until he could see the tower again. He was no more than thirty metres from the hexagonal base, a few steps from where the ground dropped sharply away by some five metres, the rim looking directly down onto where the Irish were about to complete their murderous transaction. Instantly, he could see another problem. Once any of the patrol reached the tower itself, they would have to crawl the last ten metres or be seen by the enemy, silhouetted against the clear star filled night. Sitting ducks.

But right now, the most important thing was for Des to get eyes on what was occurring down in the cut, so, the Scot, of course, did just that, got on his belly and crawled.

He silently tightened the sling on his Mp7 and pushed it around his back before dropping his body into the ground. The whole area around the tower base was wet with dew and covered in years of junk. Locals had cut various holes in the security fencing and discarded everything from old rusting drinks cans, broken bottles and condom wrappers to impede the Scot's progress. He also had company. Live company. He couldn't see them, but he could hear the rustles and squeaks of rats either side of him, as he disturbed their peace. He shivered at the thought. Rats had always been a pet hate of Cogan's, but he couldn't let that put him off his stroke now. He moved slowly, controlling his breathing, pushing his body forwards with his feet until he reached the edge of the ledge.

Finally, he could see down into the cut.

As he expected, the four bikers had formed an outer cordon and were set at intervals along the length of the road that bordered the flat area where the players were gathered. They were looking outwards, backs to the transaction, peering out onto the moonlit landscape, towards the man-made boating lake and the rough ground that they themselves had negotiated to make the scene. They had their weapons slung over their shoulders, one was smoking, comfortable, confident.

Maria was standing next to the black Merc 4x4. It had its tailgate open, and she was in deep conversation with a weather-beaten, well dressed guy who just had to be Abbas. He had an equally well attired bodyguard standing with him, a massive black guy with a shiny bald head. George McCaul and Walsh were leaning inside the back of the Transit, obviously checking the goods. Fennel stood close to the action, carrying a short machine pistol, a Mac10 or Uzi, it was hard to tell, wrapped in those huge hands of his. One thing Des could see though, was that he never took his eyes from Maria, or Abbas' bodyguard for that matter. That left the kid who had collected Walsh and Fennel from the Bury flat. He seemed uninterested in the proceedings, kicking out at unseen debris in the dirt, hands in pockets, and one other player, probably the black Transit driver, standing by his vehicle, smoking. Despite both these guys seemingly casual stance, they both had those trusty M4's slung across their shoulders, so couldn't be discounted once the action started. Right now, however, Cogan considered everyone looked casual enough.

Except Fennel, that was.

Des judged he looked anything but relaxed. He looked more like a raging bull about to be released into the ring.

"Rick, come in," he whispered.

"Go," said Fuller.

"Okay, we have twelve targets. The four bikers have formed an outer cordon on the edge of the cut but they've their backs to the tower. Directly under my position, we have Abbas and his bodyguard who is bigger than a house, plus the two drivers. As for the Irish, you were on the money. It looks like Maria is doing the deal with the Syrian, whilst Connor and George are checking the gear over. Fennel is edgy as fuck, has a Mac10 or similar in his fist and looks like he could go off any second. Oh, and as you approach, you'll need to crawl the last ten yards or so or you'll be pinged for sure."

"Is this doable?" asked Rick.

"Like fish in a barrel, pal," said Des. "Like fish in a barrel."

"Roger that, on our way," said Fuller, then. turning to Jerry. "Okay, pal. You take the right flank and nice and easy on the approach, eh? Jacko… you okay?"

Shenton nodded. Rick thought the kid looked pale. He knew how he felt. Jobs like this gave you time to think, time to ponder the worst possible outcome.

"Stay close to me, son," whispered Fuller. "And don't forget, we take the main players first, okay?"

"Yes, Mr Fuller," said Jack. "I'm on it. Honest I am."

Rick slapped him on the back.

"Come on then," he said. "Let's get this done."

As Rick, JC and Jack edged their way to Des' position, the Scot continued with his commentary on the movements of their targets.

"O'Shea is still with Abbas. He's pulled some bundles of notes from her cash bag and the big bodyguard is testing them with a UV light. The bikers are half asleep on the outer cordon, but the two drivers, the ones closer in, are beginning to look twitchy. They're holding their M4's now... standby... right... Walsh and McCaul are pulling something from the van."

Rick was down in the crawl, doing his best to avoid some rather unpleasant deposits left by the locals.

"Two minutes," he hissed.

Moments later, Fuller could just make out the silhouette of Des Cogan, peering over the edge of the cut at the targets below. He turned his head so he could see Jerry behind him and pointed over to his right. Commons gave him the thumbs up and began to crawl away towards the far flank. Then Rick stopped and waited for Jack to catch him up. Once the young Liverpudlian was within touching distance, he got in his ear. Comms were one thing, but Fuller knew, when you had a raw recruit, a new lad to this kind of operation, the personal touch settled some nerves.

"I want you there," he pointed. "Between me and Jerry, yeah? And steady away, son," he hissed. "Be really careful at the edge and wait for my command, okay?"

Shenton swallowed hard and nodded before crawling off into the night.

Rick was just feet from Des when the Scot got back on his comms. His voice quiet but incredulous.

"You are not going to believe this, pal. But that box the two boys just pulled fe the wee van has Russian markings, now excuse my French here but it says... Ruchnoy Protivotankoviy Granatomyot and then a code... T tango, D bravo, 7, G Golf."

"RPG's," hissed Jerry.

"Worse than that pal," whispered Des. "The TB7G has a thermobaric warhead."

"What the fuck is that?" asked Jack, still edging his way to his allocated point.

Des wanted to explain to the young lad, that a Thermobaric weapon, or vacuum bomb was designed to kill its living targets in a unique and most unpleasant way. When you used an RPG with a thermobaric warhead, it wasn't the explosion that did the damage, it was the pressure wave, and more importantly, the subsequent vacuum, which ruptured the lungs, popped eyeballs or burst your liver. Even if the fuel in the warhead combusted but didn't detonate, victims would still be severely burned or inhale the burning fuel. And since the most commonly used fuels, ethylene oxide and propylene oxide, are highly toxic, the undetonated gasses proved as lethal to personnel caught within the cloud as with most chemical weapons. Either way, your chosen victims died in agony.

However, Des didn't have the time for the chemistry lesson, so he simply managed,

"It's a fuckin' nasty piece of kit, son."

Finally, Rick made the edge of the cut and took a quick recce.

Walsh was opening the crate with the Russian lettering on it whilst McCaul examined something in another metal box.

"Plastic explosives. C4 maybe?" whispered Fuller. "Fuck me, these guys aren't playing around."

Rick twisted his frame slightly in order to get his Mp7 into a firing position, still taking care not to point the suppressor over the edge of the drop, therefore making it visible to the enemy.

"Okay, lads," he hissed. "Sort yourselves out and wait for my command. Remember, the main players are our priority."

No one acknowledged him. There was no need. Every man knew his job. There would be racing hearts and damp palms, but also a clarity, a transparency and precision that only came with the level of expertise and experience of such accomplished fighting men.

"Standby, standby," he whispered.

One slightly less accomplished player was Jack. He too needed to lift himself slightly to get at his H and K. He rolled a couple of inches to his left to free the weapon from under his arm. Next, he carefully extended the stock and settled himself back into a firing position. He could just see Fennel's head. The huge Irishman was pacing up and down muttering to himself. Jack thought he looked like his nerves were getting the better of him.

Shenton knew how he felt.

"Fuck's sake, Maria," suddenly bawled Fennel. "Are we ready or what?"

"Shush, why don't yees," hissed O'Shea. "Keep yer hair on and yer eyes peeled."

Fennel spat on the ground and continued to pace, throwing the odd hate filled glance towards Abbas and his guard.

Jack lifted his weapon carefully into the aim and slipped off the safety, selecting single shot as Rick had requested.

He was ready. He took in a long deep breath and began to exhale, settling himself.

But in that moment, in that split second, he felt his elbow catch something on the ground. With his heart in his mouth, Jack turned his head. He hadn't noticed anything close by, he'd simply felt the resistance as his body touched something solid. Then he saw it, a bottle, an empty glass bottle, and it was rolling slowly towards the edge of the cut. Agonisingly, it rocked on the lip of the precipice as if undecided on its fate. Jack knew he needed to stop it falling down the sheer five metre drop into the cut. He released his right hand from his weapon and made to grab it, but even with his lightning reflexes, he was too late, the bottle slipped through his gloved fingers and fell, clattering down into the darkness, before shattering on the ground below.

It wasn't the loudest of sounds, but to Jack, it was an explosion.

As for Fennel, who had been on edge all night, it was the only excuse he needed.

With his machine pistol set to fully automatic, he blindly turned towards the sound and strafed the top of the cut where Jack was positioned. His Uzi was wild and off target, the inaccuracy of the old gun making his job even harder, but it was enough to set off the two Syrian boys, the two drivers, who instantly let go with their M4's.

They too were firing blindly, nerves getting the better of them.

O'Shea was about to scream at them to hold their fire. After all, the noise could have been caused by a feral cat or fox. But deep in her gut, she knew differently.

"Fuller," she hissed, grabbing at her own SLP. "It just has to be you."

Walsh and McCaul began to hurriedly load their precious cargo back into the black Transit as Abbas' bodyguard pushed his charge inside the Merc 4x4 before he too, turned and let go with his own sidearm at the unseen enemy above.

It was carnage.

The ground directly in front of the team exploded in a hail of red hot 9mm and 5.56 rounds. Shards of glass and tin flew into the faces of Rick, Des, Jack and Jerry, driving them backwards, forcing them to use the ledge as cover.

Yet this was not a time for the faint-hearted and Fuller knew it.

Rick pulled two M84 stun grenades from his coveralls and lobbed them over the edge towards the main players. Des did the same with a pair of L83 smoke canisters.

The second Rick heard the flash bangs detonate he bawled at his team. They were words he thought he'd never have to use in battle, yet, as he dragged himself to his feet and powered himself forwards, he couldn't think of anything more appropriate.

"Over the top, boys," he shouted. Jumping feet first from the ledge.

As he dropped, his heels dug into the soft earth of the cut, slowing his descent. He slithered downwards, steadying himself with his left hand whilst letting go with his Mp7 clutched in his right, his rounds disappearing towards his smoke cloaked enemy.

Des was next over, opening up with his own H and K on fully auto as he too slid down the muddy bank. He could hear his shots clattering into the van and the Merc, the specialist armour defeating rounds of the Mp7 easily defeating standard vehicle bodywork. But he could hear engines revving too. Engines and screaming.

Jerry and Jack hit the bottom of the cut together.

Jack was deaf from the enemy gunfire, and his eyes streamed from the billowing smoke, the steady sea breeze carrying it back towards the team. Dozens of rounds peppered the ground around him, some so powerful he could feel the earth tremble as they buried themselves deep into the earth beneath his feet. They seemed to be coming from all directions. It was near on impossible to identify where the enemy were until they fired. Then, and only then did they give away their position, their muzzle flashes cutting through the dense smoke.

A rather disorientated Shenton felt Jerry grab his shoulder and pull him downwards.

"Keep yer head down, son," he shouted over yet another barrage of 5.56. "And listen up. We're going to fire in bursts of three, okay? Fire and move, fire and move…Got it? On me son."

Jack did as he was asked. Keeping the former Det man on his right, he crouched as low as he could, aiming towards the white and blue flashes that peppered the smoke filled night in front of him. Jerry was like a man possessed. He screamed at Jack every few seconds.

"To your left. Straight ahead. Left again. There, to your right, come on son, fire, fire now."

Jack had never been as scared in all his life.

Fuller could just make out Des to his left. He was edging his way towards the Merc.

"Cover me," bawled the Scot, lifting his Mp7 into the aim and stepping up his pace.

Rick did just that, peppering what he could now see was the outline of the Merc. His rounds clattered and flashed as they found their target, whilst the Scot stepped ever closer.

Rick saw one of the drivers with an M4 pop out from behind the Merc and try his luck, but Rick slotted him with a single shot before he could get his own rounds away.

Despite the danger, Cogan kept moving forwards, firing as he went. He could see that the door of the Merc was wide open, and that Abbas' huge bodyguard appeared fatally wounded. He had fallen face down across the front seats. Taking no chances, Cogan stepped sharply around the door and put a single round into the back of the giant man's head. He then grabbed at his collar, and, using all his strength, heaved him out of the Merc, dropping him onto the dirt. It was only then that he could see Abbas himself. The huge CPO had done his very best to protect his charge, throwing his body across the Syrian as he'd cowered in the footwell under the team's hail of bullets.

Abbas lay on his back, shaking with fear, hands covering his face.

"Please, please," he begged. "They make me do this. The Irish, they make me."

Cogan put two in his chest and one in his head then moved around the Merc in search of his next victim.

Despite the ever dispersing smoke, Des could still only hear moving vehicles.

He shouted into his comms. "JC? Jacko? Can you see the van? The Transit?"

Neither man had a clear view. And to make matters worse, the motorcycle boys, or what was left of them, were giving as good as they got, keeping the pair pinned down.

"We're taking too much fire," shouted Jerry. "Can't see shit here."

Luckily, Rick could see their problem and began to take aimed shots in the direction of the bikers. His extra firepower seemed to quieten them, but the Transit van, and the goods, were getting ever further away and out of range of his Mp7.

He dropped his H and K onto its sling and slipped the far more powerful Israeli made ACE31 assault rifle from his shoulders.

Just as he was about to make the weapon ready, Fuller heard a noise off to his right. A half groan, half curse.

"British bastard, yees…"

It was, of course, Fennel. He lay on his back, gasping for breath, yet still pointing his Uzi directly at Rick. Fuller twisted his body, stepped sharply to his left and kicked the weapon from the Irishman's hands.

Fennel let his head fall back onto the dirt. He even managed a guttural laugh, which quickly turned into a hacking cough. Rick saw the blood pouring from the Irishman's mouth. He'd taken two rounds to his chest and didn't have long.

"It was feckin' empty anyways, ye bollocks," he gurgled.

Rick tore his eyes from the dying Fennel and looked across the cut. One single biker was making off, following the taillights of the Transit as it bounced along the uneven road.

Des was dragging Abbas from the Merc Jeep.

"We need to get after those fuckers, pal," shouted the Scot, blowing hard under the exertion. "I'll get this thing started and see to that bastard, Fennel. You grab JC and Jacko, eh?"

With the smoke cleared and the enemy's gunfire silenced, the night turned eerily quiet. Rick peered over to where Jerry and Jack had been fighting.

"JC?" he said into his comms, staring into the darkness.

"Off to your right," said Jerry. "Here, pal."

Moments later, Rick found the Det man. He was on his knees, working on Jack.

"Leg wound," said Jerry. "Femoral artery is breached. He's bleeding like a stuck pig."

Rick knelt by Jack's side. He was conscious, but only just.

"Sorry, Mr Fuller," managed Jack.

"What on earth for, son?" said Rick.

Shenton winced in pain as Jerry added more pressure to the inflatable tourniquet wrapped around his leg.

"The bottle. It was me who knocked the bottle off."

Fuller stood.

"Des, come in."

"Go," said the Scot.

"Leave Fennel and bring that Merc here, pal. Jack needs the hospital and fast."

Rick heard the Merc turn over and fire. And within seconds Des had the German marque's tailgate open at the side of the moaning Shenton.

Rick and Jerry lifted the lad carefully into the back of the Jeep as Des found a morphine pipette and punched it into Shenton's arm.

"You drive, Jerry," barked Rick. "Des will work on Jacko en route. The nearest hospital is Aintree University, ten minutes away." He checked over his Mp7, changed the mag. "And call that arsehole Casey too. Tell him to pull out all the stops on this one. No messing, we want the best medics and no trouble from the local cops, okay? I'll clear up here and we'll RV back at the layby soon as you have the kid sorted."

Des was hunkered in the back next to Jack. He was cutting his coveralls away to get a better look at his wounds.

"What d'ye want te do with this bag here?" he asked, gesturing towards a blue rucksack at his feet.

"What's in it?" asked Fuller.

"Bout quarter of a mil, I'd say," said Des, grimacing at the sight of Shenton's damaged thigh.

"Call it a bonus," said Fuller. "Go on, get Jacko on the table. I'll see you at the RV." He leaned into the 4x4 and rested a hand on Jack's chest.

"You'll be fine, son," he said.

Des gave Fuller a look that told him Jack might be anything but, then gestured over his shoulder.

"Give that baw face Fennel my regards," he spat, and pulled the tailgate closed.

As Rick watched the Merc drive away, he pulled off his hood, ran a hand through his sweat soaked hair and began the gruesome task of ensuring no one was left at the scene to tell any tales. It took him less than five minutes to find all the players and put a single round in each man's head, breathing or not.

Last came Fennel.

The huge Irishman hadn't even attempted to move and still lay on his back, gasping for every breath.

"Get it over with, Fuller," he said.

Rick dropped down on his haunches and looked into the Irishman's face.

"She told you then. Told you who I was?"

"Some of it."

"Some?"

"Yer name and that you were once SAS, no more. She plays her cards close that one."

Rick nodded.

"Whatever, anyway, it looks like you drew the short one, Fennel," he said. "Your boss Maria, Connor and Georgie boy are all on their toes."

"They get to see the fireworks," managed Fennel. "Shame I'll miss 'em."

Rick let out a long slow breath.

"Y'know something, Seamus… you don't mind if I call you Seamus d'ya?"

"Like I give a fuck."

"Thought so… well, Seamus, I always figured that if I got gut shot, or took a couple in the chest like yourself, that someone like me would come along and finish the job, y'know, show some mercy, put me out of my misery. See, I've never been frightened of dying, but when my time comes, I want it to be quick. I don't want to be like you, lying there in a pool of my own claret gasping for breath."

Fennel closed his eyes a moment, then looked Fuller in the face.

"So just finish me then. One soldier to another."

Rick smiled, nodded.

"Soldiers… hmm… yeah course. Now, you're a good Catholic boy, aren't you, Seamus? You drank the wine, broke the bread. Bet you were even an altar boy, eh?"

Fennel turned his face away.

"None of yer fuckin' business."

"True," said Fuller, pointing a gloved finger. "But it must be a worry for you, eh? See, I don't believe in the hereafter, heaven or hell. I don't believe that there will be a penance to pay for my sins. I won't be knocking at the pearly gates hoping for absolution. But you…"

Fennel coughed, winced, "What the fuck are yees talking about."

"Well, I was thinking, y'know, as you have very little time left, you might want to at least try and make peace with your maker, so to speak."

Fennel's eyes widened, flashed with hatred.

"I'll tell yees nothin' of the operation if that's what ye are suggestin'. I'm a freedom fighter so I am, and, unlike yerself who murders fer money, I kill for a united Ireland. In the name of the righteous. They'll be no debt to pay on the other side fer me, no atonement, no need fer repentance."

Rick nodded slowly and pointed his H and K at Fennel's forehead, he sniffed.

"Someone once asked me if I ever see the ones I've killed in my dreams. Do you see them, Seamus? The people that you've shot, bludgeoned to death. Do you see them…still see them?"

Rick knew the Irishman was in tremendous pain, but he was a tough boy, a genuine hard case. He gritted his teeth, eyes darting this way and that. Then managed, "And what was yer answer, Fuller? What did yees say? Do yees? Do yees see 'em? The ghosts?"

Fuller nodded.

"I won't lie to you, Fennel. I see some, yeah."

There was silence a moment, before the Irishman nodded.

"Aye, I suppose," he said. "So do I… some."

Rick flicked off the safety.

"You sure you don't want to say a hail Mary or somethin'? Just for old time's sake, like?

Rick had watched Fennel's eyes change. The moment he'd heard that safety click off, they switched from defiance to dread.

The Irishman finally nodded.

"Well, if that's what yer offerin'. I'll take that, so," he said quietly, then rummaged around the collar of his shirt with a blood-soaked hand. Finally he found what he was looking for, grabbed at a small gold cross hanging from a thin chain and closed his eyes.

"Just a minute," said Fuller.

Fennel looked up.

"What now?"

"I've changed my mind," said Rick, and pulled the trigger.

Fuller examined Fennel's corpse for a moment, head cocked, and considered what he had just done. Given a man hope, and then taken it away.

Had he eliminated any prospect of everlasting life, for Seamus Fennel? Forgiveness or clemency?

No matter how tenuous or fragile the prospect, believer or no, had he truly snuffed out another man's last opportunity for absolution?

Would Fennel now burn in hell for his crimes?

Well, if so, Fuller was certain of one thing.

He would see him there.

Rick strode over to the silver Peugeot that O'Shea and Walsh had arrived in. It appeared undamaged and at least he knew the car was clean with no markers, which would be a bonus if he came across any cops sent to investigate all the noise out by the tower. He opened the tailgate, dropped his Mp7 and ACE31 in the boot, checked over his Kimber K6S and lay it on the roof and removed his covert comms. He then pulled off his coveralls and folded them on top of the rifles, pushed the Kimber in his Levis, comms set in his pocket and took in a few lungfuls of the chilled night air. There was still a hint of cordite there, that lethal aroma that had followed him around all his days. He blew out his cheeks, stretched his back, then rubbed his face with both palms. In that moment, Fuller felt every day of his age.

He was tired of the life, tired of the death.

Moments later, he edged his powerful frame into the driver's seat, then adjusted it to accommodate his long legs. Finally, he turned the key in the ignition. The French car fired up as it should, and Rick sat a moment listening to the diesel engine as it rattled away.

As the misted windscreen cleared, his thoughts turned to Jack. Would he lose another member of his team? One so young? He pulled his burner from his pocket and called Des. The Scot answered on the first ring.

"Any news?" asked Fuller.

"Too early, pal," said Cogan. "The boy's lost a lot of blood and from what I could see, there's quite a bit of internal damage around the groin."

"The round?"

"Still lodged in there. They've got him on fluids now and he'll be prepped for surgery in the next hour. Casey's sending a couple of suits up here to deal with the polis. Me and JC are leaving for the RV now."

"See you in ten," said Fuller, and closed the call.

He sat a moment longer and considered what Jack would be going through. Fuller had been there himself, he knew just how painful a groin wound was and how long it took to recover from such an injury. Of course, Shenton was a tough boy, young and exceptionally fit. Even so, a wound like that could cause long lasting disability and Fuller wondered if tonight's events may have just put an end to Jack's burgeoning boxing career. That would break the kid's heart for sure.

He liked Shenton. And Des had been right, he saw a lot of himself in the boy. Probably brought about by the same lack of parenting, the same poor upbringing. He recalled something that Jack had said to him in the pub back in Aigburth. Something about how, he wouldn't have minded Fuller as a father.

How that comment had thrown him.

Fuller had always walked his own path, and bad luck or fate had ensured that there would be no heir to his considerable wealth. There would be no son or daughter to spoil, to teach and to keep away from the life he had chosen. Losing Cathy and Lauren had made sure of that. Maybe that was his penance, maybe that was his own personal version of eternal hell.

Fuller shook his head, forced himself back to the present, pushed the Peugeot into first gear and slowly moved away.

The ageing French car groaned as it negotiated the rough ground, its suspension complaining with every pothole and rut it found. Yet there was another noise, one from inside the car, a definite shuffling sound that emanated from behind him. Fuller was about to turn and investigate, when he felt the unmistakeable coldness of a barrel against the back of his neck.

"Drive steady now, Richard," said a female voice.

Rick selected second and took a look in the rear view.

"If you wanted a date, you only had to ask, sweetheart," he said.

O'Shea lifted herself fully upright and edged closer to him, her lips almost touching his ear, pistol firmly in place.

"Well, I'm asking now... nicely. Take me sailing."

"Sailing?"

"I like the water," she said almost absently. "It's romantic. Especially in the moonlight, don't ye think?"

"I suppose it is. It might get a little chilly tonight though. And I really need a shower and shave, so if you don't mind..."

"Oh, I do mind," she said sharply. "I mind a lot. And don't worry about the temperature, I'll make sure ye get a sweat on. You'll be doing the rowing."

"If I'd known, I'd have packed my stripey blazer."

"I think ye'll find that's fer punting. A rowboat is more... casual. Now, just up here on the left is the boating lake. Keep going until you see the first jetty."

The rough track that the players had taken to the radar tower was bordered by the manmade Marine Lake. This was used by Crosby Sailing

Club and Sea Cadets. It boasted an adventure centre and kids playground and was a popular haunt for those who preferred life on the water. Not, however, in the dark and near freezing temperatures, no matter how prettily the moon shone.

After a couple of silent minutes crawling along the lane, Fuller could see the outlines of the first small boats tied up alongside the jetty.

"I have to say," he offered. "I'm surprised you're not on your toes with what remains of your team. I take it you know Fennel's dead."

"Casualties are inevitable in our business, Richard," said Maria. "You know that. Besides, I had pressing business here that couldn't be put aside for another day."

"Pressing business?"

"Aye, you Fuller."

"I'm touched you think me so important."

"Pull over," snapped Maria. "Here. Yeah, just here, and throw the wee revolver ye have in yees belt on the back seat. Nice and easy."

Rick did as he was told.

"Phone too," she said. "Same script. And then the car keys."

Rick pulled out his burner but left his personal phone in his pocket. He held it, two fingered, behind his head."

"Throw it on the back seat," hissed Maria. "I don't feel the need for personal contact."

"And here's me thinking you were going to be an easy lay," he said, defiantly dropping the phone and keys at her feet and turning his head.

Maria rapped him sharply on the back of his skull with the barrel of her gun. The blow was hard enough to draw blood and fill Fuller's peripheral vision with stars.

"Face forwards," she barked. "And do as yer told."

Rick felt warm claret run down the back of his neck and seep inside his collar.

"And listen," said O'Shea. "No more wise cracks. I'm going to step out first, then you. I'll tell you when to walk and what to do. You follow my orders exactly... understand me?"

"Did you train at Auschwitz?" said Rick, keeping up the irritating bombast.

"Bergen-Belson," quipped Maria, and stepped from the car. "Now, out," she snapped.

Rick pushed open the door of the Peugeot and got his first proper look at his captor. She was much as he remembered her from the pub. Stunningly attractive, yet starkly dangerous. He also noticed that she was bleeding. It wasn't a serious wound, but she'd obviously been clipped by a round just above her left elbow.

"I said, step out," she said. "Nice and slow and keep your hands where I can see them."

Fuller did as he was asked and stood directly in front of O'Shea, hands raised, eyes locked on hers.

"What's all this, about?" he asked.

"Turn around, Fuller," she said. "Now, see that little white rowboat there. That's all ours… off yees go."

Rick began a steady walk to the water's edge.

"You're in first," said Maria. "Get settled, untie her and ready your oars."

"Aye Aye Captain," mimicked Rick stepping aboard. "I don't suppose I'll need a life vest?"

O'Shea didn't bite. She simply waited for Rick to get onto the craft and make it ready. Finally, with her gun firmly pointed at Fuller's chest, she joined him aboard, Maria at the stern, the pair sitting opposite each other for the first time.

"Row," she said.

"Anywhere in particular?" asked Fuller. "I believe Southport isn't far."

"How about the middle where it's quiet," she said. "Where the sound won't carry."

Fuller began to edge the small boat away from the jetty. If he were honest, rowing was not his forte. He'd used a machine in the gym, but he couldn't ever recall attempting to row a small boat. It was harder than it looked.

Finally as the craft bobbed further out into the lake, away from the ambient light of the quayside, Fuller began to find his rhythm.

Maria was resting both her elbows on her knees, her pistol pointing directly at Rick's chest. With less than five feet between them, she couldn't miss.

"I hope you're going to tell me what this is about," said Fuller, slowing the pace slightly. "I'm the curious type."

"Just row," she said. "I'll tell yees when to stop."

The minutes passed slowly, Rick never taking his eyes from O'Shea's.

Finally.

"Bring in the oars," said Maria. "Nice and steady now, don't you be foolish."

The boat rocked slightly, the gentle lapping of the water against the hull the only noticeable sound. Again, Rick didn't look away from his captor, he examined her, scrutinising every small detail. Her green eyes flashed as the moonlight radiated off the water, illuminating her beautiful pale face.

She edged herself backwards on her bench, putting just a little more distance between them, right arm extended, pistol in the aim.

"The sixteenth of February nineteen ninety two," she said.

Rick turned down his mouth, shook his head.

"You brought me all the way here to tell me I missed your birthday?"

"I was born May eighty six, Fuller."

Rick shrugged.

Maria's eyes widened. She snorted in disbelief.

"Are ye tellin' me that date doesn't mean anything to yees?"

"Should it?"

O'Shea curled her lip, gripped her pistol tighter.

"Oh aye, fucking right it should. St Jude's church, Granville, Dungannon."

Rick shook his head.

"I'm sure it's very nice, but I'm not religious and I've never been to Ireland."

"Liar," she snapped.

"You shouldn't believe all you hear from your pal with the silver hair. He's prone to exaggeration," said Fuller. "He likes to gild the lily, so to speak."

"You mean Paddy?"

Fuller nodded.

"Well, I'll tell yees this about Patrick there, he's more of a man than you'll ever be Fuller. And he knows all about you and your pal Cogan. He's one of the best intel men we have."

"Had," said Fuller. "Past tense. He went for a swim earlier. I thought the river was a bit rough for that kind of activity myself. Maybe he gets his love of the water from you, sweetheart?"

Maria's pale skin appeared just that little more ashen, her beautiful petal shaped mouth twisted into an ugly sneer. Fuller could almost smell her rage. He was pushing all the right buttons and he knew it.

"I don't believe you," she snapped.

Fuller shrugged.

"Please yourself, darlin'. And look, although you make for company that is easy on the eye, and I'm not adverse to a romantic interlude on a moonlit lake, how about you get on with whatever you are planning to do eh?"

He leaned forwards a foot or so. Testing the water. O'Shea simply clicked off the safety, pistol dead centre in Fuller's chest.

"Not yet," she hissed. "Not until you tell me why."

"Why what?"

"St Jude's, the ambush. You and your patrol killed eight men that night. But what yees didn't know, and have never known, is that there was a ninth. A priest. Inside the church setting up for midnight mass. He saw you slaughter seven good souls on the car park of that holy place and then watched the eighth man throw down his rifle and run away. Run away into the night, into the pouring rain. An unarmed man. Then he saw a soldier run after him. And that soldier was you."

Rick shook his head.

"I told you, Maria, I've never been to Ireland."

She ignored his defiance.

"And you ran across those bog filled fields, didn't you? Slipping and slithering your way through the mud, bawling after him to stop. But he wouldn't. He wouldn't because he knew what would happen if yees caught up with him. He knew that you would murder him, the way yees had with the rest of the unit. But he grew tired. He was exhausted, soaked to the skin and freezing cold. Whereas you, oh yes, the mighty Richard Edward Fuller, you had more in the tank, and finally you came across him, coughing his guts up, unarmed and too wearied to fight. You could have taken him prisoner, but no, you shot him down like a lame horse, didn't yees?"

Maria's voice began to crack.

"You executed him. The hanging judge, and jury, all rolled into one. And then, to cover your crime, you put a gun in his hand."

She swallowed down a mouthful of anger and grimaced.

"And how do I know this? Because the East Tyrone Brigade only carried rifles that night, and that man, the man you shot down, was Frank O'Shea, my father."

Fuller let his head fall a moment.

It was pointless keeping up the façade and he knew it. How the Provos had ever found out his identity was anyone's guess, but he'd been at the forefront of so many operations over the water, both in and out of uniform, and for so many years, there had to be some comeback someday. Had he lost sleep over what happened that cold wet night? Of course he had. But the guy had given him no choice, and no doubt would have shot him down without a second thought had the roles been reversed. Sometimes it just came down to simple facts.

He ran a hand over his mouth. It was enough of a movement for O'Shea to grip her SLP just that little tighter.

Rick looked into her eyes and saw tears had fallen, just a few, but tears, nonetheless.

"That picture he had in his hand. The one he reached into his coat for, the one I thought was going to be a gun, That was of you and your mother, wasn't it?"

Maria didn't answer. She gritted her teeth, lips trembling.

"I challenged him," said Rick quietly. "I gave him the chance to surrender... more than once. It was dark, pissing down, like you said, and he... he slipped a hand into his jacket and..."

"And you murdered him."

Fuller eased his body backwards, tucked his feet under the wooden slat that he sat on, hands on knees.

He ran his tongue across his teeth.

"I shot him, yes. And as a result, you became the Black Widow. Did you know that's what they call you?"

O'Shea sniffed, managed a thin smile.

"I've been called worse."

"Ain't we all, darlin'. But me and you, we're different, see? You think we're the same, but we ain't. We ain't, cos after you put a bullet in me and push me overboard, you'll go on to kill innocent women and kids."

She shook her head violently, curled that lip again.

"Don't give me the rhetoric, Fuller. All our targets are genuine military installations."

"What, like the 207 Field Hospital in Bury? Civvy doctors and nurses, real hardcore, that is."

He saw that he'd hit home, so went for more.

"Thought you had all your lips sealed tight, didn't you? No traitors in East Tyrone? Come on, Maria, the 207 is a soft target by anyone's standards." He moved his feet wider, ready to spring.

"IED or RPG? What's it to be? I mean the thermobaric warheads are a nice touch. Your idea, were they? Not happy with blowing the poor sods to pieces, you have put them through unimaginable agony in the process."

It was Fuller's turn to grimace, to sneer.

"You're not the fucking Black Widow, you're a sinful, iniquitous, depraved piece of shit, just like your father was. He and his little band of freedom fighters had gone out that night to murder men in their beds. What was brave about that eh? And where's the courage in dropping a pipe bomb over a wall for some kiddie to find and play with? Tell me that? In fact, no, don't fucking say another word. Just get on with this and slot me."

"You smug fucker," spat O'Shea. "You think you know it all don't ye? But ye know fuck all. Know nothing about fighting for freedom, fighting for the return of your country. Ye think that a rocket attack on a training hospital isn't legitimate? They fix you bastards up so you can kill more Irishmen. That's what they do… and that makes them a valid target."

Fuller had heard enough. He powered forwards with his feet planted and went for O'Shea's pistol.

Of course, stripping a handgun from your enemy is always a dangerous activity. It requires speed and accuracy, as well as a fair smattering of good fortune.

The technique is to lean away from the weapon, bat the gun with the back of your left hand, then twist your body and simultaneously grab the underside of the barrel with your right, palm up, tearing the gun upwards and out of your assailant's grasp.

Rick had trained for this moment hundreds of times. But that was back then.

As he sprang, he swiped at the gun with his left and was arching his right over to grab at the barrel, just as O'Shea fired.

He felt the round tear into his flesh, knocking him off balance, felt the burn. It was like being hit with a red hot lump hammer wielded by a twenty stone man.

But where exactly was he hit?

The shock and the spread of the pain made it hard to tell. Upper chest somewhere, left side. Yet despite the searing agony, he could breathe… for now.

Somehow, he'd still managed to grab the barrel of the pistol and rotate it skywards, but Maria was clever, she knew what to do. She didn't fight the upward movement, didn't resist, just kept a firm hold of the butt and fired again. It was an instinctive reaction rather than a desperate one, a reminder to her foe that she was still in control.

Fuller felt the gun kick in his hand and spun his head away from the exiting round which mercifully flew past his face and up into the night sky. However, he was too late to prevent the muzzle flash searing his cheek, rendering him near blind.

Rick held on with all his might, twisting O'Shea's weapon away from his body and leaning into his enemy. Yet Maria was equal to him, the Irishwoman being both immensely strong and determined. She tore at Fuller's fingers with her free left hand, desperate to keep hold of her weapon, kicking out at him with her feet, raking his legs with her boots.

Bright lights blurred Fuller's vision and his left side was close to useless. Even the smallest of movements jangled every nerve ending, sending blistering rivers of pain across his chest and down his arm.

Being so badly injured, Rick knew his only hope was to use his superior weight against O'Shea. He had to smother her blows and somehow gain the upper hand in close. Using his powerful legs, he pushed his bulk forwards again, falling on top of her, as both continued the fight for control of the gun. The boat rocked violently, and ice cold water splashed over his back. Maria cried out in rage and twisted herself from underneath him, lifting her knees, pumping them into his midriff, desperate to land a blow to his groin.

Using all his strength, Rick tore the gun upwards with his good right hand then slammed it down, smashing O'Shea's wrist against the edge of the craft.

She screamed in pain but didn't let go. She was snarling at him, teeth bared, snapping at his face, his ears, kicking his shins. She fought like a banshee, bellowing insults as she did so.

Rick slammed down the gun a second time, then a third, and finally, he heard it fall from her grasp and drop into the lake.

It was a hard fought victory, and it had taken its toll on him. He was blowing hard, running on empty.

O'Shea wasted no time, scrabbling free from his weakened grasp, rolling to her left. She elbowed Rick in the face, raked his cheeks with her nails, gouged at his eyes. She was on top of him again. In control. He tried to fight her off, one handed, but was bleeding badly and he knew it. He could feel the warmth flooding down his chest to his belly. He felt sick, weak. Time was running out.

Risking further agony, he grabbed a handful of Maria's hair with his damaged left and swung a rather desperate right to try and land a blow of his own. He heard O'Shea grunt as he made a glancing contact, but she shrugged off the deflected punch and fought on, kicking and screaming as the boat rocked violently from side to side.

Rick rolled again, desperate to gain the advantage and overwhelm

O'Shea, to pin her down, but with the combined weights of both combatants now concentrated on one side of the craft, the small boat was close to capsizing. Water poured over the edge as Rick tired badly. He arched his back, lifting his body just enough to get in a single punch, bringing it down with all he had left, but Maria dodged it easily and he struck the wooden bench she had been lying across sending rivers of pain through his hand, up into his wrist. As he cried out in agony, O'Shea pushed him off her and rolled him onto his back.

He had nothing left.

Rick lay there, breathing hard, his chest covered in blood, face burned, scratched, bitten, his left side now all but paralysed, his right hand swelling by the second.

Maria lifted herself to her knees, then stood and steadied herself in the still rocking boat. Fuller didn't move.

"So, ye fuckin' coward," she hissed, picking up one heavy wooden oar and resting it over her shoulder. "This… is for my Daddy."

Fuller examined O'Shea through slitted eyes. The bright lights that had invaded his vision had subsided and despite his swollen face, he could see every detail of her. She was framed in the moonlight, the glow picking out every detail of her long raven curls that fell around her shoulders. She was still breathing heavily as she gripped the oar in both hands, but knew she could take her time. She steadied herself, feet wide apart before allowing herself a broad smile, raised the makeshift weapon, let out a cry and brought it down with all her might towards his head.

Fuller watched the oar as came down upon him. He knew he had to time his move perfectly or he was a dead man. At the last moment, that final millisecond, he rolled his shattered body, and the oar came down inches to the left of his head.

There was a crack as it struck the wooden bench and he heard O'Shea curse her luck. Not only had she missed her target, but she was now off balance in an already unstable boat. Fuller kicked out with his right leg, catching Maria on the left knee. He felt the contact and intuitively knew he'd done damage. She cried out again, this time in pain rather than frustration, and began to fall. O'Shea had no choice but to lose the oar and tossed it overboard as she tumbled atop Fuller once more.

This time, Rick had readied himself, pulling up his knees, ready to fight her off. With his legs as his only truly functioning weapons, he pushed them out and upwards to meet the falling O'Shea, slamming them into her midriff. She grunted, fell backwards and rolled away, scrabbling around at the stern in an attempt to regain her footing and control of the situation.

Fuller went for broke.

As Maria lifted herself to her haunches, he threw himself at her, grabbing her by the throat with both hands. The pain receptors in his brain were screaming at him to stop. It felt like his left shoulder was being sliced away from his body piece by piece, his right hand, so swollen he could barely move his fingers. Rick knew that he wouldn't have the strength to strangle O'Shea, however if he could get her head in the water, things may be different.

Using all his reserves, he pushed her towards the stern, her arms flailing in a desperate attempt to stay upright, but it was futile. She teetered and fell, her lower back striking the edge of the craft. Rick fell on top of her, desperately holding onto her neck. She tried to wriggle free of him, but with the majority of her body hanging out of the craft and Fuller's weight on top of her, she was helpless.

They were face to face now, he gripping her throat, pushing her head closer and closer to the freezing water, she punching his head, tearing at his face with her nails, eyes wild, cursing him with every breath. The boat rocked precariously, so badly that Fuller considered it may capsize at any moment.

Rick knew that if that happened, he would drown. He would have no way of swimming to shore or climbing back into the craft. This was the final throw of the dice. It was simple...her or him.

Maria was struggling with everything she had, trying to kick Fuller off her lower body so she could slip into the water away from his grasp, but she had no purchase, he simply used his bulk to smother her struggles, wrapping his legs around hers as he pushed her head down, lower and lower.

She could feel the cold water on her head, her long hair was immersed in it, and it lapped against her scalp. She tore at Fuller's fingers that held her throat so tightly and forced her body upwards using her tremendous core strength, desperate to keep her head out of the depths just for those few seconds more. The instinct of survival all consuming.

But it was pointless. Fuller knew he had her.

He looked into those beautiful green eyes again, his own no more than slick, black, heartless coals, locked his elbows, took the deepest breath, and squeezed her neck with all he had.

Leaning forwards as much as he dare, he forced O'Shea's head and shoulders lower, ever downwards, inch by terrifying inch into the lake.

His face was badly swollen, his hands, arms and cheeks were lacerated from her clawing nails, and blood still poured from his gunshot wound, flowing down his left arm. There was so much claret on his hands that his fingers slipped and slithered on her skin, painting grotesque shapes on her pale throat as they did so.

Yet any pain he'd felt had long gone.

In fact, Fuller didn't feel anything at all.

He grimaced and his eyes widened as he pushed her under for the first time. It was only a matter of inches, yet her reaction was unsurprisingly instant. She grabbed at his wrists, twisting her body with every last sinew. She glowered at him, fierce, defiant.

Oh yes, he could still see her under the water. He could see her perfectly. Her ashen skin, ruby lips, emerald eyes, all framed by her raven hair, which floated eerily around her shoulders, licking at her cheeks like a rare and beautiful sea anemone.

Yes, the moon and the stars had seen to that. The moon, the stars and the crystal cold water would do nothing to hide what evil he was about to do. The heavenly bodies and the freezing lake, determined to leave him with all the material he would ever need for his future nightmares.

Small bubbles formed around her nose, then larger ones at her mouth, but she kept those eyes open. They stared into his, flat calm now, all signs of any fear pushed aside by... by acceptance. The moonlight once again picked out her alabaster cheeks and highlighted her mouth. Fuller watched on as she parted her lips to release her final breath. It seemed to him to last a lifetime. And in all that time she kept staring.

Finally, she blinked, once, twice, then mercifully closed those lovely eyes forever.

He fell back against the hull of the boat, holding onto O'Shea's leg. He took a moment, then gritting his teeth against his returning pain, pulled her corpse back into the boat. Breathing hard, Fuller rooted in her jeans, found his burner phone and dialled.

"Where the fuck are you?" snapped Cogan.

"Can you see a lake from where you are?" he said.

"I can see boats."

"Well find the fuckin' lake they float on. I'm in the middle."

ROBERT WHITE

FIFTEEN

Cogan and JC helped Rick from the small boat and lay him on the jetty. They had towed his craft to shore using an almost identical vessel. Both men had struggled with the art of rowing, especially with the weight of Fuller and O'Shea's dead body aboard the second boat, and Des was still blowing hard as he cut away Fuller's shirt in order to inspect the damage to his chest. Rick winced as the Scot prodded around the wound.

"Dinnea ever ask me te row another fuckin' boat," said Des. "Now, ye need fluids, an IV. Maybe even a transfusion. And yer lucky it wasnea an inch or two lower or ye'd be a goner."

"You always did have the best bedside manner," said Rick quietly.

"And an X-ray," added Cogan ignoring his friend's chatter. "If that round has fragmented, it will have te come out. I say we take ye te the same casualty as wee Jack."

"And I say, it stays in me, like all the rest. Just patch me up. I'm going nowhere."

"Oh aye," said Cogan, unable to hide the incredulity in his tone. "Ye'll be all fine and dandy in the mornin', eh? Dinnea be so stupid, pal. Ye need the hospital, proper care, no a patch up fe me."

Rick grabbed at Des' with his right hand and flinched.

"Look…"

"Never mind, look," spat Cogan. "That's bollocks. Yer right hand is busted too. I don't even need a doctor te tell me that one. And as I'm about te put yer left in a sling, what de ye think yer gonna fight with? This job is over for you, pal."

Cogan found a pack of rapid haemostatic gauze and taped it across Rick's wound.

"Right, that will stop yer bleeding fer now. I'll give ye some morphine to…"

Rick grabbed at Des again. This time harder. And this time he didn't flinch.

"No morphine. Just bandage me up and give me a few co-codamol."

Des knew it was pointless arguing. He sat resignedly on the ground next to his oldest and dearest friend, rummaged for his pipe, filled the bowl and lit up.

"Richard," he began, blowing out a plume. "We have no way of knowing if McCaul and Walsh will continue with their plan, or if they'll simply run fe home. We have Jacko in theatre, you shot te pieces and nowhere te even start te look fe the fuckers. I say we call Casey, let him clear up his own shite, keep what's in the blue bag in the Merc and fuck it all off."

Rick eased himself painfully into a more comfortable position.

"The 207 in Bury is a definite target," he said. "She as good as told me so. That's a place to start."

"Aye, and maybe ye are right, pal. But what if we sit on that plot and they go elsewhere? What if there's more than one target?"

Jerry had been pulling Maria's body ashore.

"Don't know why you didn't just shove the bitch overboard," he moaned.

At that, all three men heard a phone ring.

"It's in her pocket," said JC, rolling her over.

"Get the number, quick," said Rick, lifting himself.

JC rummaged in O'Shea's jeans.

"It's a mobile," said Jerry clocking the screen. "0778853... Aww, it's gone off... and the screen's locked"

Fuller gingerly got to his feet.

"Give it here," he said. "And come on Desmond, where's them happy pills?"

Des pulled a blister pack from his med pouch and handed it to Rick.

"No more than four in twenty four, okay?"

Rick popped out two tablets, dropped them into his mouth and took the now silent phone from JC.

"Yes, doc," he muttered examining the screen. "Now, is that Merc Jeep you're in an automatic?"

"Aye," said Des.

"Then I'll drive," said Rick. "I drive, you two fight. That's the deal. Now, let's get what weapons we have left together and move."

"Where te?" asked the Scot.

"Eggheads," said Fuller. "I'll call him, give him the heads up... And fuck

Casey, this is still our mission."

"What about her?" said JC nodding down at O'Shea's body.

"Check the rest of her pockets and push her in the lake," said Fuller.

"Now you tell me," said Jerry, shaking his head.

Rick did manage to drive, but Des and JC could see that he was struggling. His dressing had already begun weeping, and he was in shocking pain. They stopped at a service station halfway to the Rossendale Valley, bought him a hot sweet tea and forced him to have a break.

Just after one in the morning, with Fuller barely conscious in the back seat, they arrived at the rather forlorn looking farmhouse that was the home of the team's technical brain, Simon Small.

Rick stood on the front step as Des dutifully hammered on the door. JC wandered about the garden examining the various items of junk that littered the place.

Rick caught him.

"Wait till you see the inside," he managed. "It's a palace. I hope you like cats."

"Hate the fuckers," said Jerry. "I'm a dog person, me. Labradors."

"Not yer night then," said Des, listening to Simon's heavy footsteps as he plodded down the stairs.

There was the sound of locks turning and the front door was finally edged open. With their prior knowledge to assist them, Des and Rick took a deep breath of fresh air and a couple of steps away from the doorway. Half a dozen mangy looking felines instantly made their bid for freedom out from behind Simon's bare legs and into the garden. The heady smell of cat pee, mixed with what could only have been some kind of Indian takeaway wafted out behind him, leaving JC with his hand over his mouth.

"Jesus wept," he muttered.

"Ah, Mr Fuller," offered Simon with a beaming smile. "You're just in time for some grub. As I mentioned earlier, the Old Crone is away on her travels at present, so, knowing you were en croute, I've taken the liberty of ordering in from Abdul's in the village. I hope you like it spicy?"

Simon took a better look at Rick.

"Although, I do have to say, Mr Fuller, that I've seen you looking perkier. If you don't mind me saying, like."

"Can we get inside," said Fuller wearily.

"Of course," said Simon pulling the door fully open to reveal his fluffy pink dressing gown. "Mi casa es su casa as they say en Français."

The three followed the barefoot Egghead upstairs to his workspace. Jerry stepped in something unpleasant on one of the treads and cursed cats in general.

"Hard to train," shouted Simon from the landing. "When you have so many, as my old mum does, a litter tray is like spitting in the sea. Don't fret mister, they aren't allowed in my rooms, just leave your boots at the door, there's a good chap."

Finally, all were safely in Simon's computer room.

"So, Mr Fuller," began Egghead. "As I understand it, you need to know where a certain mobile phone is?"

"Correct," said Rick, wincing as he dropped into his chair.

Simon held out a hand.

"And you have the set that this person called earlier, the one with the number logged in its memory."

Rick handed over Maria O'Shea's phone.

"It's on there, but the screen is password protected," he said.

Simon plugged the phone into his desktop.

"Easy peasy lemon squeezy," he smiled, opening a new tab. "So, let's have a quick look see, now.... on this set are just seven numbers logged in the memory, but no names attached to any of them. Not a very popular chap, eh?"

"It's a burner, and she was female," offered Des.

"Ah," said Simon pointing an index finger upwards. "Then a person of the criminal underworld, am I right?"

"Maybe," said Rick.

"Then," offered Egghead, typing furiously. "It is highly unlikely that any of these numbers have been registered on the 'Find My Phone,' network, but it's worth a look... and, umm yes, they aren't, so, now, Mr Fuller, stop me if I'm teaching you to suck eggs here, but the actual tracking of cell phones can be done in two ways. Triangulation, which covers them all, even the old bricks, the Nokia's etcetera, or GPS, which is standard in modern smartphones, aka this one. With triangulation, three cell phone towers are used to approximate the location of the set in question. However, these towers are constantly pinging cell phones to provide services, so a user's whereabouts and path of travel are easily traceable. GPS, on the other hand, is able to pinpoint a cell phone's exact location. All of this data is constantly recorded and resides with the wireless providers. In this case, T Mobile."

"What if the GPS is switched off?" asked Des. "We were always told te do that, fe security reasons like.

Simon tapped some keys on the set.

"Aye, that can slow the process, but as with the modern computer, the mobile phone is one of the least secure items man has ever produced. As a rule of thumb, if you don't want to be found, don't carry one. You see, the major providers retain all kinds of info every time a phone is used. What sites you subscribe to or visit regularly, call records, cell towers used, text message details, including content, pictures, IP details, and payment histories. This is the big brother of all big brothers, guys. They say this info is used to improve services... but."

"But?" asked Jerry.

"They sell it to the cops for one," said Simon rubbing his thumb and finger together. "Make millions a year."

He swivelled in his chair and tapped a black box on his desk.

"Hence people are investing in these. This is a King Fish, a man portable interrogation and direction finding unit for the CDMA waveform."

"English," barked Fuller, finding two more co-codamol.

Simon turned again to face Rick.

"In plain speak, Mr Fuller, you ring this mush, or he rings you... you keep him on the line for more than ninety seconds, and I tell you where he is."

Rick gave Des a look. The Scot raised his brows.

"Who d'ya think called her?" asked Cogan.

"Had to be Walsh," said Rick.

"I agree," said JC. "They were close, sleeping together."

"Give me the phone, Simon," said Rick, holding out a hand.

"You sure, you don't want a few poppadom's and dips before you get started, Mr Fuller," said Simon, rubbing his ample belly. "I was hoping for supper about now."

"Phone," snapped Fuller.

Egghead dutifully handed over the set, then swallowed hard.

"Of course, you do realise that these King Fish units and the relevant software cost an extraordinary amount of money, Mr Fuller, and..."

"How much do you want?" said Rick, doing his best to open the phone.

"Call it two bags," said Simon quietly. "Mates rates, like."

Rick took a deep breath and handed the phone to Des "You dial," he said, "My hands are playing up."

Des did as he was asked, dialled, selected speakerphone and handed back the set.

The number rang and rang until almost a minute passed. Finally the call went to the standard T mobile voicemail message.

"You want me to call again," said Des.

Rick held up a hand.

"Give him a minute."

All sat in silence as the seconds ticked away. Jerry stood and looked out of the window into the darkness, hands clasped behind his back. As an ex Det man, he was used to waiting, used to being patient, but even he knew the significance of this one call.

"He'll ring," he muttered. "He's in love."

Moments later, JC was proved right.

Rick almost dropped the set in surprise as it vibrated in his hand. He painfully swiped the green answer button and once again selected speakerphone.

"Maria? Maria?" said the voice, full of concern. "Maria, fer fuck's sake, where the hell are yees?"

Rick didn't answer. He simply began to count down the seconds. One, two, three...

Walsh sounded rattled.

"Maria? You there?"

Five, six, seven, eight...

Finally.

"That you Connor?" asked Fuller flatly.

"What? Who the fuck...?"

Twelve, thirteen, fourteen...

"I take it, it is you, son," said Rick. "Connor Walsh, born New Lodge, Belfast. Twenty seven years old. Arrived into England last night on Stena Lines, in the company of one Maria O'Shea. A fine looking thing if ever there was one."

"Who the fuck are you?" spat Connor. "Put Maria on the phone the now. Don't be messin' with me. I'm warning yees."

Rick waited, still counting down the seconds.

"Hold the line," he said.

He counted another ten.

"Connor? You there?"

"Of course I'm fucking here. Who the fuck are you, and where's Maria?"

"She can't come to the phone right now, son."

There was silence for a few more precious seconds. Rick thought Walsh had hung up, but Simon gave him a quick thumbs up to say otherwise.

"You know who I am, don't you?" said Fuller.

The whole room could hear Connor breathing.

"Aye," he said, a venomous edge to his tone. "I reckon I do."

"Then you know why Maria can't come to the phone then eh? But listen… Connor, you are still listening, aren't you?"

"Yeah… I'm here, yeah."

"She was brave till the end," said Rick coldly. "I don't know if that means anythin' to you. Does it Connor? Were you close? In love? Or was she just a casual fuck? I mean, perhaps… perhaps you worshiped her, idolised her, knew of her courage. But that's as maybe. I'm tellin' you now, she had bottle that one."

"What are yees sayin'?" hissed Connor.

Fuller licked his dry lips as he recalled O'Shea's last moments.

"I'm saying that even as I wrapped my hands around that pretty throat of hers, even as I pushed her head under the water, she showed no fear. She looked me in the eye as she took her last breath. Imagine that Connor."

"You bastard," screamed Walsh. "I'll fuckin' kill you, I mean it, kill you, yees murdering swine."

Simon held up a hand. He had what he needed.

Rick nodded.

"Connor… Connor," he soothed. "Calm down son. Listen, you and your geeky bomb maker pal, McCaul have two choices. Are you listening, son? Connor? Are you listening? You run… or die. Just like O'Hare, Fennel and your pretty little bitch. Stay on English soil and you're both as good as dead."

Walsh cut the call.

Simon sat open mouthed.

"Sometimes, Mr Fuller, I get the impression that you have anger management issues."

SIXTEEN

"I'm going to see to these bastards," growled Rick.

Simon had traced the call to Luther King House, a budget hotel in Longsite. Fuller already knew where the premises were, he'd driven past them many times. He also knew, that just across the road from the accommodation was the 6th Military Intelligence Unit and Army Reserve Centre.

Was this their second target? Well, as far as Rick and his team were concerned, it was too much of a coincidence to be otherwise.

Jerry drove whilst Des cleaned Rick's wound and changed his dressing. Cogan had pinched a couple of bags of frozen veg from Simon's freezer and they sandwiched Rick's right hand on the back seat.

He rooted in his med pouch.

"Here," he offered. "Ibuprofen for the swelling and some antibiotics, we don't want ye going down with sepsis now, do we?"

Rick popped them, swallowing them dry.

He grimaced.

"Okay, where are we up to with weapons and ammo."

"I did a quick check," said Jerry. "We still have the ACE31's and plenty of 7.62, but we are really short of ammo for the Mp7's. I've still got my Browning, like."

"And me," said Des.

"Okay," said Fuller. "Swing by the lockup. We'll ditch the ACE31's. and Mp7's and pick up three Mp5k's and some nine mil. And we need to clean up and change, or we ll stand out like spare pricks at a wedding. We're all covered in claret... most of it mine."

"And Jacko's," said Des, pulling out his phone. "Which reminds me, I need the give Aintree a call, see how the boy's doing."

Minutes later Rick hobbled gingerly from the Merc and unlocked the heavy metal door that led inside the team's lockup. JC drove the German flagship 4x4 inside and went straight to the shower room. Rick rooted in the med cabinet for something stronger than off the counter pain killers, whilst Des stepped out onto the pavement, smoking his pipe, waiting to be connected to Aintree hospital's intensive care unit.

Fifteen minutes later, with clean clothes and the blood and grime washed away, all three were far more presentable, even if Fuller's face looked like he'd been in a fight with a sabre tooth tiger.

"So Jacko's awake then?" asked JC.

"Aye," said Des, stuffing a pack of hastily heated rations into his mouth. "From what I can gather, they're pretty happy with him for now."

"Early days," said Rick.

"True," nodded the Scot, licking his fingers before pushing two spare mags in his clean jacket. "He'll be a while convalescing fer sure. But he's young. Ye heal a wee bit quicker at his age."

Rick stood and began to lay weapons out on the old, gnarled table that had served him and his team so well over the years.

"Okay, one Mp5k each, and three mags. You both have your personal sidearms and spare rounds and I've put new batteries in all the comms sets. Now, Luther King House is student accommodation that rents un-used rooms out to the public. That poses problems within itself. There'll be stoned kids coming and going even at this late hour, so any contact will have to be contained within the targets' room or away from the premises.

"How do we find their room number?" asked JC.

"We persuade the night porter to tell us," said Cogan.

"Desmond can be very persuasive," said Fuller.

"I'm sure," said Jerry.

***

McCaul was hard at work.

The plan for the pipe bombs was long gone. For a start, they had no pipe, and no grinder to cut it with. But George wasn't fazed. There was more than one way to skin a cat. He had explosives, det cord, batteries and two spare mobile phones.

The plan to detonate the charges at two sites, whilst simultaneously attacking the third with the RPG's was still possible. All it needed was clear thinking and guts. And despite his shaking hands and sweat soaked shirt, George still had both those in spades, didn't he?

All he needed was a new host for his IED's, and Walsh had just better come good with that little task.

Connor had been no help at all the last couple of hours. He'd lost the plot. The minute he'd found out about O'Shea, he'd become worse than useless, wailing like a fish wife.

George had pointed out the error of his ways.

This was a once in a lifetime opportunity. Be a hero or die trying.

The plan may have changed, but that was to be expected in war, wasn't it? Shit happens and you had to be able to think on your feet no matter what the adversity. When it came to their line of work, people died.

And if George had his way, many more would.

He'd tasked Walsh with finding a vehicle, preferably a builder's van, something with lots of nails, tools and nuts and bolts laying around inside it. From there on it would be simple.

The Syrian had come good on his promise of providing military grade C-4. It was packed in demolition bars called M112's. Rectangular blocks roughly 11 inches x 2 x 1.5, wrapped in an olive coloured Mylar film. One block was easily enough to manufacture a pipe bomb, but George didn't have that luxury. He would need more power, more kinetic energy to send white hot shards of metal flying across Manchester's streets. So, for this little job, he had formed six blocks into one single charge using two priming assemblies and three metres of det cord, capped at each end with boosters. Then, he'd connected a battery to fire the cord and finally, a mobile phone to trigger the battery... simple.

One car bomb here, just across the road from the hotel, repeat the process at Belle Vue later this afternoon, before a drive over to Bury for the piece de resistance. Oh yes, the icing on the cake. This very evening, just as each reservist centre opened their doors to their volunteers, Walsh would fire the RPG's from the window of the Bury flat, whilst George dialled the two phone numbers that would detonate the car bombs.

McCaul smiled to himself as he worked.

Child's play.

***

Rick lay across the back seat of the Merc. Although his pain was easing the new drugs made him feel edgy and a little sick to the stomach. Des drove whilst JC lolled in the front passenger seat, eyes closed, seemingly oblivious to the monumental task that lay in front of them.

Cogan edged the Merc out of the city centre, along Princess Street and onto the A34, running parallel with Oxford Road towards Longsite, before taking a right into Norman Road.

He crawled past Langdon House, the home of 6 Military Intelligence Unit, Royal Signals

842 Troop, 33 Signal Squadron and 37 Signal Regiment. It was essentially a large Army Reservist Centre that held regular drill nights for those already signed up, but also, on those particular evenings, it opened its doors to anyone who may be interested in joining any of those regiments as a part timer.

Drill nights were held once a week, and as Cogan trundled past the front gate, he saw the sign which told all and sundry that Langdon House held these very events every Wednesday between 1900hrs and 2145hrs.

"What day is this?" asked Rick quietly.

"Well, I suppose we are into Wednesday already," said Des.

"Thought as much," said Fuller. "So tonight it is then."

"Not if I have my way," said Des.

Rick let his head fall back against the seat and closed his eyes. *Tonight. Fucking tonight.* It just had to be then. The same night that Simpson would be at Naomi's house.

Cogan caught a glimpse of his dearest friend in the rear view.

"You okay?" he asked.

Fuller curled his lip. The meds had kicked in enough for him to slip his left arm from Cogan's makeshift sling, and the anti-inflammatory's, paired with the ice had brought down the swelling in his right hand.

He flexed his fingers, wincing slightly.

"We can't miss these fuckers, Des. This has to end now."

JC, who had obviously been awake throughout, lifted himself upright and stretched.

"Sound by me," he said pulling his Browning from his belt and making it ready. "I'm in the mood to make a mess."

***

"So where did yees park the van then?" asked McCaul.

Connor sat on the edge of one of the two single beds in the small room. He still couldn't believe that Maria had been killed. In the heat of the battle, he'd tried to persuade her to leave the handover, to escape in the van with him, George and the goods, but she'd been insistent. She had been determined to stay, and he was certain that it had something to do with that bastard, Fuller. The one on the phone, the one from the pub, the one with the scar, the one Paddy had identified as SAS. It was obvious to Connor now that MI6 had been on to them from the beginning. The whole operation should have been called off…delayed, postponed, whatever. But oh no, Maria wouldn't listen. And that night, the night of the meet with the Syrian, she was as wild as he'd ever seen her. He believed that she knew this man Fuller would come for them, knew that he would try and stop the mission. Yet even as the bullets flew, she wouldn't leave. She wanted that man dead more than any other human being on earth. But why? Connor was convinced that there was something… something from the past that had made her stay behind at the tower, something to do with him… Fuller. Whoever he was and whatever he meant to her had made her behave irrationally, foolishly, left half the team dead and The Firm on their tail.

And now, McCaul had gone the same way. He wouldn't listen to reason either. Connor wanted to bury the explosives somewhere out on the moors and somehow get back to Ireland, regroup, lick their wounds and go again. But George seemed to be suffering from the same irrational, absurd, senseless behaviour as Maria.

He rubbed his tired eyes with his palms. "It's in the car park," he muttered. "Blue Berlingo. A builder's van like yees asked. Sign written, Shaws or somthin' like that."

George edged the curtains open and peered into the night. Their ground floor room looked out onto a pleasant, secluded courtyard with wooden tables and chairs dotted around for guests to sit at. The carpark that served Luther King House was around the front of the building.

"Which car park?" hissed McCaul. "Where? I can't see from here."

George zipped up the holdall that contained the first of his newly constructed bombs, peered out of the window a second time, then drew the curtains a little too hard. Connor noticed he was sweating.

"This is crazy," said Walsh. "Look at the state of yees. Ye look like a man possessed so yees do."

McCaul wiped his forehead with his palm and threw down the bag containing the bomb at Connor's feet.

"Don't start that shite again, ye fuckin' soft arse. Best yees go and drop this baby in the back of that van the now, then park the fucker closer to the barracks like I told yees."

"It's not a feckin' barracks," spat Walsh, eyeing McCaul. "It's a reservist centre. And get this. Tomorrow night, when they have their drill sessions, guess what? They rent one hall out, to a feckin' yoga class. So now what eh? We blow up a set of middle aged women in leotards? How fucking macho is that?"

McCaul's eyes darkened. He curled his lips to reveal his brown, stained uneven teeth.

"Now you listen to me, Connor. This job goes as we planned it. I don't give a fuck about collateral damage. Old mums, wee bairns. It's all the same to me." He pointed in the general direction of the reservist centre. "That place recruits soldiers. Men and women who will be trained to kill the freedom fighters of Ireland." He got in close to Connor and gave him a shove in the chest. "Now get the fuck out of me sight, before a put a bullet in yees myself."

Connor eyed McCaul a moment, noted his rapid shallow breathing, the reddening of his eyes. The beads of sweat had already returned to his forehead and top lip. The man was on the edge. All rational had left him. But what was he to do? If he walked away now, the Brigade would find him. Hunt him down as a traitor to the cause. No, Connor would rather die from an MI6 bullet or of old age in Belmarsh prison, rather than suffer what the Brigade would have in store for him.

He stood and faced McCaul. Walsh was taller, heavier, fitter and despite his grief, from what he could assess, in a far better mental state.

"I'll take yees wee box of tricks to the van, so," he whispered, mouth twisted, eyes narrowed. "And I'll no doubt drop the next. But yees listen to me the now, Georgie boy. If yees ever touch me again, I'll snap ye skinny neck like a twig, so I will. And hey...when this is all done and we're back in the homeland, me and you will have a private chat, just the two of us, eh? We'll find a nice quiet spot, a wee patch of grass south of the river and we'll see what yees have in yer locker. See how big them balls of yours really are."

Connor returned the push and McCaul staggered backwards.

"Now, fucking stay away from me ye here? Fix up the second device and keep yer fuckin' thoughts to yerself."

***

Rick had given JC the task of finding the black Transit that Walsh and Mc-Caul had escaped in, whilst he and Des had made to the hotel reception. It was a bright and airy communal area and despite the early hour, there were still a good few kids knocking around, some drinking bottles of beer from the vendors, some on laptops, the odd couple canoodling in the corners.

Despite his shower and clean clothes, Rick still looked like he'd been in a war, so Des made the approach and did the talking.

The guy behind the desk was double the age of most of his customers, of African origin with seemingly little interest of what was going on around him, all of his attention taken up by whatever he was watching on a small TV behind the counter. He was more of a security guard than a porter, and as a night operative, probably an agency worker rather than employee of the university. He wore a freshly ironed white shirt with lapels on the shoulders, a standard clip-on tie and had a cheap shortwave radio fastened to the belt of his smartly pressed black trousers. He was a big lad too. Gym fit, well-muscled with plaits in his hair that ran across his head from ear to ear finishing with a tight bun at the back of his neck.

"Morning," said Cogan, managing a smile.

"We're full," said the guy, without looking away from his screen.

"We don't need a room," countered the Scot.

"The bar is for residents only," said the guy, still glued to his program.

Cogan leaned over the desk and pulled the plug on the TV.

"We don't want a drink either, pal," he said flatly, the smile all but gone.

That got the guy's attention. He pushed his chair back, stood, then ran a hand across his plaits as he weighed up the situation, first taking a better look at Rick, then another at Des.

"Your friend doesn't look too well," he said. "Maybe you should try the Royal Infirmary."

"Maybe you should learn some customer service skills," said Rick, taking a step closer.

"We don't tolerate aggression towards our staff here, sir," said the guard quietly. "So why don't you take a step away. It's never a good idea to invade a man's personal space."

"We don't want to invade anythin', son," said Des. "We just want a wee bit of information, and we'll be on our way."

The guard rested his hand on his radio.

"I don't have any information to give you gentlemen, so if you don't mind, I'll ask you to leave the premises."

Rick ran a hand across his mouth and gave the guy the once over.

"Where did you serve?" he asked.

Once again, the guard's eyes flitted between the two men.

"What's this about?" he asked.

Des' eyes went flat cold. There was no time to pussyfoot about. He took a deep breath, went for broke.

"We believe that you have two men in a room in this building currently constructing IED's, and I'm a pound to a pinch of shite sure you know all about those."

The guard furrowed his brow. "ID?" he said, holding out a palm.

"They tend not to give out those fancy cards in our line of work, pal," said Des.

Rick looked again at the way the guy was turned out, took a guess at his age.

"You were army," he said. "Let me guess, you did a tour or two in Iraq. Am I right?"

The guard nodded.

"Princess of Wales's Royals, drove a Warrior. C Company, 1st Battalion. Before that it was Kosovo."

"Ireland?" asked Rick.

"Three months… I was a kid. It was all over by then anyway."

"Tell that to the two fucker's who are about to plant a bomb across the road," said Des.

Once again, the guy looked unsure.

"Look, gentlemen. I don't book folks in and out of here. The guests are already allocated their rooms before I start my shift. I'm just here to stop the kids from stealing the beer and shagging in the corridors."

Des handed over two photographs depicting McCaul and Walsh.

"They are what is left of an NIRA Active Service Unit. They were driving a black Transit van last we saw them."

The guy took a deep breath in through his nose. He pointed at the picture of Walsh.

"I can't be a hundred percent, but I think I saw him earlier. He was leaving the hotel."

"On his own?" asked Rick.

The guy nodded.

"On his own."

"When was this?" asked Cogan.

The guy shrugged.

"Maybe an hour ago. I didn't see him come back, but I have rounds to do, so that doesn't mean he's not here."

Rick looked across at Des.

"Maybe he went back to the Transit?"

"Let's check in on JC then," said the Scot.

***

Connor trod the narrow corridor from his room towards reception carrying McCaul's bag full of death and destruction, his head still bursting with the events of the last few hours. As he pushed at the double swing doors that would take him to the communal area, he stopped in his tracks.

Standing at the desk, in deep conversation with the security guard, were two men, and one of those was without doubt, Richard Fuller, the man with the scar, the man that had murdered the love of his life. He allowed the door to close slightly, holding it open just enough so that he may still see his nemesis.

The guard was handing back what appeared to be some sheets of paper to the shorter of the two men. Documents? Photographs? Whatever they were, the guard was shaking his head. Connor had booked him and McCaul into the hotel using an online service and fake names. Payment had been taken using one of the Brigade's many untraceable credit cards and the woman on the desk had barely looked at him when he'd collected the room keys. The guard had come on duty later and had never set eyes on either he or McCaul, he was certain of it, but what to do now?

Every sinew in his body was screaming at him to push open the doors walk up to the two men and shoot them down, there and then. Oh how he would love to do that. But then, of course, the plan would be ruined completely.

Reluctantly, he let the door close and turned back towards his room.

Connor had spun around blindly, not expecting anyone else to be there. But this was student accommodation, and these kids were awake half the night. As he turned, he walked straight into two young men, one of whom was much the worse for wear.

The unsteady guy was taken completely off guard and tumbled backwards, hitting the floor hard.

"Whoa!" shouted his pal, who'd managed to remain upright. "What's your hurry, mate?"

Connor didn't need the noise, or the conversation for that matter and made the instant decision to get back to the relative safety of his room.

"Sorry," he mumbled and made to move on.

The standing youth, however, was having none of it and grabbed Connor by the elbow.

"Hey, hey, where do yer think you're goin'?"

The Irishman glared at the kid. He was tall and rangy, maybe twenty at best. Mixed race with short, cropped hair, a thick Mancunian accent and the standard street wear of the day.

"Leave it lad," snapped Walsh.

The kid stepped away. Not in fear, but to give himself a little room should he need it.

"Leave what?" he asked, bouncing a little on his toes. "What d'ya think yer doin' like, eh? Just knocking my friend down like that?"

The 'friend' was now on his hands and knees.

"You fuckin' tell him, there Paulie," he slurred. "Think I've bust summat."

"Yer fine, so," hissed Connor. "Now, I'm sorry okay. I didn't see yees." He made to move again. "And, like I said, let's leave it at that eh, son."

Paulie wasn't having any of it.

"I'm not your son," he sneered. "You're a white boy fer a start." He gestured over to the swing doors just feet away. "And what were you up to there eh? Peepin' through them doors? What's so interesting? Spying on some young meat were yer? Some teenage piece of ass? Bit of a perv are yer? Nonce?"

Connor was beginning to lose it. Could they be heard by the guard? Would he come to investigate? Would Fuller and his pal follow on?

Walsh was more than capable of dealing with the kid, and his friend for that matter, but he couldn't risk it. Not here, not in such a public place.

"Look," said Connor. "Okay, I'll level with you. I was checking to see if the guard was there. I haven't paid for my room see. I was going to do one, but took a look and saw he was at reception with what looked like a couple of cops. I turned around and bumped into you guys. Like I said, it was an accident."

At that, the guy on his knees made a grab at Connor to try and lift himself upwards. He went for his arm, but instead pulled at the handle of the holdall containing the explosive device. Walsh instinctively snatched at the bag with both hands and tore it from the kid's grasp.

"Hey man, what the fuck," said the kid, finding himself back on the deck.

Paulie eyed Walsh, then the bag.

"What yer got in there, man?" he asked, lips pursed. "You doin' some dealin' in here or what?"

"Like I said..." began Connor, his pulse rate now hitting max.

"Let's see in the bag," said Paulie, making a grab for the holdall. "I could go some weed, man."

Connor took a step away, dropped the rucksack on the floor and with lightning quick reactions, smashed his left elbow into Paulie's face. The kid staggered and Walsh followed that blow with a sharp right to the chin, flooring the lad. He then turned his attention to the boy on his hands and knees, raised his right leg and brought it down with sickening force on the back of his neck. Walsh heard the crack, heard the kid exhale and knew in the very instant, he would never inhale again.

Alive one second, dead the next.

Despite the ease in which he'd dealt with the boys, Walsh was near blind with panic. He looked in desperation down the corridor. There was an emergency exit just yards away. It had to be that. He had no choice now. Connor picked up the still breathing Paulie, wrapping his arm tightly around his throat, dragging him backwards towards the exit door. He squeezed at the kid's neck as he went, tighter and tighter, cutting off the blood supply to the brain.

By the time he'd made it to the door, Paulie too had breathed his last.

Walsh jogged back to the second kid, dragged him alongside his friend, then kicked out at the locking bar. The emergency exit opened as it should, and he pushed both bodies out into the night, closing the heavy doors behind them as quietly as he could.

Connor blew out his cheeks and picked up his bag. He and McCaul needed out of this place, the sooner the better.

Meanwhile, back at the reception desk, ex Lance Corporal Ian Obulae of the Princess of Wales's Royals, instantly noticed the emergency exit door alarm light up on his panel. He selected camera seventeen, the device that covered the pathway directly outside it and panned around. Exit door alarms were a regular occurrence on his shift. Pissed kids that couldn't be bothered to walk around the building to the courtyard often pushed open the doors to go outside and smoke a little weed. Some just nipped for a piss, but not this time. Obulae had seen enough dead bodies in his life to recognise another two. He grabbed his shortwave comms and sprinted out of the front door, just yards behind Fuller and Cogan.

"Gents! Gents!" he shouted. "I think we have a problem."

Rick and Des turned towards the burly guard.

"This way," snapped Obulae. "Follow me."

The pair did as they were asked, Rick struggling to keep up, each hurried step jarring his shoulder and sending jolts of pain through his body, but he gritted his teeth and powered forwards. The guard pushed open the very doors Connor had been peeping through moments earlier and jogged along the corridor towards the emergency exit. Des noticed a blood splatter on the wall just inside the door.

"Looks new," he pointed.

The guard stopped at the exit doors, pushed at the bar and they swung open. There, lying on the path were the twisted bodies of Paulie and his friend. Des and Obulae knelt and checked them over.

"This one's neck is busted," said the Scot.

The African gave Paulie the once over, lifting each eyelid in turn.

"Blood vessels around the eyes are weeping. I'd say he's been strangled."

Cogan stood.

"Well, they're both still warm."

"They were dumped less than a minute ago," said the guard. "This door is alarmed, it showed up on the system and I checked the CCTV."

Des stepped back into the corridor and walked over to the blood splatter he'd seen earlier. Fuller and the guard followed him.

"It happened here, and you can see the drag marks on the floor tiles... look."

"You know these two?" asked Rick.

Obulae nodded.

"They're students. They both live in. The mixed race lad is called Paul. Bit of a boy, but nothing heavy."

Des' comms crackled into life. It was JC. He sounded excited.

"I've found the van, the Transit. It's in a back ginnel close to the reserve centre... Olivia Grove. Looks all secure, engine's cold."

"Get yersel in cover, pal," replied Des. "Walsh may be out and about and there's been an incident here, and it just has to be our guys. I reckon they'll be on their toes soon as. They may even be on their way to you."

"Roger that," said Jerry and edged his way around the corner out of sight.

Rick turned to the guard again.

"You sure you can't help us with a room number, pal?"

Obulae shook his head.

"Best I can do is look which rooms have been sold out to external guests on this corridor. But listen. I need to call the cops."

Des stepped forwards.

"Give us the room numbers, then ten minutes, and ye do what ye have to from there, eh?"

The guard looked at both men in turn.

"Who are you guys?" he asked.

"Put it this way," said Fuller. "Help us out now, and I promise you won't be sitting behind that desk on minimum wage next month."

"Come on then," said Obulae. "I'll need to look at the computer."

"You did fuckin' what?" shouted McCaul.

Connor was pushing what remained of George's workings into a plastic bag, spare bits of det cord, electrical wiring, slivers of tape.

"I had no fucking choice. Six are here the now. Fuller and another. Heaven knows how many more. We need to get out of here. Cut our losses."

"And what about the plan? What about the Brigade?" snapped George.

Walsh grabbed McCaul by his shirt and slammed him against the hotel room door.

"Fuck the plan you dumb bastard. That was the old plan. The plan before this lot turned up. The plan before we were ambushed, ye hear? Now listen to me. We have two devices here. Two perfectly good working bombs. We fire this room, climb out into the courtyard, take the two bags and the Berlingo I just stole... then...then," Connor was thinking on his feet. "Then once we get to safety, we call the Brigade and ask for instructions." He grabbed at George's chin, squeezed it hard. "Listen Georgie boy," he spat, nose almost touching McCaul's. "Do yees want to die here? Shot down like a dog? We can still have our day, eh? Still make a splash. You can still be a feckin' hero if yees please. But we have to go... and go now."

McCaul nodded rapidly.

"Okay, Connor. I'll follow yees so I will. But we can't leave those RPG's. We have to pick them up on the way out."

Walsh knew that he needed George, needed his gun, needed his loyalty.

"Okay," he said releasing his compatriot. "We'll get the feckin' rockets you love so much. Now… help me fire this place."

***

Obulae had identified four possible rooms. Numbers eleven, seventeen, twenty nine and thirty three, all situated along the ground floor corridor where the two students had met their fate.

Fuller nodded to the guard.

"Thanks for your help, there. I won't forget it."

"Do you need another pair of hands?" asked the big African.

"Ye have done enough, pal," said Cogan. He took a look at the remaining undergraduates still slouched around the communal area. "Just make sure no one comes into the corridor behind us, eh? Then give it ten like I said, and make yer calls, do what ye need te do."

"Good luck lads," said the guard. "I'll lock the doors behind you."

Cogan and Fuller edged their way into the corridor and drew their weapons, Des with his trusty Browning, Rick with his latest toy the .357 Kimber K6S.

They reached the first door, number eleven, one man either side of the opening, backs to the wall weapons at the ready. Des reached across and knocked.

"Do you know what fucking time this is?" came a very irritated female reply.

Rick gave the nod to move on. As they edged their way quietly along the corridor, Fuller raised a hand.

"Smell that?" he whispered.

"Burning," said Des.

The pair bypassed seventeen, following the smell until they reached twenty nine. Des dropped to his belly and sniffed at the bottom of the door. He lifted himself and gave Rick a thumbs up.

Cogan raised three fingers and looked Rick in the eye. Fuller didn't wait for the countdown, he lifted a leg and smashed in the flimsy door with his boot. The room was in darkness and filled with smoke. Even so, the pair could immediately see it was empty. The sash window leading out onto the courtyard had been left wide open.

Rick was on his comms instantly.

"JC come in."

"Go," replied Jerry.

"They're on their toes and could be coming your way. Heads up pal, we'll be with you in five."

Fuller gingerly stepped through the open window, followed by Cogan.

"What about my signal?" asked Cogan as they made their way across the courtyard. "My countdown?"

"I'm getting impatient in my old age," said Fuller.

Des strode around the perimeter of the building with Rick doing his best to keep pace. Once they reached the entrance gate, Rick checked up and down the street for the Irish, but all was quiet.

He rested himself against one square brick pillar and pushed his pistol back in his jeans.

"Can't believe we've lost them again," he muttered.

Des held up a hand.

"Hear that?"

A diesel engine had clattered into life somewhere towards the far end of the car park. It was unrefined, agricultural almost.

"Taxi?" suggested Rick.

"I'll have a look," said Des.

Fuller pushed himself upright. He was still moving cautiously and Cogan could see how much of his usual drive was missing.

"Why don't ye wait here, pal," he said. "This will only take a minute."

Rick nodded. He knew he needed to conserve what strength he had. There was no point in playing Billy Big Bollocks at this point in proceedings.

"I'll wait here by the gate," he said, feeling in his jeans for more meds.

Des strode towards the rattling diesel engine. The carpark was all but full, yet he could easily see a plume of white smoke off in one corner. It was coming from a small dark coloured Citroen van. As he drew closer, it began to reverse from its space and, even in the half light, he could see it was sign written, white on navy blue, 'Shaws and Sons.' The driver finally put his side lights on as the van edged out between two other cars and began to turn towards the Scot.

The first thing Cogan noticed was that the door lock on the driver's side was missing. The whole mechanism was gone. Suspicious, but he really needed to clock the occupants before making any move. Equally shady was that whoever they were, they had decided not to wait for the windows to fully demist, so it was hard for the Scot to identify anyone inside.

Des felt his hackles rise.

"Knock off motor fe sure," he muttered, pushing his hand into his jacket, grabbing the butt of his Browning High Power pistol.

No sooner had the Scot felt the reassuring coldness of his SLP in his grip than the driver of the van switched straight from side lights to main beam headlights and hit the accelerator. Cogan was instantly blinded. He heard the van's engine scream and a squeal of tyres. That was enough for the Scot.

He knew he had no choice but to jump to his right or be run over. He leapt between two parked cars, rolling as he did so, his right shoulder hitting the tarmac hard.

Even though he was winded, Des was on his feet in seconds, weapon in the aim. But those few moments, that ten seconds, meant that the van had already passed by him and was careering for the exit.

Rick had heard the commotion and got himself in some degree of cover, leaning behind that same gatepost at the exit. Fuller steadied himself, drew his weapon and aimed at the van's screen as it screeched towards him.

"Have we a positive ID?" he shouted into his comms.

"Negative," bawled Des, sprinting back towards Fuller. "I couldn't get a look, but..."

Before Des could finish, any doubt as to who the occupants were was settled when George McCaul leaned from the passenger window and opened up at Rick with his own sidearm.

Nine millimetre rounds popped and flashed off the gatepost in front of Fuller, close enough to send him scuttling for better cover. The sheer barrage of George's fire forcing him down on the floor, his already damaged body slamming onto the concrete behind the low wall to his right. The pain was so great, Fuller actually cried out, rivers of pain coursing down his left side.

The van screamed by him and did a right out of the gate, the driver losing control of the rear end, clipping a parked car as it did so. Fuller twisted his body, and despite being flat on his back, managed to fire at the van as it slewed down the road. Moments later he was joined by Cogan who added to the party, letting go with his Browning, his rounds clattering and flashing as they struck their target.

Despite the direct hits on the vehicle, the van carried on its manic path along Norman Road and out of sight.

"Fuck, fuck, fuck," cursed Cogan.

Rick sat up, his back against the low wall, one arm raised.

"Gimmie a hand up pal, will yer?" he said.

Des did as he was asked and examined his great friend as he sat on the wall, pale faced, chin on his chest.

"You need the hospital, pal," he said quietly.

Rick lifted his head and looked Des in the eye.

"Another day," he said, blowing out his cheeks. "What I need is one more day, mate."

JC pulled the Merc up alongside Rick and Des.

"I think you scared 'em off, lads. I've put in a call to Casey," he said. "A team are going to collect the Transit. Are we ready to rock or what?"

Fuller was already on the phone to Egghead. He switched it to speaker as he stepped into the Merc.

"Simon," he barked.

"Ah, good morning, Mr Fuller. I'll tell you what, you missed a real treat with that curry. You can't beat Abdul's for a good Rogan Gosh."

"So I take it you haven't been to bed?"

"Night owl me, Mr Fuller, besides, you asked me to keep track of that mush you were talking to earlier."

"As it happens," said Fuller, edging his way gingerly across the back seat. "That is just what I was hoping you'd say. We appear to have lost him, and I'm a tad pissed about it."

"One sec," said Simon.

"Quick as you can," snapped Fuller.

"Hmmm, well… it appears our friend is mobile."

"I fuckin' know that…whereabouts?"

"Anson Road, Mr Fuller. He's heading for town, and you are in luck."

"I am?"

"Yes sir. Your pal is using Google Maps, he has his GPS on."

"Stay on the line, Simon. I need you to help us catch this fucker."

"Erm, well yes, I suppose I could continue with the commentary. Of course, I couldn't condone the use of any violence."

Des grabbed Rick's phone.

"Just stay on the line and direct us to the bastard, ye fuckin' tube."

***

"I'm shot, I'm fuckin' shot, look, I'm bleedin' bad, Connor. I need the hospital. Get me to casualty the now."

McCaul had taken a round to the arm and was in blind panic.

"Take it easy, George," snapped Walsh. "It's a flesh wound. Yer not goin' to turn up yees toes just yet."

"Aww but it hurts like fuck. I can't move it. I need a doctor."

Walsh had slowed the van so as not to draw attention to it. He steered with one hand and took a hold of George's good arm with the other. He shook him.

"Now you listen to me, Georgie. You were the one who wanted to go out in a blaze of glory."

"But I'm shot, Connor," he whined. "I could bleed to death."

"Ye'll not bleed to death, yer bollocks, an' stop bein' so soft about it."

George looked across at Connor, wide eyed.

"Are yees goin' to call the Brigade? Tell 'em we've lost the rockets? Tell 'em Maria and Fennel are dead? What do yees think they'll say? Will they do our knees or what?"

Connor was in turmoil. He knew Fuller and his men would be on their tail soon enough. And if they went to ground now, they'd be found by Six before the day was out. The whole plan would be scuppered. His knees were the least of his worries.

"Look, we have two bombs here in the back of this van. I say we plant them tonight and blow them at rush hour first thing. We go really old school." He handed George his phone. "Just feast yer eyes on Google there and direct me to Piccadilly Station, it'll take yees mind off yer pain, so."

George looked at the screen a moment, then back at Connor.

"Piccadilly?" said George, brow furrowed. "Are yees sayin' we go fer civilian targets? I mean, what do yees think the Brigade will say to that?"

Walsh curled his lip.

"Is that all yees can think of George? The fuckin' Brigade this, the fuckin' Brigade that. Well they aren't here, are they? We are. We're the ones bein' shot at. We're the ones taking the risks. Now, I say we drop one bag in a litter bin at Piccadilly, and then leave this heap with the second bag at Oxford Road." He grabbed George by the arm again. "It will be carnage, Georgie boy…. Just like you wanted, eh?"

McCaul looked across at Connor, his eyes wild.

"Aye, fuck, aye…We'll be heroes eh Connor? Just think, we'll put the fear of God into them."

Connor snorted, swallowed some bile.

"Aye, fuckin' heroes, course we will," he managed.

George had never been one to notice irony, and he'd missed Connor's attempt at it. He even managed a smile.

"They'll make a fuckin mess, Connor," he gushed. "They're the biggest I've ever made."

Walsh gazed out at the road in front. Traffic was limited to the odd taxi or delivery van.

Quiet, normal.

Just folks going about their daily lives, finishing their shift to pay the rent, feed their kids. And here he was, in a stolen van full of explosives, about to ruin those lives. After this morning's commute, there would be mothers without children, wives without husbands, sons without fathers. This had never been the plan. These were not military installations. But he had no choice. The Brigade would expect a result and, as his Daddy had always told him, *if you can't kill a soldier, ye kill his son.*

They made steady progress along the A34, past the Manchester Royal Infirmary. He saw George look longingly at the entrance to A and E as they drove by. He'd found an old t shirt in his door pocket and had managed to tie it around his arm. That had seemed to stop the bleeding, and mercifully, thought Connor, his complaining.

They took the slip road that would guide them under the Parkway, less than a mile away from their first target, where in just four short hours from now, at the height of the morning rush, George would call the first of two mobile phones that would detonate each device and decimate all around it. Dozens would die, hundreds would be injured, some would lose limbs, their lives changed forever. And those that witnessed it would never forget.

Most importantly, they would never forget the New Irish Republican Army.

Connor took the van along London Road to the junction with Fairfield Street. It was where the cabs pulled in, where the main entrance to the station was, and where two pedestrian crossings would feed their victims directly past the site of the bomb.

This was a dangerous ploy all around and he knew it. Dropping a device at a main station in a major English city, even though the trains had long since stopped running for the night, was risky. Cabs were still dotted around, their drivers standing outside their vehicles, smoking, chatting, waiting for the early trains to begin to bring in their first commuters. And it wasn't just cabbies either. Cops were around too. As Walsh steered the van closer, he could see a marked police vehicle parked under the apron with two young officers standing by it. They were both drinking coffee from Styrofoam cups, casual, sharing a joke.

The other daunting issue was McCaul's favourite subject, the Brigade, the hierarchy. This operation had been months in the planning, the targets carefully chosen at the highest level. Connor knew that there would be those within the organisation that would never agree to what he and George were about to do. They would dread the political fallout of hitting civilian targets, worry about losing support from both within, and the Republican faithful public. He knew that if he called this in, he would never be given permission to carry out such a mission. However, he also knew what losing half the team, all the explosives and cash and walking home empty handed would mean too. At least this way, some of the top table would have a degree of sympathy. They had improvised under extreme pressure. That had to count for something, didn't it?

The last time a litter bin had been used as a receptacle for an explosive device by the IRA was on the 20th of March 1993, when two bombs, exploded on Bridge Street in Warrington, one outside a McDonald's, whilst a second detonated outside Argos. The area was crowded with shoppers who fled from the first explosion directly into the path of the second. Three-year-old Jonathan Ball died at the scene, whilst twelve-year-old Tim Parry, was gravely wounded. He died five days later when his life support machine was turned off. Fifty-four more people were wounded, four with life changing injuries.

Connor sniffed as he recalled the history of it all. Over twenty years had passed since that day. Of course, what no one remembered this side of the Irish sea, was the retaliation.

Four days after the bombings, the Ulster Defence Association shot dead a Sinn Féin member in Belfast. The next day, it shot dead four Catholic men including an IRA member in Castlerock, and hours later, a 17-year-old Catholic civilian.

No one read about that in the Liverpool Echo, eh?

Even so, despite the history, despite the rhetoric, his guts churned with hesitation.

As he stopped the van next to one of only two cast iron bins left close to the entrance to the station, he pulled out his wallet and opened it to reveal a photograph of Maria O'Shea. She was the most beautiful thing he'd ever seen. The love of his life. He took a long, deep breath and kissed the picture.

If he'd had any doubts around what he and McCaul were about to do, at that very moment, it was clear to him. If Maria was still alive, he knew what she would choose. She wouldn't run home with her tail between her legs, she'd go out in a blaze of glory.

"Georgie boy," he snapped. "Go shove the first bag in there. That second bin, the one with the wider opening, and be quick about it."

George turned and looked Connor in the eye. He was sweating again, hands shaking.

"We'll burn in hell fer this," he said.

"That's as maybe," hissed Walsh. "Now, get on before them coppers notice us."

***

JC was not taking the drive steadily. He had his foot firmly to the floor and the Merc screamed along the same route just taken by the Irish.

Rick cradled his phone in his right hand. It had begun to swell again, and this time, no amount of pain killers or ice would help him. He felt light-headed and sick to his stomach, his left side where his wound still wept blood, was virtually paralysed. Even trying to raise his left arm was agony.

"They've stopped," announced Simon. "Right outside Piccadilly Station."

"There's no trains at this time of the morning," offered Des. "Nothing for another half hour at least."

"Hang fire there, Mr Cogan," said Simon. "Let me see if I can take a sneaky peak at the station's CCTV."

The seconds ticked by, with all those in the Merc hoping against hope that the computer genius would come good.

"Aye… right, so," began Egghead. "They're parked up alright, just by the main entrance, hazards on. The passenger door is open, and one mush is standing by a bin with a bag in his hand."

"Jeezo," said Des. "You don't think?"

Rick shook his head.

"No way they would hit a train station. It would be political suicide."

"Maybe they ain't thinkin' straight?" said Jerry, easing the Merc left onto the slip road. "With Maria gone, they are a rudderless ship. Fuck knows what they'll do."

"Only one way te find out," said Des. "Come on JC, keep it pinned."

JC pulled the Merc to a halt within feet of where the Irish had been parked minutes earlier. Rick leaned forwards in his seat so he could get a better look at the station's apron. The police van was still there, the two cops, still in deep conversation over their coffee.

"We can't hang around here, Des," he said. "By the time we finish explaining ourselves to those boys, we'll lose the Irish for good."

Des grabbed Fuller's forearm. "Just give me five," he said and slipped out of the Jeep, casually walking by the first bin.

"Slot is too narrow on this one," he said into his comms, strolling as casually as he could muster to the second container. Cogan felt in his pocket, removed his pipe and filled the bowl. He found his PTT again. "Hold up, yeah, it's in here, there's a zip up bag in the second one," he said.

"What's the plan?" asked JC. "If I don't move this motor in a minute, those boys over there are going to be snooping about and we are going to be answering questions till doomsday."

Des walked around to the tailgate of the Merc and opened it, to all intents and purposes, looking like an early morning traveller, lifting out his luggage, all the time keeping an eye on the two cops.

One took a casual glance over, then obviously decided that at such an early hour, the parking violation could wait.

"Ideally," said Cogan into the back of the Merc. "I'd like to cut the bin open, then the bag, so I could get a look see."

"But?" said Rick.

"But," said Des. "We all know I cannea do that, so I'm going te have te pull out the bag and work on it in the car."

"What if there's a tremble switch?" asked Jerry.

Des lifted out his satchel of tools, draped it over his shoulder and closed the tailgate. He then took a look at the closest vehicles to the bin, then their drivers. If he made an error this day, it would be touch and go for some. He was taking a massive chance.

"Then it will go bang," he said. "So why don't you guys park across the road whilst I have a wee smoke and think about this one."

Rick wound down the rear passenger window.

"I'm staying here," he said.

Des gave Rick a dark look.

"Drive him across the way, JC," he said flatly. "I'll be with ye in a minute."
Jerry did as he was asked.

Cogan lit his pipe and blew out a long plume. He'd disarmed several IED's in his time, done the training, walked the walk. But this was different, there was no time, no handbook, no back up.

"Well, well, well," he muttered to himself. "I didnea see this one coming, that's fe sure."

He looked across at the cops again and walked around the bin, a full three sixty. As he did so, he noticed that the door used by the council workers to change the internal bag was open, only a smidge, but open. After another glance at the cops, he knelt and eased it fully open. The holdall had been dropped into the clear plastic sack that sat inside the cast iron container. It was there alongside various other discarded items, Costa cups, fast food wrappers, general rubbish. The easiest way would be to take the whole sack, but, as JC had eluded, if McCaul had fitted some kind of boobytrap, and Des was well aware of the IRA's love of those, he would be blown sky high. He stood, lit his pipe again and got on his comms.

"Ask Egghead if he can get on that CCTV again and run it forwards. See if Georgie boy just shoved this bag into the top of the bin, or did he open the side all careful like."

"On it," replied Fuller.

Then.

"That is a positive," said Rick. "He stood around a bit then pushed it through the opening."

Des knelt again.

"Well I reckon, if he can shove it in, I can pull it out," he whispered, licking his dry lips, feeling sweat run down the small of his back. "In fer a fuckin' penny, pal."

Des unclipped the plastic bag from its fixings and the weight of the holdall caused it to clatter to the floor.

Cogan looked across at the cops again, allowed himself to breathe, grabbed at the plastic sack and pulled it from the bin.

He strode across the road, swinging it as he went.

"Piece of pish," he said, wiping his brow. "Piece of fuckin' pish."

***

"What the fuck are yees playin' at? Why are yees stopping?"

George was in blind panic. The Berlingo van had rolled to a halt, just half a mile from Piccadilly and

Connor was hastily trying to restart it.

"Shut the fuck up, George," he barked. "I'm doing my best."

"They'll be behind us, Connor. Six, that Fuller fella, I'm tellin' yees, they'll be close."

Walsh shot out his left arm and cuffed George around the head.

"And I said, be quiet whilst I fix this."

McCaul leaned over and looked at the French van's dials.

"It's out of fuckin' juice yees fool," he spat. "Only you could steal a van with no fuckin' diesel."

Connor slammed both palms on the steering wheel in frustration.

"Well, we'll just have to walk then, so. It's only ten minutes from here to Oxford Road."

George twisted his thin frame and took a look in the back. It was a jumble of tools and unused materials in there, however, lurking amongst the muddle, was a black fuel can. He reached over, picked it up and waggled it in Connor's face.

"We ain't walking anywhere, yees bollocks," he sneered.

***

Des had the holdall across his lap. He had cut it open alongside the zipper and was peering inside. As he did so, he let out a low whistle.

"Jeezo, boys. These two really do want te make a mess eh? There's enough C-4 here to take out a row of houses."

"Can you defuse it?" asked Rick.

Des nodded.

"Aye. The boy's made it in a hurry, like. It looks pretty crude. I just need to cut the battery connections before I remove the phone. But I'd still like Jerry te pull over and you two take a walk rather than do this on the move with your good selves fer fine company, like."

"He's right," said JC, steering the Merc into a side street.

Jerry stepped out, walked to Rick's door and opened it.

"You coming?" he said.

Fuller took a deep breath and swung his legs out of the Merc. He grimaced as he pushed himself out of his seat with his right hand.

"Meds worn off already?" asked JC.

"I'm okay," snapped Rick. "Come on let's go for a stroll whilst Scotty has his fun."

"Thanks fer fuck all," called Des from inside the Merc. "I'll give ye a shout once I've saved the world."

Jerry strode away, leaving Rick to try and keep up. After twenty yards or so, he stopped and waited for him.

"You need a Doc," he said as Fuller hobbled closer.

"Everyone's a fuckin' expert," said Rick, dropping more tablets into his dry mouth.

Commons knew he was on a loser so changed the subject. He nodded towards the Merc.

"So how long have you two been pals then? I mean, I know you were both over the water in '92."

Rick turned down his mouth.

"Probably ten years before that... you lose track."

Jerry knew men like Fuller didn't 'lose track'. His mind wasn't working as it should. Pain does that to a man, dulls his senses, makes even simple tasks difficult. Commons could see that Rick was on his chin strap, all but finished. Most would have given in by now, but not him. That's why he was one of the best, why Casey wanted him.

"We did selection together," added Rick. "We'd both done tours before that. Just a pair of daft lads really. Two completely different people thrown together that somehow found common ground." Rick's eyes lost their focus. "Tough little bastard he is. And the best shot I've ever seen."

"Seems a grand lad," said JC. "I see he wears a wedding ring."

Rick managed a wry smile and snorted.

"Yeah, Anne. Fuck me, they were together from school. The perfect couple."

"I sense a 'but' coming on."

"Aww, it's ancient history, Jerry. She ran off with some bloke years ago. Got fed up with Des being away. She divorced him. Broke his heart."

"Happens," said Jerry.

"It does, a lot, but Des took it really hard, as did his family. Big Catholics you see. Not the done thing. Anyway, she's gone now... cancer. He was with her in the end, I believe."

Jerry went quiet a moment, then asked, "What about you, Rick? Did you ever marry?"

Fuller gave JC a look that told him to mind his own business.

"Just making conversation," said Jerry, taking the hint.

"Sorry pal," offered Rick. "Yes, I was married… Cathy. The best thing that ever happened to me. I lost her in '96. The Provos murdered her."

JC was wide eyed. Anyone who had ever been connected to Special Forces in the nineties knew about the murder of a Trooper's wife.

"The Hereford killing? That was you?"

Rick nodded. "In one, pal. They came to my house… looking for me of course. It was just after 22 had done a little covert op over the water. Someone on the inside bubbled me. But I was out at the shops buying paint. We were doing up our house see. They missed me and shot her."

"You ever find out who dropped your name?"

Rick closed his eyes a moment.

"Now that is a long story, Jerry."

The headlights flashed on the Merc.

"Looks like Desmond has worked his magic," said Rick. "And saved me from telling you the rest of my colourful history."

"I'm sure we'll have a beer or two when this is all done. You can tell me the rest then," said Jerry, giving Rick a pained smile.

"I'm sure," said Rick. "Well, a beer at least."

Fuller once again slid painfully across the back seat. Des tossed him a mobile phone.

"He didn't set a timer. He just needed to ring that, and… bang." he said.

Rick rolled the phone around in his hand.

"Same make and model as Maria's," he mused.

"All burners probably," said the Scot.

Rick turned his attention to his own mobile. "Simon," he barked. "Give me an update."

"Sorry Mr Fuller," replied Egghead. "I just needed to point Percy at the porcelain so to speak. Now, this mush was stopped for a bit. Not far from where you are yourselves, but he's on the move again now. Looks to be headed for Rusholme… oh, hang fire, no, he's turning towards Oxford Road. Close to that pub you and Mr Cogan are so fond of."

"Get ye foot down again Jerry," said Des. "They're going fer Oxford Road Station next."

JC slammed the Jeep into drive and the Merc squealed away, leaving rubber on tarmac.

"Do a left here, Sackville Street," said Rick. "Now right, right, right, Charles Street. Come on Jerry, foot down now."

The Merc jumped a red light at the junction with Princess Street and careered over the canal, past the famous Lass O'Gowrie pub to the junction with Oxford Road, where it slewed right.

The city was just beginning to wake. The early delivery drivers, the dawn starters, going about their business. One truck blaring its horn at the speeding Merc.

"Left here," shouted Rick. "New Wakefield Street. Pull up by the arch." He lifted his phone closer to his mouth. "Come on Simon, where the fuck are they?"

Simon didn't need to answer.

"There," said Jerry pulling his Browning. "Outside that pub."

The Berlingo was indeed parked not twenty yards away on the opposite side of the arch, outside the front door of The Salisbury and at the bottom of the steps where in just a couple of short hours, hundreds of commuters would descend from the station, on their way to work.

Walsh was walking away from the van, towards Oxford Road. McCaul had the back doors open, head inside the cargo area.

Rick pushed open his door and stepped out. As he did so Connor looked across and saw him. Fuller could see in his face he was torn. Fight or flight? What was it to be? Risk everything to avenge the death of the woman you love, or live to fight another day?

Walsh turned towards his compatriot who was still oblivious to the arrival of his enemies.

"Come on... fuck's sake George," he shouted.

"A minute. I need a fuckin' minute," shouted McCaul, head still buried in whatever was taking all his attention in the back of the van.

Rick made to walk towards Connor. He responded by firing a couple of loose rounds in Fuller's direction before twisting his lithe frame and sprinting across the street towards the Palace Theatre.

Rick had no chance, he could barely stand. He stumbled forwards, revolver outstretched, but it was pointless firing, Walsh was too far away.

He rested his weight against one of the benches that served the customers of the Thirsty Scholar, his whole body racked with pain.

"Go get the fucker," he said to Des and JC. "I'll deal with George."

Des didn't need telling twice and sprinted past his friend, Jerry at his heels.

Connor had made it across the road and was running back the way they'd driven, towards Princess Street. He was much younger than both

Cogan and Commons, but years of endless tabbing and keeping in the best possible shape was on the side of the ex military men.

They were gaining with each stride, but now found they had another problem. It was five in the morning and there were people on the street. The city was awake. Some were strolling along whilst looking at their phones, checking their social media, reading the news, some, simply heads down, dreading another long day. Either way, it meant that Des and JC were unable to engage Walsh. They needed him off the street.

Seconds later, the Irishman gave them their wish and darted to his right down a narrow alleyway.

Des was first to the opening. He stopped holding up a hand to indicate to Jerry to do the same. Both men listened for the heavy steps of a grown man running, but there were none.

Cogan pointed to the far side of the opening.

"Cover me," he hissed.

JC nodded and readied himself.

Des sprinted across the narrow gap that led down the alleyway, head down. As he did so, Walsh opened fire, rounds sparking off the brick walls, narrowly missing the Scot.

Jerry twisted his frame, and, nicely tucked in returned Walsh's fire.

With a man now either side of the opening, Walsh was in deep trouble. He couldn't move and couldn't fight his way out.

"It's over, Connor," shouted Cogan. "Give it up, son."

"I'll not go to jail," bawled, Walsh. "Never. And if either of yees comes fer me, I'll shoot yees down."

Des could see that Conner was hiding behind a large cylindrical bin. It was on wheels, as tall as a man and well over a metre wide. He considered firing at the floor, just beneath the bin, the rounds hitting the deck and sitting up just high enough to hit Walsh around his feet and ankles, but in the half light and with the streets getting busier by the second, he discounted the idea.

The bin was on JC's side of the alley.

Des looked across at the ex Det man. He pointed at the container.

"Keep him pinned," he whispered. "On my signal," and held up three fingers.

On this occasion Cogan's instructions were followed to the letter, and as he dropped the third digit, JC opened fire, his nine millimetre rounds slamming into the metal bin, sparking off its metal exterior, some piercing it and rattling around inside.

Due to Jerry's rate of fire, Walsh couldn't move. He had no choice but to cower behind the only cover he had.

Des edged his way forwards, Jerry's rounds flying dangerously, but accurately past his right shoulder. Within seconds he was within sight of Walsh. He had the angle, the time and the accuracy. The Scot punched out his Browning, took one more step, spreading his feet as he did so then fired twice, a double tap to the chest, and the night went silent.

Jerry jogged over to Cogan who was kneeling by Connor's body.

"He's gone," said Des.

Fuller had staggered to within shooting distance of the van. He could feel his legs shaking. He was so weak now, he thought they may just give way. His hands so numb he could barely feel his revolver, his mouth so dry his tongue felt huge inside it, stomach churning from the drugs.

George McCaul had straightened himself and slammed the rear doors of the van. Both had heard the shooting from a few streets away. Both knew of the probable result of that fire. He turned to Fuller, eyes wide, sweating profusely. In his right hand was an SLP, in his left, a mobile phone.

He shakily pointed his gun at Rick and held the phone up in the air like some bizarre trophy, its screen lighting one side of his thin face.

"Walk away, soldier," he shouted. "Walk away and live, or take another step and die."

"Very fucking dramatic," managed Fuller, slowly lifting his own weapon. "What do you think this is, a spaghetti western?"

"You fire at me, soldier, I press the wee green button on this phone, and we all get blown to hell. Come on, even someone as stupid as you will know, I could manage that before I go. Even before yees pull the trigger. Look at yees, yer all shot to pieces, yees can barely stand."

Fuller nodded, staggered slightly.

The Irishman was right, he was indeed on his last legs. His hands shook as much as his legs, meaning the chances of a head shot to stop McCaul triggering the second device was nigh on impossible.

Still, Fuller was in no mood to give up.

"You don't look too good yourself, son," said Rick. "Bit on edge are we? See, you know what your problem is, Georgie boy? I'm prepared to die. I don't give a flying photograph. I'm ready. I've been ready for so long, you wouldn't believe it. But are you, son? Are you?" Rick cupped the butt of his revolver with his damaged right hand. "Did you hear the shooting, George?

You did, didn't you? Your pal Walsh is dead, no danger. He'll be lying in a pool of his own claret. And now, you are the only one left."

Rick edged ever closer, shuffling along the cobbles with the last of his strength.

"And you know what Georgie boy? I reckon, that if you were going to blow us up, you'd have done it by now."

McCaul forced a smile. He was manic, close to hysterical, shook his head wildly.

"Ah, yees know it all don't yees? All clever. But yees don't know me, soldier. Don't know anything about me, so don't push yees luck there. I'm quite prepared to go down with this ship. I'm not scared."

"You look like you are," said Rick, doing his best to steady himself. "Shitting it, is how I'd describe you."

McCaul lifted the phone higher.

"I'm...."

George was cut short by the sound of running feet. Des was first around the corner, JC just in behind.

At that very second, the Irishman, knew it was over. He closed his eyes, whispered a prayer to himself and hit the call button.

Cogan and Commons instinctively hit the deck.

Rick, however, didn't move.

He stood as still as he could manage, holding out his pistol, staring into the face of George McCaul.

Struggling to stay upright, visibly rocking from side to side, he reached into his pocket with his free hand and pulled out a vibrating mobile. The same phone Des had handed to him in the Jeep, the same phone that Cogan had removed from the first device.

Rick broke into a rare beaming smile.

"Wrong number, Georgie," he said. And shot the Irishman dead.

Des and Commons were instantly back on their feet. Fuller, however, had collapsed.

They lifted him and helped him into the Merc.

"Come on, mate," said Cogan. "It's the hospital fer ye and ne arguments."

"No...no...tonight," mumbled Fuller. "Simpson...tonight, Des. No...I need..."

But whatever his message, he was unable to finish it.

Fuller fell unconscious.

SEVENTEEN

Jerry and Des were in the air. They'd been collected by helicopter from a small airfield close to the Trafford Centre and were en route to be debriefed by Casey at the SIS building in Whitehall. Rick had travelled via Medivac and was already being prepped for surgery at the Queen Elizibeth Hospital in Birmingham. The Bomb Squad had been scrambled to take care of McCaul's second device, and despite dozens of men in suits clearing up the carnage caused by the team, rumours were already circulating within the Manchester press agencies that a covert Special Forces operation had foiled a terrorist plot in the city.

"Casey says they will move Jack down to Birmingham tomorrow," said JC. "Bit of company for Rick."

Des nodded, but he was deep in thought.

"What d'ya think he was on about, y'know, when he was saying about 'Simpson' and 'tonight'?"

JC gave Des a sideways glance.

"Well, we all know what he's been up to recently. Maybe he had plans in place."

"Hmm, maybe. And there's something else that has been bothering me."

"Go on."

"Well, why did O'Shea stay behind at the ambush. I mean, from what he told me, she hid in the car waiting for him. Him, not the team...him."

JC took a breath.

"You recall, at the office, I said that there was a connection between your team and the Irish crew, well, that was it. Rick and Maria. We never considered that he would actually be identified, and how that happened is still a mystery, but it happened and..."

"Hold on, pal," said Cogan. "You're losing me here. What connection?"

Over the next few minutes, Jerry went on to tell Des about the fateful night in Dungannon. Frank O'Shea, the picture of the woman and child, the gun, all of it.

"Jeezo," said Des. "He never mentioned it. I mean, he was quiet after the op, I remember that, but I put it down to Jimmy getting wounded."

"I still believe he blames himself," said Jerry.

Des shook his head.

"Bollocks to that. The boy had just shot one of ours. He reached into his coat. That would have been enough fer me."

"Different times," said Jerry quietly.

"Aye, and good riddance to 'em n'all."

"I'll drink to that."

Des perked up.

"That's the best idea ye have had all week, JC. Soon as Casey has finished with his whining, I say we go out and get royally pissed."

***

Naomi had been waiting for Stephen to call. The arrangement had been that he would already be in the house waiting when Larry Simpson arrived. But she hadn't heard anything from him, even after her text. And now, his phone was switched off.

All this had added to her already cold feet.

Maybe this was for the best?

Did she really want to be an accessory to murder? Even for so much money?

Well, she would just have to deal with Larry as she always did. She knew what he wanted. Give it to him, take his cash and worry about the mysterious Stephen Colletti and the fifty grand sitting in a case in her spare room later.

By the time Larry was due to arrive, she was made up in her standard gothic sub style, thick black eyeliner, black lipstick, and dressed in Simpson's favourite PVC outfit. It had metal hooks on the sleeves and collar, to make it easier for him to restrain her. Torn fishnets and black patent five inch spike heels completed the look.

As she gave herself a quick once over in her full length mirror, the door bell rang. Larry was exactly on time, just as he always was.

Naomi opened the door and put on her best submissive look.

"Good evening master," she said.

Larry looked her up and down before pushing her roughly back inside the house. It was his way, his dominance over her had to be complete, from the moment of his arrival, to the second he ejaculated inside her, he had to be in total control.

Unusually, Larry carried a case with him and he dropped it on the coffee table.

"You brought something special?" purred Naomi. "Tired of my old whips and chains?"

He turned to her, his pale blue eyes examining her face.

"This will be a night like no other," he said. "I hope you are prepared."

Naomi's breathing deepened. She was playing the game.

"Show me," she whispered, her lips touching his lobe. "Show me… hurt me."

Larry leaned down and opened the brown leather briefcase.

He removed a pair of latex gloves and made a show of pulling them onto his large hands.

"Mmm," said Naomi. "Now that is different."

Simpson held her chin a moment, squeezed it painfully hard.

"Why oh why, Naomi?" he said wistfully.

She pulled away.

"Hey, tiger. Not so rough so soon."

Larry rummaged in the case again, this time he removed a thick square clear plastic bag. He looked into Naomi's face and twisted his mouth into a vicious sneer.

"What?" she managed, just before, with a flick of the wrist, Larry opened the bag, and in one swift, practised movement, plunged it over her head.

She grabbed at his wrists as he twisted the edges of the bag tight around her throat.

Naomi was in an instant panic, gasping for breath, she took the last of the air in the bag with her first breath, but as she inhaled again, the plastic fell in on itself, sealing her nose and mouth.

As he dragged her backwards, pulling the bag ever tighter, Simpson caught a glimpse of himself in Naomi's full length mirror. At times like these, he lost himself, he didn't recognise the man looking back at him. At these moments, just like the time with Lauren and all the other times the authorities had never discovered, he had indeed lost himself. It was during these, 'moments' his strength came from somewhere dark and evil. It flooded his body, coursed through his veins like wire in his blood. He gripped the bag so hard now that he lifted Naomi from her feet, twisting at the bag with everything he had.

"Stephen Colletti," he hissed in her ear.

Naomi blew out some air and the bag inflated for a second, giving her some respite, some hope. But the second she inhaled, the plastic bag sealed her mouth and nose again. She was terrified, stars danced around in her vision. She was trying to kick out at him with her heels, twist herself free, but he was too strong. He was dragging her towards the kitchen.

"Stephen fucking Colletti," he bawled. "A...K...A Richard Edward Fuller."

She was crying now, there was no air left, she could feel herself going into the darkness, down, ever down.

Once Larry Simpson was convinced Naomi was unconscious, he went back to his bag and found a roll of Gaffa tape. He wrapped several layers around her neck, sealing the bag, just for good measure, then sat her up against one of her kitchen units.

He looked at her twisted body, straightened her legs then found a shoe that had fallen off and replaced it. Still not quite happy with his work, he rested her hands together on her lap, then cocked his head quizzically.

"There," he said. "You look all pretty now...just one last thing, though."

Larry went back to his bag one last time and removed a Polaroid camera. He took three shots.

"One for me," he said smiling. "One for you," he offered laying the developing shot on Naomi's lap. "And one for Richard," he said, slipping it into his jacket.

"That will fucking teach him."

END

Printed in Great Britain
by Amazon

86690427R00123